Wicked Sweet

Other great reads you may enjoy

My Life Undecided	Jessica Brody
Paradise	Jill S. Alexander
The Poison Apples	Lily Archer
The Stalker Chronicles	Carley Moore
Flirt Club	Cathleen Daly
52 Reasons to Hate My Father	Jessica Brody
My Invented Life	Lauren Bjorkman
Just Flirt	Laura Bowers
The Karma Club	Jessica Brody
Pizza, Love, and Other Stuff that Made Me Famous	Kathryn Williams

Wicked Sweet

Mar'ce Merrell

SQUARE
FISH

FEIWEL AND FRIENDS
NEW YORK

SQUARE
FISH

An Imprint of Macmillan

Library of Congress Cataloging-in-Publication Data Available
ISBN 978-1-250-02737-5 (paperback) / 978-1-4668-1599-5 (ebook)

Square Fish books may be purchased for business or promotional use.
For information on bulk purchases, please contact the Macmillan Corporate
and Premium Sales Department at (800) 221-7945 x5442 or by e-mail at
specialmarkets@macmillan.com.

Originally published in the United States by Feiwel and Friends
First Square Fish Edition: May 2013
Square Fish logo designed by Filomena Tuosto
Book designed by Ashley Halsey
macteenbooks.com

2   4   6   8   10   9   7   5   3   1

LEXILE: HL700L

For Callie

Wicked Sweet

Chantal

· · · · · ·

C is Only for Cupcake.

When Jillian slips off her T-shirt, I swear I break out in hives. She must know I'm not prepared for my best friend in a string bikini. Suprises like this are for spontaneous people—not for me. Now I need more than cupcakes. I need an antihistamine.

It's midafternoon, school is out for the year, and girls and guys from our class carry coolers of beer down the hill, looking for towel space near the water. Jillian and I sit at the top, under the tree we've claimed since the third grade. Everyone else wants to be close to the lake, the sun, and each other. I concentrate on the pattern of beach umbrellas and towels: circle, rectangle, circle, rectangle. I try not to stare at Jillian's bikini triangles.

"Chantal, quit staring," Jillian says.

"I didn't expect . . . a bikini." I stare down at the small hills in my one-piece. I am so lacking in this department. "But it's . . . nice. It fits." *Barely.*

"Good. I was worried you'd think it was too, well, you know." She unzips her shorts, lets them drop to the towel. Two strings connect her bikini bottom pieces. Silver studs situated, uh, strategically, sparkle. She smoothes down the fabric while she waits for my response. "Isn't it hot?"

I nod. I smile. I look to see how many people are gawking at us. Well, her. But the surrounding girls and guys are spreading on tanning lotion, opening their drinks, laughing with each other. My skin prickles. I scan the hill and mountains around us for signs of impending disaster, but Williamson's Lake is the same. For nine years, it's always been like this: Jillian, me, and a day to plan our summer project.

While Jillian adjusts the triangles over her parts, then brushes her hair into perfect blond waves, I unpack my beach bag. I need a cupcake. I open the grocery store cello pack: chocolate cupcakes, white frosting, silver balls of sugar. The signature summer sweet.

I hand one to Jillian.

"Oh," she squeals. "We match." She holds the cupcake next to her right boob. "White and silver."

Next time, I'll definitely buy a different combination.

She takes the tiniest bite of chocolate and vanilla, sets the rest of her cupcake down, rubs tanning oil over her flat belly. "We should get you a bikini, too."

I open my mouth to protest.

"You can tell your mom it's mine."

I reach for my sunscreen, SPF 50. "She'd know that you couldn't fit into an A cup."

"I think she'd be okay with a . . . modest . . . bikini. We'll go for playful instead of sexy, but you need padding. Cleavage is bikini success."

I stare at the shadows between Jillian's breasts. I have seen way more of her C's this year than I expected; tight sweaters, low tank tops. I thought they were the only hand-me-downs from her Vancouver cousin that fit. I thought that Jillian's new sexy was, almost, unavoidable. I thought reusing was better than buying something new. Practical, that's me.

"Remember the first principle of design? Form follows function.

I can't wear a bikini. I like to dive off the platform. And swim, really swim."

"But what if you had two different functions, and, therefore, two different forms?"

It's the way she looks at me when she says it—her eyes unsure, her mouth sort of between a smile and a frown, her jaw tensed. I swallow. My eyes narrow with suspicion. Two months ago she started rating guys—few got above a seven and Jillian said she wouldn't date anyone below a ten—and now she shows up in a bikini, just when the town is about to be overrun by eligible guys without shirts.

"Tell me you're not going for maximum exposure to get a guy's attention." Summer romances don't work, she should know that. Last summer a girl from our class hooked up with a lonely sixteen-year-old from a tourist's family and stowed away in the back of their RV. They sent her back four states later.

"You need a different bathing suit."

"Because?"

"It's the summer? We're going into our senior year? We're both good-looking?" She hits me with the same sort of intensity I see when she's practicing the points and counterpoints for a debate. "We can attract attention without compromising our principles." Jillian rolls her eyes, just the tiniest bit. "Wearing a bikini doesn't mean we're on the dessert menu."

I tilt my head as she goes on to list, again, how much potential my features have. My un-blond and untamed hair needs short, straightened bangs. Dyeing my eyebrows darker will frame my eyes, even when I'm wearing my glasses. And her favorite: a shopping trip on victoriassecret.com will be *our* secret. I'm lucky, she says, runway models have androgynous shapes like mine. This is the fourth time she's called me androgynous since she started running like a fiend. My head aches. I could use another cupcake, but I look at Jillian's.

She's taken two tiny bites. Even with all the preservatives, the frosting is beginning to melt.

"I'm only five-three. And I like cupcakes. I'll never be a model." I've offered this point before. Back then, it stopped her argument.

"Brain surgeons can be hot, too." Clearly, she's been practicing.

"I guess." I imagine my future as a brain surgeon, what it would be like having guys whistle at me in my white lab coat, my hotness startling them like Jillian's does now. "But I think neurosurgery is pretty hot all by itself."

"Think about the surgeons on TV."

"They're all old."

"Exactly. And they're still not bad, are they? We can be young, hot neurosurgeons." Jillian's pink fingernail glides along the top of her cupcake. She licks the frosting from her finger, reaches for her sunglasses, and shifts to catch the sunlight.

I tell her that when we're in med school the last thing we'll need are boyfriends. I detail how I ended up trapped in a girls' bathroom stall during last period today, stuck listening to a whole my-boyfriend-dumped-me drama. I remind her that we made a pact in ninth grade that we'd never put a guy above (a) our friendship and (b) getting good grades. "Remember?"

"Yeah."

She stretches out on her towel and I pop the last of my cupcake in my mouth. As it dissolves on my tongue I detect an aftertaste I'd missed before and almost tell Jillian not to finish hers. But there's no point, she's abandoned it to the ants anyway. This is not how our first day of summer is supposed to go.

Jillian

. . . . . .

Reality Check.

$\mathcal{I}$ should have started preparing Chantal sooner. If my upgrade from a one-piece upsets her this much, a meet-up with guys could end in a meltdown. I convinced myself that the subject matter, our all-A's physics study group, would put us in Chantal's comfort zone. Now I know she's not there yet. But time is running out, next year we'll be seniors.

In ninth grade the "no guys" rule made sense. I mean if you had a mother like mine who popped out boy babies every time a new guy text messaged her, you'd tell your best friend you didn't want to have a boyfriend, either.

But you grow up. At least I did. A couple months ago I was coming out of Cooper's grocery store carrying three heavy bags, struggling not to drop them, when I heard a voice.

"Need some help?" A deep voice with an accent, maybe French or Italian.

I didn't turn around. I mean, we're a tourist town; nearly every girl in my class has a story about an older guy hitting on her. Last year a guy who was old enough to be my father stopped to ask for directions to the farmers' market. I helped him and I was about to leave when he put his hand on my shoulder and asked what I was doing later. I still remember his slimy palm. Girls don't forget their first encounter with slime.

So that's why I didn't turn around. But I dropped a grocery bag. And Mr. So-Not-What-I-Expected picked it up and followed me to the minivan. He was young. Like, my age. With shocking dark hair. And great teeth.

Hockey equipment fell out when I opened the trunk. As we piled it back in, I snuck looks at him and I caught him doing the same to me. I imagined him asking what a hot girl like me was doing in a grocery store parking lot in the middle of nowhere. I was about to say *something*, suggest we go for coffee even, when I realized he was staring into the grocery bags. Diapers. Formula. Baby wipes. He looked up at me and tilted his head. I guess he was a Mr. Right for a few seconds.

"Thanks for your help," I said. I slammed down the hatch door.

"Yeah, no problem," he said in his sexy accent. He was gone before I could give him one last look of longing.

I made a critical assessment of myself in the rearview mirror. My knotted hair was pulled back in a light gray headband bleached out from being washed in hot water with crib sheets. No makeup. I wondered if my breath smelled like the only thing we had left for breakfast—peanut butter on leftover garlic bread. And still, he saw something in me. I needed to refine the something. And get away from the teen-mommy image. Fast.

I haven't told Chantal about this turning point because she'd call me out as shallow. I'm still trying to figure out if that's what it is—my shallow, vain side trying to edge out my common sense side. And I guess I thought this meeting with Parker and Will would be a good test.

I know they aren't interested in us, really. We've known them since grade school and even if Parker is one of the hottest guys in our class, he's been Annelise's boyfriend forever. I must have imagined the chemistry between Parker and me when he said he wanted to meet up today; I thought he checked me out and that our eye contact was longer than usual. The guys say they want to talk about our study group and it's possible that's all it really is.

I knew I was guilty of a minor case of best friend betrayal when I carried the bikini into the changing room. But shallow girls don't get top grades in physics, I need to remind Chantal. And potential neurosurgeons can have fun, too.

Chantal
• • • • • •
Crushing on Abnormal.

"So . . ." I unzip my backpack; take out my spiral notebook and pen. "Summer projects." I turn to the first clean page. This is the best part of the first day of summer, meditating on the productive potential of free time. Brainstorming ideas. Harmonizing options. Making the list. Happiness dances in my brain while buttercream frosting slides on my tongue.

"The lake. Parties. Camping." Jillian doesn't even sit up. She just calls them out.

I write her words. The dance music fades. Our projects are about investigation, exploration, and self-improvement. *Our* self-improvement. Jillian knows I hate camping. "Well . . . these seem more like events, not projects. And . . . there is no way I'm going to convince my mother to let me go camping, unless it's in your back-yard." Ever since we suggested hiking for a summer project a few years back, my mother started building a file of news stories about campers getting attacked by black bears, grizzlies, and cougars.

"We could tell her we'll be in my backyard." Jillian's words come out practiced.

"But we'd go . . . ?"

"Where everyone else is."

I think I get it now. She doesn't want a summer project. She wants me in a bikini on a towel next to her or in a tight T-shirt at a bonfire party or in the front seat of a car with a guy while she's in the back with someone else. I always knew that one day she'd insist we do the usual high school girl stuff. She's told me over and over I need to get out more, take a risk. But why would she pick today? The best day of my summer?

I reach for another cupcake, strip off the paper wrapper and shove half of it in my mouth. The frosting globs onto my uvula and gets stuck on my tonsils. The metal taste is overpowering now. With each breath in, I exhale a smaller amount until, the cake gone, I am trapped in my own air. I need to exhale. I start to gasp.

"Chantal? Are you alright?" Jillian slaps me on the back. "Breathe."

"I can't be allergic to cupcakes. I can't." My hands form a parenthesis on either side of my head. I get like this sometimes, all worried, and I think I'm going to have an asthma attack. Although the doctor says I don't have asthma I'm just waiting for the right trigger.

"You're not allergic. You're just . . ." She hands me her water bottle.

"I'm neurotic." She doesn't say it, but she must think it, because this is part of who I am: Chantal, girl with anxiety attacks. I silently thank her for understanding.

She waits for me to recover. We watch a swarm of junior high kids swim out to the dock in the middle of the lake, cover it with so many bodies we can't see the wood planks. Their shouts bounce off the mountains that surround us. "Do you ever wonder if we're missing out?" Jillian asks.

"On?"

"Fun."

Crud. I want to eat more cupcake, but I'm sure I'd end up in the hospital. "Our summer projects are always fun: you loved the krumping video, didn't you?"

"I hated flatland synchronized swimming."

"It would have been better if you knew how to swim."

"Remember my brothers booed us?"

"And threw pinecones at us!"

Jillian retells the horror of flatland synchronized swimming from the beginning: the research phase; our flatland adaptations; and how we wore earplugs, swimming caps, and flippers because we wanted to evoke water. I reminded her how hard we were laughing when we performed—so hard our cheeks were still sore the next day. Lifelong learners like us find inspiration everywhere.

"We were such nerds back then," Jillian says.

"It was only last year." We laugh like we love to laugh. My sides ache with happy pain.

"You're the greatest," Jillian says.

"You, too," I say.

"But I'm not flatland synchronized swimming this year."

"Only in my memories," I say. As I'm about to suggest creating a private fashion show for a summer project—thereby combining Jillian's need to make me over and my need to plan the next eight weeks of my life—Jillian interrupts.

"So . . . who was in the bathroom anyway?"

I pause.

"The girls' bathroom. Today. The whole he-dumped-me drama. What girl?"

"Annelise. Can you believe it?"

"Parker broke up with her? After three years?" Jillian picks up her cupcake and, finally, takes a decent-sized bite. And another one.

"Apparently he wanted to be free for the summer."

"You're sure?" Chocolate crumbs cling to her bikini top.

"Annelise's whine is unmistakable."

We don't say anything because we both know what the other one is thinking: we don't need that kind of drama. We have goals. Priorities. While Jillian appears to sleep, I watch the action.

Bikini girls hook thumbs into guys' waistbands—a three-legged race in slow motion. Flip-flop dust flies. They must not know how ridiculous it looks, how dangerous it is. Those girls daydream about some guy; their biggest goal is to change their Facebook status to include him. They think it's going to make them happy, but I know for a fact it won't. Goals keep girls like Jillian and me focused so that ten years from now we'll be finishing med school.

The summer after the ninth grade we were here with Jillian's mom in her long skirts and her brothers the Hat Trick (the triplet boys), the Double Minor (the twin boys), and her mom's then-boyfriend. We made flower wreaths from daisies and dandelions and put them in our hair. It was the summer of friendship bracelets. Jillian and I already had twenty-five on each arm and we were tying our newest ones onto the boys. A group of tourists stopped to take pictures of us. Amid all this flowery love, Jillian's mom left us, saying she and the boyfriend were going to get us some ice cream. They'd been gone more than an hour when one of the boys messed in his swim diaper. Jillian had to go to the car for a clean one. She came back empty-handed and furious, but she wouldn't tell me why. When her mom showed up with her hand shoved in the back pocket of the boyfriend's jeans (and without ice cream), Jillian grabbed my arm and pulled me toward an empty picnic table where no one could hear us.

"She was never even planning to get us ice cream," she said, her body vibrating with fury. "Promise me we're never going to end up like her."

And that's when we made the pact: friends first, grades second, boyfriends not on the list.

I don't know how, or if, I should remind Jillian of the circumstances of our pact. Jillian's mom is better than she was that summer, I think. She's had the same boyfriend for over two years now and Jillian even likes him. But you have to be careful with your best friend, even when you have a good reason to tell the hard truth.

Jillian's hard truth must be that I need a bikini because she says,

"Don't you think we could still be hot even if we weren't looking for boyfriends? We could like, be hot, just for ourselves."

Not again.

"Our own personal satisfaction?" I hadn't really thought of it that way.

"Well, I'm saying it's possible, don't you think, to look hot and not have a boyfriend or be on the lookout for one?"

"It might be . . . counterproductive."

"Huh?"

"Time. Money. Unwanted male attention."

"Not unwanted. Unreciprocated." It's strange to be on the opposing side of one of Jillian's debates. "It's about choice."

Jillian sits up, looks down at the watch I gave her last Christmas. It's only 2:45. The hour we have left leaves us lots of time to plan our summer project. She takes off her sunglasses, scans the hill, and then turns to me. "Chantal, we're number one and two in the class. We spend our summers on projects that are, let's face it, pretty lame. I think we need to do what the other seniors are doing."

"Joust with swim noodles in the hallways? Catch a goose and drop it into the cafeteria? Dress up like gorillas and chase people dressed up like bananas?" While I list all the things that the students in our class have done this year that we think are stupid and would never be part of, she alternately looks at her watch and then at the lake. My listing trails off when I see the catastrophe coming our way: two guys, Parker and Will.

Parker is shirtless and it's clear he's been doing more than studying. His shoulders have grown wider and he's bleached his hair. He is far from the nerdy A student he was in junior high. Will hasn't transformed much. Still average all around, still Parker's sidekick. He, too, is shirtless. Parker waves to someone at the top of the hill. I notice movement from my periphery, of sunglasses being lifted, a raised arm, and a hand waving back.

"Jillian?"

"He wants to talk about physics. The study group. That's all."

"I . . . I . . . School's over." I squint at the bottom of the hill. Parker and Will are taking the long way up, along the beach and up the other side of the hill. So they can show off their biceps and abs. I need a cupcake, but I can't eat in front of *them*.

"He specifically said physics."

I give her the look that says, do I appear to have a brain malfunction? Didn't I just say that he and Annelise broke up?

"Okay," she concedes. "It's probably not about physics. He was sort of checking me out. But, really, they just want to talk to us. It's talking."

"I knew something was up with the bikini."

"Chantal. I still want to do a summer project. Look, we can plan it after they leave. We can raise money for Africa. That would be fun." When she smiles, I feel like I'm at the doorway to her exciting life and she's handing out charity.

"As a favor, you mean?"

"I mean I still want to do a summer project," she repeats. "But . . . next year we'll be graduating . . . and, we're going to need a date for prom, right?"

"Prom?" I thought we'd decided to stand against the consumerism of prom. And no guy would see me as a potential date, not today. I didn't shower, my hair is in a frizzy ponytail, I'm in my practical one-piece, and I have never waxed. Anything. I can't be the best at fashion and looking hot and still be the best at grades. I don't have the time. And neither does Jillian. I grab my backpack, search for my shorts.

"I wasn't trying to surprise you. I wasn't. I didn't even know, for sure, that Parker and Annelise broke up. They're just coming to talk to us."

"Will picked his nose and wiped his snot on my arm."

"In the third grade."

"He tripped me in gym, almost every day . . ."

"In fifth."

"He put the fetal pig heart from seventh grade dissection in a box and gave it to me. Pretended it was a Valentine's gift. I hate him."

"He does stuff like that to lots of girls."

"No, Jillian." I want to tell her that girls who want guys to like them are like moths flickering toward a light, that third-degree burns and scars are inevitable. I want to remind her that Parker was the one who sent Annelise to the bathroom. I want to tell her that earlier this year, Will grabbed my left one while I was standing at my locker. When he's near me I fall apart inside and not in a good way. But I haven't told anyone, because it's weird. It doesn't make sense.

The guys are now five rectangles of towels and two circles of umbrellas away from us. And I don't have a plan.

Jillian

· · · · · ·

Beginning.

*O*ur friendship was immediate, that's how I remember it.

We moved to town when I was eight, moved away from the log cabin near a stream in the Slocan Valley, where my only friend had been our dog, Mangy. My parents were into sustainable living before it became fashionable. After a while my dad didn't feel like an alternative lifestyle was for him. When he left to find work in Vancouver, my mother couldn't sustain much of anything anymore.

She packed up our chipped dishes and we followed the trail of RVs on the winding mountain roads into town. We stayed in a motel at first and I used a remote control for the first time in my life. Over the noise of cartoons and *National Geographic* specials I listened to my mom talk to her parents on the phone. She told them what had happened since she last saw them ten years earlier: she could find water with a divining stick, she'd learned to play the fiddle, and she had a daughter: me, Jillian.

"I'm ready to reenter the world," she told them. I don't think they expected that she meant the world of dating. She rushed her hellos and hugs when they reunited in our motel room, and left us behind to get to know each other while she met a guy for drinks. My granddad told me stories about his old war friends and my grandmother Nona combed and braided my hair. They said I was the most precious thing they'd seen, more beautiful than an emerald lake or a sunrise on the prairies. They let me drink hot chocolate with my dinner and eat ice cream for dessert. My mom and her new friend opened the motel room door as the sun was coming up the next morning, and Nona begged for me to stay with her and Granddad a little longer. The new boyfriend took me for a walk while my mom argued that she wouldn't let them take me away from her. My grandparents left after breakfast.

The guy stayed with us in the motel long enough that my mom said I should call him Dad. "He can be Dad Two," I told her, sure that she'd get mad and walk away. Instead she called the guy in and told him the story of me saying the cutest thing. Dad 2 looked at me sideways when he hugged my mother.

"She's a real charmer," he said. "She could tame a grizzly bear, couldn't she?"

We moved into our house on Columbia when it was 85 degrees outside and Mom complained she was hot and sick. She walked in the front door, opened the freezer, and stuck her head inside. I carried my one box (containing colored pencils, sketchbooks, my collection of *Mrs. Piggle-Wiggle* books, and an empty piggy bank) to the top of the creaky stairs and set it in the corner. I had my special things—I was moved in. I opened the window and leaned out to see what the world would look like. That's when I saw Chantal in her backyard, crouched in the shade, staring at a glass bottle glinting in the sun. A sprinkler waved over the flowerbeds on the steep incline.

"Hey!" I yelled. "Hey!" She didn't hear me. I got louder. "Hey you, in the backyard." She still didn't look up. I pounded down the stairs, stopped to watch my mother run past clutching her stomach, vomit in the toilet. "Jesus, I'm pregnant," I heard her tell Dad 2. "I just know these things," she said.

When she had her head back in the freezer, I approached her.

"Mom. I'm going to meet my best friend next door." I *just knew* Chantal and I had a shared destiny.

"Hey." My shadow stretched over the glass bottle in Chantal's dandelion-free grass. I could see the bottle had strips of duct tape markings all up the side. "What are you doing?"

"Watching evaporation."

"Cool. Can I watch, too?"

"It takes a long time, evaporation. You have to be real patient."

"Oh, I'm patient," I said. "Dad Two says I'm charming, too. He says I could tame a grizzly bear."

"Whoa," she said. "I'd like to see that."

We were made for each other: two geeky girls with shared time, loneliness, and dreams of being important one day. I've always believed that I moved next door to my soul sister, but maybe things have changed.

• • •

Now, I'm standing on the hill, looking fabulous in my bikini, beside the guy I want most to notice me, and I'm shouting for Chantal to come back. I have waited too long. Shocked that she bolted like she was being chased, but worried that Parker would lose interest, I did nothing. Now, though, I run after her. I don't know how to convince her, what I can say to prove that some things can stay the same.

Chantal

· · · · · ·

Swoon.

 he wind generated by my bike's velocity down a mountain road is substantial enough to carry off the choked gasps of my panic attack. By the time I get home my stomachache has traveled from my gut to all my extremities. I struggle to shove my bike into the garage, lift my legs high enough to climb the concrete steps to our house. My fingers fumble the key in the lock.

I collapse on the couch and click on the remote. I rarely watch TV, influenced by a mother who says it rots my brain. We only have a TV because my dad loves the Golf Channel, aka the snore channel. I stare at the screen, looking for a reason to get up. If my mother discovers me here, she'll start asking questions. Should she discover that I have no summer plans, my fate could be worse than a summer without a project. She likes the summer to have a structure—her structure.

The summer I was eight, my dad took my mother and me to visit his family out east. At the beginning of each driving day, my mother detailed the gifts she'd bought for my cousins, smocked sundresses from our town's seamstress who was famous for sewing a smocked sundress once worn by Princess Beatrice of York. The seamstress even had a picture as proof.

"It's an heirloom piece that can be handed down generation after generation," my mother said.

After the third time she said it, my psychologist father responded so softly I almost didn't hear, "The gifts are secondary. They want to see us."

At Lettuce Loaf (as in let us loaf—get it?), the cottage floors were transformed into bedrooms for the cousins and my parents slept in the attic in two twin beds—the penthouse, Dad called it.

I trailed after the cousins to the lake, the mini-golf course, the water park, and a daily visit to the soft-serve ice cream stand where the cousins thought the coolest things were the hottest guys.

"I'm allergic to smoke," my mother protested when my uncles invited her out to the campfire. She went to bed early and was gone when I woke in the morning, off to find a decent cup of coffee in the nearby village. She wore a sundress and espadrilles every day, with a wide hat to keep the sun off her face. It limited her, my father said, to certain activities. My mother had no interest in Frisbee, golf, or catching frogs—she thought a cottage was for lounging in solitude even if she wasn't actually doing that.

Our ten-day stay concluded with a family photo session to document our visit. My cousins held rabbit-ear fingers behind my head as we stood in the front lawn, pine branches poking our backs. I didn't ask why my mother stayed in the car. It was one of those things I knew not to do, like knowing that I shouldn't ask for hot chocolate when she was slamming cupboard doors in our own kitchen.

We were on the highway before my mother spoke the only words she'd say for hours. "There is no such thing as a loaf of lettuce.

"And those smocked sundresses, the ones like Princess Beatrice wore? I heard your sister say that the girls thought they were hideous. Old-fashioned."

My dad should have said something like, I'm sorry or you're right or they have very poor taste if they don't like something that the queen of England's granddaughter wore. I almost said something myself.

Their conversation ended, finally, when my mother announced

that was our first and last trip to the cottage. I was carsick for the rest of the trip.

I knew then that family vacations were doomed to fail. Luckily, I found something else that day. I went outside with my canning jar and my duct tape, ready to try a different experiment. That's when I met my best friend . . . until today.

I breathe deep and hold it for as long as I can. I think my lips might even be turning a bruised blue. Like all only children, I know how to throw a tantrum to get what I want. I feel one coming on.

Jillian

· · · · · ·

The Surprise Ending.

I didn't get very far in chasing Chantal, once I realized how little support my bikini top offered. I climbed the hill to grab my stuff; my towel first, wrapped around me. Parker took a few steps back to give me some space, but Will stood close and watched me, wolflike.

"Well, that was weird." Will slouched as he shoved his hands into the pockets of his board shorts. I stopped what I was doing and stared at him. He looked like every guy my mother brought home, dark stubble on his face, indifferent eyes; his fingernails were probably dirty. Why did I think Chantal would even sit next to him? Will took off his ball cap, smoothed his hair back, checked to see who was checking him out. Maybe a few tenth-graders.

"Jillian." Parker's voice was soft.

I looked up. His eyes. Eyes like those have never looked at me that way. Even if you saw him from across a playground, Parker could melt your resolve with his good looks and the way he stands with just enough tension in his shoulders, square on as if you were about to slow dance. Standing there, the rest of the world disappeared, including Will. Until he spoke.

"So . . . summer. You and Chantal got any plans?"

"Not really. Not yet." Parker was never this cute when he was dating Annelise. "Maybe some physics."

"Right. About that," Will said. "Straight up. We don't need any physics tutoring."

"What?" I sort of knew it wasn't about physics and, still, I felt a little betrayed. More proof, I guess, of what I didn't know about the guy-girl world. They could have at least asked a few vector questions. If I walked into a debate that unprepared, my team would dump me.

"Hey." Parker took a step toward me and lowered his head, then his eyes grew smoking hot. "There's a party at Mia's on Saturday night. You both need to come."

"Um . . ." I shouldered my beach bag. "I don't know."

Will kicked at the grass, shook his head.

"Chantal doesn't really go to parties." I didn't tell them that I didn't, either.

I don't think he meant for me to see, but I witnessed Will jab Parker in the ribs with his elbow.

"But Jillian, we'll play Cranium," Parker said. "Chantal kicked ass at it in career and life management class last year. Remember?"

"Cranium." Will nodded his satisfaction. "It'll be fun. I love that game."

"Well, maybe if there's Cranium. I'll have to see." I searched the ground to make sure I hadn't left anything behind.

"You have to come," Will said. "Both of you."

"I gotta go." I turned for a final potentially meaningful look with Parker, waved good-bye, and headed for my bike with a plan to go to Chantal's house.

For a second, or maybe less, I wondered why Will was suddenly so interested in Chantal. Maybe his torture tactics were his way of saying "I liked you all along."

Chantal

· · · · · ·

Tantrum.

The television numbs my pain. Maybe TV viewing could be my solo summer project. I flip through the channels: soap opera, soap opera, game show, news about a war, old movie, gardening, cop show, cop show, building, redecorating. I think I'm hungry. One smushed cupcake remains in the plastic cello case, the silver balls askew. The chocolate crumbs that litter my chest provide more evidence that I am not allergic to cupcakes. I need to develop some sort of aversion, though, or I'll be shopping for a one-piece bathing suit with a skirt attached to it by the end of the summer.

A few hours of TV might successfully blur the image of Parker and Jillian. How she sucked in her stomach, swept the hair from her face, blushed when he said, "Hey." Will looked my direction a few times as if he thought I would suddenly welcome attention from someone who has always taunted me.

Blood pulses in my head, acute, dangerous. I'm like my mother; I want to keep things inside until I can't bear it. I can't. I want to do something, like smash a hole in a wall, kick in a door—hurt myself. Or maybe, swear.

"Shit," I yell.

"Damn.

"Shit.

"Shit.

"Shit."

It feels phony, like words filtered through a swimming pool of Jell-O. The words become squiggly, laughable. Me. This would be hilarious for anyone but me.

Damn.

My life plan is a series of photos: next year, my valedictorian picture will be on the front page of the newspaper, in color, with the red of my lip gloss an exact match of the red graduation robe (this is important, according to Jillian). Four years after that, it will be a Harvard hat and tassel in crimson. By the time I'm thirty, it will be a picture of Jillian and me in front of the United Nations in New York. We'll be doing important work in the most exciting city on the planet. (She picked the city and I picked the job—neurosurgeons committed to world health.) I can't live in New York without Jillian. She is my GPS.

Damn.

"Get your life together," I yell out loud, to myself, I guess.

I am able to move my right pointer finger.

"Screw Will."

My wrist flickers.

"Screw Parker."

I create a fist, open it.

"Jillian is *my* friend."

My arm moves. I have achieved flexibility.

The TV kitchen is painted a light gray and pastel blue, visual pain relief. Ceramic bowls sparkle with precisely measured ingredients. I reach for the final cupcake, free it from its paper liner. Let the taste of chocolate soothe me. The woman on TV with dark flowing hair and a British accent is in love with her blue bowls. Or cooking. Her hands float over the bowls, grip them delicately as she pours the contents into her mixing bowl. Caresses butter, sugar, and vanilla with her white spatula.

"Baking is one of the sheer delights of being alive," she says. "A chocolate cake is a sensual delight of chocolate that melts in one's mouth and infuses the soul with happiness."

The woman, I'm sure now, is obsessed with food, maybe even more than I am with grades. With my future.

The woman giggles, a deep throaty sound, as she pours the mixture into three cake pans, tells me the oven temperature, the way to test for doneness. How can anyone love to cook that much? My mother complains that it's a chore designed to keep women tied to the home, but I know that it's because she hates any mess and she's terrified of ingesting more than twelve hundred calories per day. I suspect her figure is one of the reasons I'm an only child.

"One taste of this fudgy delectable and your guests will swoon. It's that perfect."

I wonder if I'll find any organic dark chocolate bars in my mother's secret stash. I start at the cupboard above the refrigerator.

The memory of Jillian's face, her sharp blue eyes observing me, judging me, appears on the cupboard doors. I open the cupboard and her voice pipes up, "Come on, Chantal, it's not a big deal. They only want to sit here."

I dig for chocolate behind spices and boxes of salt and cornstarch. Maybe my mother hides her treats in a different place each time hoping she'll forget where she hid them.

I imagine what I looked like, my towel and sunscreen clutched to my chest, covering my one-piece as if I was afraid I was going to be attacked. Scared. Pathetic.

Damn.

Behind the bag of wild rice, I find the chocolate bar. It's mocha flavored and I don't drink coffee, but I'm still happy for the treasure. I unwrap the chocolate, admire the perfectly lined-up squares.

I remember, now, how I heard Jillian's voice call my name, more than once.

Breathe.

I break off two squares of cocoa, fat, and sugar, and slip them onto my tongue, trying to imitate the dark-haired woman on TV, letting my taste buds do their job on the brown molecules that dissipate, dissolve. This. Is. Relief. At least for the next six ounces.

Jillian

· · · · · ·

Choices.

*N*ow I push my bike along our street. The chain fell off after I left Chantal's house. Chantal says she's giving me her old bike, which is five years newer than mine, when she gets a new one. That's the least of what might not happen now.

Chantal wouldn't even come to the door when I knocked. I could hear the television blaring. I looked in the window and saw her on the couch, but she ignored me. I tried to walk in, but she'd locked the door.

It's 86 degrees outside and I'm pushing my bike. If it had been any other day, I'd have taken her bike and left mine in its place—she would know why and she wouldn't care, not at all. If her mom complained that I was always borrowing her stuff, she'd say, "She's my sister."

Girls like Chantal know they can have whatever they want and can be whatever they want to be. They come from families with two parents who work, where the parents believe their happiness is dependent on the success of their children. Girls like Chantal aren't allowed to fall or fail.

Girls like me are different.

Girls like me know that wishing on our birthday candles will not result in the delivery of a horse, that lists for Santa should be short and that most conversations our mothers start begin, "I need you to help me." Girls like me know that our parents are never going to come to our rescue, no matter how much we hope.

I'm pushing the piece of crap that Dad 2 rescued from the landfill. He replaced the brakes and the front wheel and told me I was worth his time to fix it up. Dad 2 put in lots of time; he cleaned the house and took the triplets to hockey. He's the one who started calling them the Hat Trick, referring to when a hockey player scores three goals in one game. "I got myself a Hat Trick," Dad 2 said the night the boys were born as he handed me a cigar. "Now, save that until you're older. And don't tell your mother I gave it to you."

When the twins were born he took parental leave from the railroad to take care of them. But when his nine months were up he didn't go back to work as a brakeman. He decided he'd worked as a union man since he was seventeen and he needed a life. My mom threw him out once she realized the life he wanted was smoking pot all day long. She says she told him he could come back if he was clean and had a job. Dad 2 said things were so screwed he couldn't live with us anymore. He moved to Vancouver. I wonder if he ever runs into Dad 1 there.

Our street is downtown now. We had to move from Columbia once Dad 2 wasn't making any money. It's okay. The houses are close together, but we live on a dead end, so the boys have a place to set up their hockey nets. It makes it easier to babysit a set of seven-year-old triplets, almost-three-year-old twins, and a one-year-old. Chantal and I chill under the tree and read or do our projects while the boys run around with hockey sticks and eat popsicles. Chantal says the time between diaper changes is great. But everyone's favorite part of the summer is the end, when we put on our summer project performance. Despite the boys booing our flatland synchronized swimming last year, they loved watching us, being part of something that felt like a real family thing, minus the parents. We made lemonade and cookies and we had music, and those flippers and our nose plugs. I couldn't breathe, I was laughing so hard.

I remember the look on Chantal's face right before she ran away. Then I remember the way Parker looked at me, the way no one else has, and I wonder if I was imagining it. "Maybe we can go for ice cream tomorrow," he said when he met me at the bottom of the hill as I was getting on my bike. I told him I'd have to take the boys with me because I was babysitting. "No problem," he said.

But it is a problem. What happens when he finds out who I really am?

Parker

· · · · · ·

Keeping Score.

"Dude. You're serious? You're going to her house tomorrow? And taking her baby posse out for ice cream?" Will holds out his fist.

I make sure we're alone before I pound it. "You got a man challenge, you gotta send a man to do it." I watch Will as the words register. The comment is fresh meat for a starving piranha.

"Dude." Will throws his towel at my head but I catch it, throw it back at him. "Don't go thinking you got one up on me. We handicapped this one, remember?" As predicted. If he wasn't my best friend he'd probably say he wanted to kick my ass.

"Right. When I'm winning it's all about luck." I click the automatic unlock on my key. The Mustang clicks in response. "Who remembered Cranium? Brilliant. Say it, Will. Brilliant."

"Whatever." Will opens the passenger side door. "I'm laying it out there. It's going to be harder for me to kiss my target than it is for you. Not that I'm bitching. 'With the greatest effort comes the greatest reward.'"

I tune out Will as I slide the key in the ignition. Jillian in the bikini. It's like I never really saw her until today. And, damn, she's fit.

"Dude, are you listening to me?" Will interrupts my private movie. "You know who said that, don't you?"

Sometimes I'd like Will to shut up. "Said what?"

"'With the greatest effort comes the greatest reward.'"

"Gandhi."

"Shit, no. Mario Andretti, man."

The engine growls when I start it up. Satisfaction. "Andretti?"

Will nods his head, turns up the volume, and the car rumbles with hip-hop.

"Yes you can. Yes you can," Will shouts to the radio. He lowers the window, and hangs his arm outside. I think he's making the Mario Andretti thing up because Will's like that. Meh.

Even if I get Chantal to the party, and Will works his magic, I know I'm definitely ahead on this challenge.

Sunroof open. Radio on. I wonder if kissing Jillian will be much different than kissing Annelise.

I check my reflection in the rearview mirror—hair, sunglasses, and a smile.

"No kidding," Will says. "That was funny."

He thinks he knows what I'm thinking.

"Damn." He slaps the side of the car for effect. "That Chantal can *run.*"

Chantal

· · · · · ·

Hope.

As my chocolate euphoria crashed and my dejection descended a million times deeper than Cinderella's, I Googled "British TV chef" until I found her. Nigella Lawson. Despite the absence of magic wands or spells, I knew minutes later that Nigella was my virtual savior.

It was the episode of "Totally Chocolate Chip Cookies" that convinced me that she had been waiting for me.

Nigella: (Close-up of her concerned face with those killer eyebrows and hair that's a little out of control.) You've probably guessed that was a sobbing girlfriend on the phone.

How does she know?

Nigella: A small bit of tea and sympathy is required.

I love Earl Grey. With milk. And a shot of vanilla syrup.

Nigella: But I think an express batch of chocolate chip cookies will administer all the comfort that's required. (Her voice as smooth and husky as a full moon in September.)

Therapeutic baking. Of course. I don't have to eat it to feel better, I just have to create it. Like being a mother to myself.

Jillian

. . . . . .

Home.

I push my bike though the mess in our front yard. The toy cars Dad 2 picked up at a garage sale, the hockey sticks Dad 3 complains about taping, the goalie nets that lean sideways, and the hockey padding that reeks.

I hear the boys although I can't see them when I walk in the house. They must be in their rooms on time-out or put-yourselves-to-bed duty. All I want is a glass of ice water and a fan blowing on me, but I have to face Mom first, without revealing that Chantal's mad at me or that I have made consistent eye contact with Parker.

I realize, when I see them from across the room, that I didn't need to worry about them picking up on anything I was thinking. Mom and Dad 3 are at separate ends of the couch. Kid toys litter the space between them. They each have a short glass with a single ice cube. It's Thursday and Mom is cutting loose.

"Jillian," she says. "I thought you'd be home at dinner. Had to do it all myself." She takes a drink, her hand moving sloppily toward her mouth, the glass dipping, slipping, before it reaches the arm of the couch again. It's clear this isn't a routine Thursday night.

I remind her that today was the last day of school and the first day of summer holidays and I went out to the lake, like always. My nerves twitch. "What did you eat?"

"Tacos," Dad 3 says. "Again."

"Everyone eats tacos. That's the important thing." Mom picks between her front teeth with her pinky nail. "And hamburger is cheap."

I wait for the conversation to continue or end, and subject myself to watching Mom and Dad 3 exchange slanted glares. Something is going down.

"Well, I . . . uh . . . need to go to bed." And get out of this room. "I'm on kid duty tomorrow, right?" I know Mom is working this weekend and Dad 3 spends his days off with "the boys," but he means the guys from work. Maybe only one of the six boys sleeping upstairs is *his,* but the Hat Trick and Double Minor think they belong to him, too. The only men Mom seems to marry are the ones who love their man friends as much as they love her.

"About that." Dad 3 leans forward, and I notice, again, how ugly facial hair is—bushy eyebrows, mustache, beard stubble. I don't share my mother's taste in men and I see that as a positive sign for my future. Dad 3 drains his drink, wipes his lips with the back of his hand. "I'm heading out of town . . . for . . . a while. And you'll need to be helping your mother out a bit more."

Not again. The tone of his words, too familiar, carries all his apologies: I always liked you, thought you were such a good kid, you've got a real promising future, if you ever need anything you can call me. I stare at Mom. How can she pick the same guy over and over?

"He's visiting his brother." Mom shrugs as if the end result of his talk doesn't matter.

"In Vancouver, right?" I force myself to keep my voice steady, keep eye contact.

Mom lasts exactly three heartbeats before she drains her glass.

Dad 3 goes on about how he's going to do the electrical and the plumbing on some house for his brother. "He's flipping it. You know what that is, don't you?" His energy increases as he talks about his freedom. "You buy low, fix it up, and sell high." He doesn't realize how ironic his words are, how he's not impressing me, how anything worthwhile he's done in the past two years is shit now, how when Chantal asks me about Dad 3, I'll tell her the asshole left.

I walk past the couch, up the six stairs that lead to our bedrooms.

"Jillian," he calls. "Jillian."

"Let her go," my mom says. "I told you she wouldn't understand."

I undress and pull my old T-shirt over my head, all thoughts of the past few hours gone. I climb into bed and squish my body against the wall. I know Mom will be camping out on the other half of my bed tonight.

Chantal

. . . . . .

Chocolate Chip Hope.

The world is full of words.

"These wonders are quite good at mopping up tears," Nigella says as she melts the chocolate for her chocolate chocolate chip cookies.

I watched an hour of her videos before I decided to make them. I wrote out the list of ingredients and biked to the grocery store. The money came from my savings account—money my parents award me for great grades. I've been saving for a long time, waiting for a reason to spend it. My mother would choke on her coffee if she knew I was spending her reward money on fat and sugar. Muffins are the only thing I've ever baked with my mother, and only for school bake sales or to give away at Christmas. But I can do this on my own. I'm good at following directions.

We don't have a mixer—my mother says doing it by hand burns more calories—so I cream the butter with the brown sugar and white sugar the way my mother taught me, with a wooden spoon. I measure out flour, cocoa, baking soda, and salt into a bowl. I add vanilla, then the melted chocolate into the butter mixture. An egg and the flour mixture landslide on top of the creamed butter and I stir with the wooden spoon. The surprise ingredient is two packages of chocolate chips. Thankfully, my mother is working. Probably until late.

I drop the batter onto the cookie sheet and eighteen minutes later, I have my first batch of what Nigella calls "top-class comfort."

• • •

I hope the cookies will be the words I don't know how to say to Jillian. This is what I think as I pedal my bike to her house the next day with a shoebox of Totally Chocolate Chip Cookies in my bike basket. One taste will make her cry with gratitude, Nigella assures.

I'm hoping the pound of chocolate chips, a molten lake of chocolate, butter, and sugar will prove I'm a loyal friend and will say, I'm sorry I'm unchangeable and a lifelong nerd. Even if the guys are a mistake, my friendship with Jillian is more important. At about twenty chocolate chips per cookie, it cost me three A's to make them, but Nigella says she doesn't put a price on alleviating human suffering. I can't, either.

Jillian

Friday.

I've picked up the phone to call Chantal a dozen times. I know she'd have good advice, but I don't want her to know. It's happening. Again. My mother is sending away another guy.

I imagine her telling her parents at the dinner table, after they've talked through their workday and asked Chantal about the last day of school. When Chantal says, "Jillian's Dad Three took off," her mother would say, "Poor Jillian. Not again." I know her mom mostly likes me, but she also sees me as a charity case. When Chantal and I were the same size, she'd buy extra jeans and shirts and claim that she couldn't take them back.

We don't have dinner conversations at our house. At our house eating happens at kitchen counters, in front of the TV, or standing up because the last chair is already taken. Dinner at my house is a pot of goulash—pasta, ground meat, and sauce—and mismatched bowls and plates with plastic forks if there aren't any clean metal ones. Or cereal. Or pancakes. Or peanut butter and jelly sandwiches.

My mom and Dad 3 don't talk about their work, because they don't have work, they have jobs. A job is a place where you report and put in your time until it's over. Work, my life management teacher explained, is when your brain is engaged and the effort has a reward that has meaning beyond a paycheck.

One night Dad 3 told us, after a few beers, that no one in his family had ever gone to college. "I'd be real honored to help pay to get you there," he said. "'Cause, let's face it, that's what you do for family." My mom teared up and said that karma was what had brought them together.

But what will happen now that Dad 3 is leaving? Chances are my mother will go after him for child support for baby Ollie. Chances are he'll move on to another woman, another child, and he'll decide all he can afford to pay is what the law requires. And that will never be enough for a university education.

I try to stop that thought right there. I try to remember that Parker is coming over and he likes me enough to take my brothers and me out for ice cream. I need to make a good first impression so I shove the toys into the closet, run the vacuum cleaner, make sure the boys take baths, and that they put on clean underwear.

Chantal

· · · · · ·

The Effects of Chocolate.

My pointer finger hovers above Jillian's doorbell. I'm not sure I'm going to ace this test. But one thing I (as top student) battle and overcome successfully is test fear. I press the button, hold my breath, and wait for Jillian to open the door.

"Chantal!" She smiles, reaches out to hug me. Clearly this test is multiple-choice. Or true-false.

"Surprise!" I lift the shoebox lid. The aroma of chocolate slips between us. She stares at the cookies. The chocolate chocolate calls her, begs her to taste. As the first bite dissolves in her mouth I watch her shock give way to gratitude. *Oh Nigella, thank you.*

"Oh . . . these are good. Wow. They taste. Homemade." She eats more sugar than I've seen her consume in the last three months. Success. One hundred percent. A-plus. Finally, she speaks. "I stopped by your house. I tried to call you."

"I wanted to surprise you."

"Wow. Wow." She hesitates, as if she's not sure what to do with me.

"Wow is right." I nod my head. Something is wrong.

"Hey . . . come in," she says. As we walk through the living room and into the kitchen I tell Jillian I've never seen her house this clean.

The Double Minor and Ollie are down for a nap and she's paying the Hat Trick to do extra chores. She warns me not to open any closet doors. I notice she's wearing shiny eye shadow and one of the tight T-shirts her Vancouver cousin sent her. We sit at the counter stools in the kitchen, drinking tall glasses of reduced-calorie iced tea.

"So, what's up?" I reach into the box for a cookie.

She hesitates before she confesses, "I didn't know you were coming over. Parker . . ."

I almost choke as I realize, now, that the cookies aren't about alleviating Jillian's suffering. They're here to fix mine. And even with their molten chocolate lake and half-kilo of chips, they will not win Jillian back. She attempts to assure me that going for ice cream is not a real date. She even offers the ultimate insult to a dateless friend. "You can come, too. I mean, it's like a friend thing anyway."

"You, Parker, and me?"

"The boys are coming, too."

I spew chocolate crumbs across the counter. "Parker knows he's taking six boys under eight to get ice cream? He's agreed to it?"

She nods. "I know. Weird, huh?"

We chew awkwardly.

I consider the clues: the clean house, the eye shadow, the T-shirt, and the way she half-whispers his name as if it's a secret password to another life. I evaluate potential courses of action: tell Jillian to choose between Parker and my cookies and me, or accept that the three of us will be a triangle. Parker or no Parker, my life is, now, officially, different. I don't need this kind of transformation. I wonder if I will ever make cookies again.

"Your mother baked these?"

"My mother?"

She must see the look of incredulity on my face. "What was I thinking? Farmers' market, right? Your mom's allergic to fat and calories."

"Yeah, out to lunch on that one." I avoid eye contact and start in on my third cookie. Now I can't tell her I baked them. It will reveal my desperation.

We hear Ollie babbling through the baby monitor, and Jillian checks the clock again. She notes that Parker is supposed to be here in five minutes and she smoothes her T-shirt, fluffs her hair. She doesn't mention the irony of filling a baby bottle as part of date preparation.

"At least he's cute." I sweep chocolate crumbs from the counter into my hand.

She sets down the can of formula, turns to me.

"At least he's cute? Parker? What are you trying to say?"

"Jillian." I wave a cookie in the air to subtly remind her of my loyalty and friendship. "Parker dumped Annelise because he wanted to be free for the summer and then, *the same day,* he brings Will to meet us at the lake? Doesn't that sound . . . calculated? Something's not adding up."

We hear Ollie throwing his board books and teddy bears from his crib. In less than two minutes he'll be screaming.

"I guess. Or maybe he's liked me for a long time, but he's now got up the courage to act. Maybe Will's strange behavior has been masking his keenness for you."

"His keenness." She makes me laugh even when we're in a quasi-argument.

She screws the top onto Ollie's bottle. "They discovered they like us, two cute and smart girls. Isn't that even a little bit plausible?" Baby Ollie is punctual. His screams vibrate through the monitor. Jillian rolls her eyes. "I've got to get him before he finds a way to climb out of his crib."

Scientists have proven that chocolate affects your brain function. This much chocolate must be having a major impact on me. "Let me do it," I say, reaching for the bottle.

"Chantal, he needs his diaper changed."

"I can do it." I free the bottle from her hand. "And you can go with Parker."

"What? First you bring cookies and now you're going to change a diaper?" Her skepticism is far too visible. "And you *want* me to go out with the best friend of your sworn enemy?"

"You need to know if Parker's the real macaroni and the only way you'll know that is to go out with him." And I'll never win in a debate with Jillian, she's that good.

"Chantal, you're mad." She's got that concerned look on her face. I wonder if she thinks I'm angry or crazy.

Ollie's screams reach a new decibel level.

"I'll stay home with the boys."

"Stay home with the boys?" Jillian's expression changes to dismay. "No. No. You don't have to. I mean . . . you're not really . . ."

"Capable?"

"I wasn't going to say that. But, you've never watched them alone."

I remind her that the boys will lose it if they have to watch her shut the door behind her. My child psychology impresses her enough that she grabs her purse, zips up her hoodie, and walks out the door. The boys still scream, of course, because they're hungry and I'm only a notch above incompetent. But I have a secret weapon: Totally Chocolate Chip Cookies.

Jillian

. . . . . .

Falling.

*P*arker swings his key chain, catches it, swings it, and catches it as he walks up the driveway. He smiles a Prince Charming sort of smile, doesn't break eye contact. This is something new for me. Mom's boyfriends always seem to be staring at her body parts instead of her eyes.

"Hey." I meet him halfway up the driveway. "It's just us. Chantal is babysitting the boys."

"Really?" His eyes telegraph that it's great. "Not that I didn't want to hang out with the boys, but now, I get you all to myself."

"Um . . ." All to himself? Is that a pickup line?

"So . . . what would you like to do?" He swings his car keys, catches them.

"Drive."

"Just drive?"

"Yeah." I hope I sound enthusiastic because my stomach twists as I get into the car. I have never been in a car with a guy, alone. Much less a guy like Parker.

"Where do you want to go?" Parker slips the key into the ignition, presses the clutch, and eases the gearshift into first.

"Anywhere." I wish I hadn't looked out the window at our house. I see what he must have seen when he pulled up—a landfill of toys. I want to haul it all into the backyard, wipe away the evidence of my responsibilities. The ones that are going to escalate when Dad 3 moves out.

Parker heads toward Airport Road where the houses thin out and the world becomes less complicated.

Now it's like I'm in a bathtub, floating, the only place I've ever been left alone for more than fifteen minutes. I lean back, stare into the sky through the open sunroof. It's all evergreen branches and thin clouds, a hue of blue happiness. The radio is a background beat, easy rock, the only music station in the mountains. I'm thinking about Chantal saying I need to find out if Parker is the real deal. I steal a look at him.

He drives with his hand at the top of the steering wheel, his muscles perfectly sculpted in a tight T-shirt. My unfolding heart floats.

I should be talking, I guess, about people at school and classes and summer plans, but I'm not. All I think is, *thank you for rescuing me*, and any girl knows words like that will scare a guy off as fast as *I come from very reproductive genes*.

We drive twelve miles along Airport Road to a break in the trees. Here, at Twelve Mile Flats, we park in the open field that stretches into mud in the summer, floods with glacier water in the spring, and is buried in snow, of course, every winter.

Parker hangs his left arm out the window, his sunglasses set in his blond tips, and his eyes on mine. He is gorgeous, an undiscovered movie star. Would it be seductive for me to add a layer of lip gloss? "Have you been out here snowmobiling?" he asks.

"Snowmobiling? No." Wouldn't he know that? I'm not part of the party group.

"No, huh? We get a bonfire going and we drag race down the flats. It's great."

"Sounds like fun." I am tempted, but I don't go into my Cinderella story—that the only drag racing I've witnessed is my half-brothers on their sleds—because, again, no guy wants to hear all your problems on the first date.

This is a date, isn't it? And it could be the first of a few dates or many, maybe a whole summer of bonfires with s'mores and the stars, someone playing the guitar. "The sky would be incredible," I say more to myself than to him.

"You should come out sometime . . . you know . . . with everyone. You have to experience it. Just once anyway." He sucks in his breath a little as if he's worried he assumed that we'd have a sometime.

I like that he's nervous. And that he wants to include me.

"Man, what is it like with all those brothers?"

"You don't really want to know."

"Hey, look." Parker points at a hawk flying. We watch it swoop down and when it lifts again, a mouse dangles from its talons. "Cool, eh?" Does he watch *National Geographic*, too?

"Tell me about you," I say. "What do you do besides study physics with Will, snowmobile, and drive your car?" And date Annelise.

He gives me the CliffsNotes version of two parents, three astonishingly successful older brothers, and a grandma and grandpa out east. He loves the mountains, he says, even the snow. The summary? A life that is uncomplicated. We don't have that in common. I wish I hadn't asked.

Chantal

· · · · · ·

Fallout.

*Y*ou do what you have to for friends, but sometimes it's too much.

Inside of fifteen minutes of Jillian leaving, the Hat Trick and Double Minor masticated through two dozen of my secret weapon cookies. Then they devised a plan to find their favorite toys—which turned out to be at the back of every closet in the house.

Around then, the chocolate high crashed. Any ideas of playing duck, duck, goose or tic-tac-toe or having family fun time quickly disappeared. I had to confiscate every electronic gaming device the Hat Trick owned before they realized I was serious when I said they could not use Stevie as a rock in their made-up game of "boulder toss." Things were beginning to calm down until I found them using Josh as a human shield. Eventually I ordered them to brush their teeth and get into bed. It's only 7 P.M., an hour earlier than their usual bedtime.

Now, baby Ollie is heavy on my lap and my right leg has fallen asleep, but his eyes are drooping. He's drunk on the fourth bottle of formula or exhausted from my inadequate care. I need to wait it out. My whole life. Wait it out.

Twenty minutes pass with me lost in my thoughts of revenge against Parker for taking Jillian away. I memorize the scratches on the table, the whorls in Ollie's hair.

"More crackers?" Stevie tugs on my arm. He's out of bed. I look down. His pajama pants are soaked.

But he's wearing a nighttime diaper.

I want to say, "Change your own pants," but I'm not a mean baby-sitter.

"Wait," I say. "I'll put Ollie to bed and then we'll clean you up." I scoot back from the table. Ollie's eyelids flutter. I slide on my socks toward the stairs. Until I hit a puddle.

My sock is soaked. Who peed this much? No. The puddle is a lake. And the lake is at the end of a river that slides down the stairs. It must start in the bathroom where a tap is open and a sink is stoppered.

I hear it then, laughter, the Hat Trick doubled over and high-fiving each other. Josh and Stevie slosh through the puddle. Ollie squirms, his peaceful face scrunches.

This is what happens when I don't pay attention. I simply go along until some catastrophe hits. Crud. I am not a disaster specialist; I freak out when I stub my toe and it bleeds. Here, I've got six kids, one flood. This is too much. Far too much.

I want to leave baby Ollie in his crib. Leave a package of crackers on the table and walk out the door. I am an only child.

Jillian

······

Competition.

If there is one thing I am not, it's a girl like Annelise. I'm not going to ditz around with the whole how-much-do-you-like-me cutesy talk. I'm not going to write his name on the inside of my notebooks. I'm not going to imagine getting married in the first month that we're going out. I am definitely not, ever, going to give him my locker combination so that he can store his things in my locker. That is only one step below letting him keep his toothbrush in your bathroom! And, although I've never had a conversation with a guy about his intentions, I'm not above imagining it. After all, with a mother like mine plus the imminent departure of Dad 3, I am the only one who will be looking out for my virginity.

I get out of the car before he can slide over the stick shift and kiss away my resolve to figure him out. He follows my lead and we lean against the trunk drinking our bottles of water. I wonder if he's calculating his next move. I wonder which one of us will speak next, what we'll say, how I can determine if Parker is playing me. Normally I am stuck trying to negotiate around six brothers, or preparing to score points in a debate. Both skills, Chantal says, require serious strategic thinking. And thinking is one of the things I do best. That, and running.

"Let's race." I set my empty water bottle on the hood of the car.

"Race? As in run?"

"Yeah. To the first pine tree and back." I point to where we left the road to drive onto the flats.

"You're serious?" He tightens his shoelaces, untucks his shirt from his jeans. "What does the winner get?" He grins.

"The winner gets . . . to decide that when she wins." I stretch into a lunge.

"Winner's choice?" Parker jogs in place. "Okay. Hey. I'll spot you three seconds. I'm on the track team, you know."

"I don't need a head start."

We yell, "Ready. Set. Go!" and within a few seconds I'm behind by at least five strides. The distance increases by half before the turn at the pine tree. Parker slips going around the tree, though, and ends in a face plant. I jump over him and keep running.

"You okay?" I yell back. A second later I hear footsteps through the weeds and I know he's out to win. Unfortunately, the race isn't long enough for him to gain back the distance. I slap the car a second before he reaches it.

"If I hadn't fallen, I'd have beat you," he gasps.

"Oh, so that's how you play." I walk off the trembling in my legs. "A race isn't only about who is fastest. There's strategy, like knowing you have to slow down or risk falling at the turn."

"Point taken. You beat me on strategy and I beat you on speed."

I remind him that the race rules were straightforward: first one to the car wins.

"Okay. Okay." He holds up his hands. "You won. So, *winner,* what do you want?"

"Hmm . . ." I close my eyes as if I'm trying to decide what to choose, but I already know. "You have to answer one question. Total truth."

"Um . . ." Parker wipes the sweat off his upper lip with the edge of his T-shirt. Flashes me his abs. I think about changing what I want for my prize.

"It won't be too personal. I promise."

"All right. All right."

"Are you and Annelise finished?" I see the look of confusion on Parker's face and I almost regret asking. "I . . . um . . . I need to know." A good debater knows when to stay silent. If I offered my points, I'd reveal the one that embarrasses me most. My mother always seems to "overlap" boyfriends. I don't want to be the overlapped girl.

He takes a step closer and I lift my chin to look in his eyes. "I've changed my status—I am in no way dating Annelise. We don't talk on the phone and we don't text each other." Oh how I've always wanted this moment. It would be perfect if he'd reach his hand up and cradle my face and lean down and . . .

"You look like you need more water."

Was I that obviously hot?

Parker takes his time opening the trunk, pulling out two bottles of water, handing me one, going back to close the trunk.

"Okay, *winner.* Any more questions?" This feels so comfortable, so right. I think I could ask him anything.

"Well . . . no . . . okay . . . maybe one. What's up with Will? Is he really interested in Chantal?"

"Uh . . ." He fumbles the cap of his water bottle. Between long drinks, he answers my question. "It's . . . okay. We're best friends. Will and me. We do things together. And I . . . I . . . *picked you* . . . as the girl I wanted to go out with. And of course, Chantal is your best friend. And Will is mine. So that made sense." He nods that he's finished, but I don't say anything. "Does that answer your question?"

Let's face it. I stopped listening to everything past the words, "I picked you." The prince at the ball asked me to dance. I take a deep breath. If only he would kiss me. Right now. I wait. And wait.

"Hey, are you finished with that?" He points at my unopened water bottle. "It's getting dark. I guess we'd better get back."

And the spell breaks, a little. I become myself again, a girl on a first date with a guy who *picked* her. Total truth.

Parker drives with the sunroof open and the radio low enough that we talk over it. Suddenly we have everything to talk about, school and friends and I even tell him stories about my brothers. Over ice cream he tells me he knows all about brothers. His big brothers liked to play Mafia and since he was the youngest, they ordered him around and when they got bored, they iced him. This is, strangely, so romantic; me wanting my ice cream to stop melting while he tells me stories from when he was little. We don't leave the ice cream place until the stars are out.

When we pull up in front of my driveway, I'm relieved the house is dark and no one will witness a kiss. And at the moment I think that is exactly what's about to happen, Parker says, "You know what would have been the prize if I'd won the race?"

I swallow, and try to avoid showing fear.

"A second date with you."

I bite my bottom lip.

"Can I call you?"

"Sure." I manage to squeak out.

"Mia's party. Okay? I really think we should try to get Chantal and Will together, don't you? I mean it's time for them to uh . . . bury the hatchet."

"I'll talk to her." Before I die inside from all the building tension in every private part of my body, I reach for the door handle. There will be time for a kiss at Mia's party. Now it seems like it's destined.

Chantal

· · · · · ·

Blackout.

I didn't leave. I am not a mean babysitter and I'm not a negligent one, at least I didn't intend to be negligent. I should have known to check on the boys. I know them. They don't find trouble. They define trouble.

Once I discovered the waterfall, I took Ollie upstairs and put him in his crib. He cried. Of course. I turned the water off and pulled every towel from the linen closet, dropped them on the river. I couldn't find clean pajamas for the Double Minor so I stuck them in matching T-shirts and diapers. They ripped them off. I forgot how they hate to match.

"Okay," I said through my gritted teeth. "Then go to bed naked."

Ollie screamed.

I became overwhelmed, frustrated. Actually, I was furious.

Before I could count to ten, my words morphed into weapons, and I became the person I am not. I screamed at the Hat Trick, told them I was going to tell Jillian, their mother, and Dad 3 how awful they'd been.

"It was an accident," Trevor yelled through the door. "We're sorry."

When Stevie and Josh heard my footsteps stop at their door-way, their shadows shivered. I waited to make sure they wouldn't be getting out of their beds, either. Ollie pulled himself up when he saw me, gripped the crib bars. Snot ran from his nose. I gathered an armful of stuffed toys off the floor and dropped them in his crib. "I'll be right back. Stop. Crying."

My T-shirt got soaked from carrying the wet towels down to the basement. I'd never done laundry. I turned the dial a few times. Pushed it in. Pulled it out. Finally something happened. The machine started making noise.

In the kitchen I found dishcloths that sank to the bottom of the lake and I gave up. The water cleanup would have to wait for the towels to dry. My rage began to evaporate as I walked up the stairs to the boys' bedrooms. Guilt flooded in when I checked on the sleeping Hat Trick and Double Minor. Just little kids. Acting like kids. At Ollie's door, I decided I would forgive them all by morning. Then, the lights snapped off.

Ollie screamed, and I rushed to get him before he woke the other boys. I unpeeled his gripped fingers from the rail, and lifted him out. I tried to keep his snot out of my hair. Out the window, I realized the other houses had light. Jillian's was the only one that had lost power. When I was sleeping over a month ago and the lights went out Dad 3 said it was a blown breaker. "Too many demands on the system." He said it was simple to fix; throw the switch in the breaker box, in the basement. I didn't know how to do it, but I had to do something. I told Jillian I could handle this.

"It's okay, Ollie. It's okay." My legs shook as I leaned against the wall on my way down the stairs. Shock. I was in shock. I shoved action figures and plastic blocks off the couch, sat on the middle cushion. Ollie buried his face in the curve of my neck. I'd given up on the snot, smeared from my collar to my earlobe. His breath began to soothe my splintered nerves and I tried to match his breathing. In. Out. In. Out. Until I was calm enough to think. Evaluate.

Everything I know about real families, about yelling and scream- ing, and mistakes that are quickly forgotten—everything I know about blending in with the rest of humanity—I've learned at Jillian's house. I can't handle it all the time or for very long, but I get the best of both worlds with Jillian.

My mother is a perfectionist and my house is a petri dish for my future success.

It's no wonder that I got frazzled, that I yelled, that I fell apart. It's what I do now that matters, I tell myself. But I can adapt. I can make things better.

First things first, though. I thought I saw a package of mini-cupcakes in Jillian's fridge. A bit of chocolate cake would settle my nerves.

Jillian

· · · · · ·

Home.

I tiptoe into a dark house on princess toes, knowing exactly how Cinderella felt. I slip off my muddy shoes, reach for the light switch, stop. I imagine what his kiss would have been like, the soft lips and the slightest scratch from his facial hair. *Oh.* A rush of *I want* warms me.

"Jillian?"

"Chantal?" I snap back to the real world. A light beam shines from the top of the basement stairs. "What's going on?"

"Unnatural disaster." The headlamp she's wearing is mine, bought for our camping trip last summer. I thought it was buried in one of the hall closets.

"The breaker went?"

"After the flood." She nods. "And every time the machine gets going too fast. I was about to go down and throw it again."

"Huh?" I'm stunned. I follow Chantal down the basement stairs, over to the breaker box. She stands on a step stool and throws the switch.

"*Voilà! Lumiere!*"

Now that the light is on, I see Chantal's splotchy red cheeks and wide pupils, the T-shirt that's stretched and dirty, and the wild hair scrunched like a muffin top by the headlamp elastic. "What have you been doing? Where are the boys?" I press my hand against her forehead. No fever. But she looks . . . I'm going to have to help her.

"You're not going to believe it, Jillian. I am almost too good to be true." She tells me the evening's events starting with a frenzy of cookie eating, through to the flood, and her meltdown.

"Oh, Chantal. I'm so sorry." And if Will doesn't go for Chantal, where does that leave me? On the curb. Annelise will be drinking the other bottle of water.

"No. No. It's okay. Because I was sitting there, doing my times tables in my head and then, it came to me. I could fix this."

"You could fix what . . ." All of this seems so unimportant. My real life must be outside all of *this*; this house, my family, even school. My real life doesn't belong here. At least I don't think it does. If only I can convince Chantal we fit in somewhere else.

I follow her up the stairs and she begins the tour of how she's washed the main floor (the result of sopping up a lake of water) and, what's more, gone on to improve upon my system of shoving everything in closets by sorting the toys into piles of Trash Now, Trash Later, or Probably Trash Later. Plastic garbage bags wait by each pile.

"And Jillian . . ." she continues. "Before the power went out I was on the Internet and I downloaded the application for *Extreme Home Organizer.* You totally need to do this. I mean really, a set of triplets, a set of twins, and a baby, and they're all boys! If they pick you they send you off to Disneyland while they clean and organize your house for you."

"We can't go on a reality TV show. If my mother saw how pitiful we were on TV, she'd move away and I'd have to raise the boys by myself. Seriously." I sit at the kitchen counter, spotlessly clean, and wonder what I'm going to do now. My best friend has gone crazy.

"Okay, we can rule out the TV show. But, Jillian, this is totally something we can do ourselves. Organize your house. *This* can be our summer project. We can do the toys tonight and—"

I groan. "Whoa. Whoa. Whoa." I pull the headlamp off her head. I may have to call her dad for an intervention.

She smiles. "Gotcha!"

I miss a complete heartbeat before I catch on. "Chantal. I was beginning to believe . . ."

"I know. Scary, huh? I thought you were going to figure it out. There's no show called *Extreme Home Organizer.*"

"But the flood? And the power blackout?" She nods and tells me the order of tasks to come. We need to bag up the toys and label the bags and we've got a couple loads of towels to fold and put away. As she's telling me all this I can't help but wonder if she's becoming her mother—a woman who seems to think purpose equals endless productivity. "But you didn't have to do all this. You could have left it for me. It was enough that you babysat."

"I had to fix it, Jillian. I imagined what it would be like for you to come home and find the disaster."

I don't know what to say because I feel strange. I'm not sure I want to team up to fix what really is my mother's problem. Shouldn't we be sitting at the kitchen counter polishing off the rest of the cupcakes? Yet, as Chantal starts bagging the toys into garbage bags I fold towels.

I'm definitely thankful that she cares, but she hasn't even asked about Parker.

Parker

· · · · · ·

The Call.

*M*y cell vibrates in my pocket, for the fifteenth time since 7 P.M. and the fourth time in the last twenty minutes. It can only be one person.

"Will."

"Dude. Where you been?"

"You know where."

"Is she there?"

"Would I be talking to you?"

"Is that a score? Jillian and you? Chantal and me?"

"Snap." It bugs me that I can't stop thinking about her.

"You are the seducterizer, man."

"Yeah, totally." I don't want him to come over, talk out strategy, plot ways in which he can fool Chantal into thinking he actually likes her. Whatever. I'm done for tonight.

"Look. I gotta go. Talk to you tomorrow." I sign off and start the car. I turn up the volume on my electro playlist. I need sound, lots of it. I let out the clutch, press the gas, watch Jillian's house disappear in the rearview mirror. Some guys say the chase is the best part. It probably has to do with how the girls make it seem like we're perfect for each other; they talk about soccer and hockey as if they actually play it. Later though, when we're watching a game, they interrupt as Sedin is about to score, to ask our opinion of their fingernail polish. That's the girl's game: bait and switch. That's what dating is in high school, traps being set. I shouldn't feel guilty. It's nothing personal.

Chantal

Invincible.

I'm feeling a bit fairy godmother meets Martha Stewart's daughter as Jillian and I work alongside each other. It must be obvious to her, now, that I am a valuable friend. Not many friends would baby-sit six boys *and* help clean the house. Even Nigella would be impressed.

I'm labeling the second garbage bag when Jillian stops me.

"Sit." She leans against the wall, sets a stack of towels next to her that, really, she should put away before she takes a break.

"I can put those in the linen closet first."

"Chantal. Sit.

"You haven't asked me about my date." And now I see her face more clearly. That's not exhaustion. She wants more from me than tidy closets.

"Oh. Oh. I got so caught up. Tell me. Is he for real?" I laugh because this is really the only way I'm going to get through this. I mean, I don't want Parker to exist, let alone hear about her date with him.

"I think so," she says.

It's going to take longer than I thought for her to see that a guy will make her life more difficult.

"And Chantal, they want us all to hang out."

Will is Parker's best friend, she says. Parker thinks it makes sense that Will and I would be willing to at least try to get along. She tells me about the party on Saturday at Mia's house. "You have to come. It's a group thing. Totally safe."

Now I have to be entertaining. At a party. With Will as my date.

"You're not talking," Jillian says.

"Did he kiss you?"

She shakes her head.

"But you wanted him to kiss you?"

"I think you need a cupcake." When she returns from the kitchen she's got the rest of the package, a notepad, and a pen. As I eat one cupcake a second, she writes on the notepad. Finished, she slides it towards me:

If a=b and b=c, then also a=c.

"What is transitive relation? Ninth-grade math." If I had a buzzer, I'd have buzzed in.

"So . . ." Jillian says in her sweetest, most patient voice. "If Chantal (a) likes Jillian (b) and Jillian (b) likes Parker (c), then Chantal (a) will also like Parker (c)."

It drives me crazy when she does this.

"He asked me out for a second date. And I want to go. To Mia's party. And I want you to go, too." I read her mind. She feels sorry for me because I am backward. I care more about cleaning up than having fun. What if she's right? This is the wonderful thing about having a best friend like Jillian. She gently leads me through the dark when I am most afraid. And she is my best friend. I know I can trust her.

"Okay. Here are the conditions of my attendance." I try to stay calm even though I know I'm agreeing to something I would never agree to otherwise. "I'll go as long as you *never* leave me alone. *Never.* You go to the bathroom, I go. I need to get some air, so do you. We are together at all times."

"We're going to be at the same party." She laughs until she realizes I'm serious. "Okay. Okay." She crosses to my side of the hallway, lifts a cupcake from the package for each of us, and puts her arm around me. "I'll never leave you."

Will

······

Central Control.

*H*appified. With iPhone in pocket, energy drink in hand, I head up to my room: central control. Parker pulled off part one. Part two and beyond are up to me.

I fire up my laptop, log in on Facebook, and click through to the events page. Saturday Night Smash-Up. I type the words next to event name. Tagline: Everyone is going to be there. Correction: Everyone who needs to be there is going to be there. I add some emoticons the girls like and hit enter. Before I've drained my drink, everyone I've invited will accept, and Saturday night will be smashin'.

My Facebook inbox lights up with confirmed attendances. I text Mia. She texts me, asks if I'm bringing anyone. Chantal, I text. Her text back: WTF!

Chantal and me. The shock on people's faces. Killer. Parker nearly crapped his pants when I proposed the challenge and then ended up with Chantal. He said there was no way I would be able to complete it. We agreed I was handicapped so we made some adjustments to level the playing field. Adjustment one: Parker had to get Jillian to get Chantal on a double date with me. The enemy.

Stupid boy stuff started it, boogers on her arm when she told our third-grade teacher I copied the answers off Parker's math paper. The way she came unhinged was as addictive as shooting grouse in the bush. I've tortured her ever since and she is 100 percent compliant in the freakin' out department. I swear I even missed her during the summer when it was only Parker, lime popsicles, and me.

My mom bought me a bike the summer after fourth grade and I was at Parker's house from after breakfast to dinnertime, hiding out from my father, otherwise known as the Ogre. Parker's mom said I was like brother number five. Becoming blood brothers in the lean-to fort we made in the woods near his house was awesome but expected. The man challenges? Superlative.

Picture it. There we were, blood dripping off our palms because I cut way deeper than I needed to, and I'm saying, "We can't become blood brothers until we have a quest. Like the knights at the roundtable. Or Blackbeard's pirates."

"I think this is bleeding too much," Parker says. I swear his bottom lip was quivering.

"We *have* to have a quest."

We veto ideas of being superheroes or detectives or anything to do with pet sitting. But the more blood we lose, and the more gnats that hover, the more creative we get. It's Parker (I hate to admit it), who comes up with the idea.

Parker, squeezing his forearm because he'd learned about tourniquets in Boy Scouts, says, "Challenges. Kind of like Boy Scout badges, but harder."

I was all in. There was nothing I loved more than proving I was good at something. Our two rules:

1. We each had to complete the same challenge, so you couldn't make up something disgusting that you didn't want to do yourself.
2. When one of us completed a challenge, the other person had seventy-two hours to complete it or they admitted defeat.

And here we are, the end of our junior year, the last summer of challenges. Stats: thirty-nine completions, zero defeats. When we were applying to universities a few months ago we agreed that the challenges would have to end at graduation. Parker never said it but I knew he was thinking he'd end up at university for sure. It's not a done deal for me. I need scholarships. I know I need a plan, but I don't want to screw up my last summer of freedom. I want to have fun.

"Will. Will." My dad shouts. Jesus. What does he want? It's nearly the frickin' middle of the night. He doesn't comprehend that just because he's heading off to work, doesn't mean the neighbors want to be awake, or Mom, or me. He's a boil on the ass of society, my dad.

"Will." The door flies open, hits the wall behind it. I don't move. His voice pierces the room, but I hear it in dulled tones, a selective deafness I've acquired. "Your mother told you to take out the garbage. You think I want to come home to stinking garbage? Or a bear picking through it? You think I'm going to let you go out on Saturday night or do you think I'll be making sure your lazy ass needs to stay home and think about responsibility? When I was your age I was on full-time as a brakeman and you can't even take out the goddamn garbage."

I stare. This is his motivational technique? Work hard so you can be like me. Like I would ever wear a filthy baseball hat pulled way back on my receding hairline. Or striped train overalls bulging at the middle like a pregnant woman's. "I'll take it out." I log off the computer, slip my feet into my sandals.

"And tomorrow you'll mow the lawn right. I don't want to have to clean up your mess."

"Yeah." I stand. I wait for him to clear the doorway and again for him to go into the bathroom so he can't criticize me for carrying the bags wrong or setting them down in a bad spot or breathing incorrectly—in and out instead of out and then in. I drop the garbage, but when I walk in the door he's waiting for me.

"For Christ's sake. You think the neighbors want to see you in your underwear?"

I look down at my plaid boxer shorts. "I don't think they care."

"That's it. Enough of the smart mouth. You're in for the weekend. Don't even think about going out."

"Okay." I turn away.

My mom pretends there's no problem and stays out of trouble's way. I get what I want without anyone knowing. I'll be at the party Saturday night. I've got a challenge to complete.

Chantal

Spectator Sport.

$\mathcal{I}$ have always had a love/hate relationship with Saturday mornings. I love them because I don't have to go to school. I hate them because I'm at home. I wake to the crash of the smoothie machine pulverizing ice cubes, fruit, yogurt, protein powder, and whatever vitamin trends my mother has discovered. Minutes later I'm called to drink the "best start to the weekend" no matter what time I went to bed the night before. Then, the list is presented. Management of the details, Dad tells me when I complain, is part of what keeps your mother happy. We're a family, he adds, so we all pitch in, but I notice he puts his initials on more of the chores and duties than either Mom or me.

My mother lists the day's goals and objectives as I sip at my strawberry and grass-flavored smoothie. I tune out until she gets to the part, "Chantal, I'd like you to join us on our run."

"Run?" She knows I hate to sweat.

"Yes. Your father and I are concerned about your lack of exercise."

"That's not what I said," Dad interrupts. "I said I thought exercise was always a good thing. But I added that Chantal should have some say in what kind of exercise—"

"Right. Anyway Chantal, I'm . . . concerned. I've noticed that your clothes from last year are . . . well, the seams are pulling a bit. I mean . . . do they feel a little tight?"

"Are you trying to tell me I'm getting fat? You know what that does to a teenage girl's self-esteem, right?"

"No. Not. At. All. I'm trying to promote health. Body awareness. Running is good for your heart and your mood. Studies have shown that endorphins you get from running benefit you in all kinds of ways." She turns and I see how her backside fits perfectly in her exercise pants. My dad's got a deflated tire around his waist, something my mom points out when he makes popcorn after dinner. Shouldn't Mom have a bulge or two? Could she be having surgeries on the sly?

"I'm with Dad on this one. I'll pick my own exercise." I see my dad smile as he leans over to tie his running shoes.

"Fine." My mom hands me a sheet of paper. "But make sure you plan for thirty minutes a day. We'll be back in a couple of hours. I'm training for a half-marathon."

"Have fun." I rinse out my smoothie glass and put it in the dishwasher. The only way I'd run a half-marathon was if something was chasing me.

My list requires that I clean my bedroom and bathroom, sort through my summer clothes and create three piles labeled: I Will Wear It, I Might Want To Wear This Someday, and I Will Not Wear This. Didn't I just do this at Jillian's? But that was different, this is just one closet.

I have to find some way to cope with the party and the fact that my mother thinks I'm turning into a chub. So . . . I spend the next half-hour on YouTube with Nigella. Within four videos I find my inspiration.

Nigella: Chocolate and cheesecake are the two things vying for the top spot in the dessert hall of fame.

Impressive. And I like to impress.

I make a list of ingredients. I bike to the grocery store, which is the exercise I chose. There's a difference. And because it's so efficient, I should have enough time to make the cake while they're running.

My laptop is on the kitchen counter. Nigella fills the screen. I thwack the graham crackers into submission, hitting a large plastic bag of them with a rolling pin. I add cocoa and butter to the bag and thwack it some more. It's not until a spray of crumbs hits the floor that I realize there's a hole in the bag. Doesn't extreme heat kill floor germs? My feet crunch. The rescued crumbs form a crust in the springform pan. I press play.

"The second part: the luscious chocolately custardy interior." It's not until I get the packages of cream cheese into the bowl and try to stir them with the wooden spoon that I realize cheesecake must have been invented after electric mixers. Nigella explains that room-temperature cream cheese is essential. How could I have missed that the first seven times I watched the video?

It takes three minutes on low power to get the cream cheese gooey enough to stir. And parts of each block are a bit on the melting side. But it's not like I can start over. And I'm not a quitter. My arm muscles burn as I add sugar, cornstarch, vanilla, and three eggs plus three more yolks. Does this count as exercise, too? I add sour cream. I stir. Stir. Stir. I look at the clock. It's taken me over an hour. I hope they're going for a latte after their run. The lumps are impossible to get smooth and I know Nigella's is perfect and mine is not. I move on.

The chocolate infusion begins with some cocoa dissolved in hot water and a huge pool of melted bittersweet chocolate. I add both ingredients to the cheesecake mixture.

Nigella tells me to fold it patiently and dreamily. I close my eyes and stir. "Sooner or later," she says, "everything gives way to choco-late." I stir and stir and when I open my eyes I realize that my stirring has caused a whirlpool and that the bowl is not large enough to contain it. The chocolate cheesecake filling, though perfectly match-ing Nigella's in color and consistency, runs along the countertop, drips onto the floor, pools with the abandoned crumbs.

I salvage what I can and pour the rest onto the crumb crust. My cheesecake will definitely be shorter than Nigella's, but it will still make a major statement at the party.

I'm so afraid of making another mistake that I play and rewind the next steps several times, wasting precious minutes of time. Finally, I wrap the pan with aluminum foil, set the pan in my mother's deep rectangle dish, add boiling water to halfway up the sides of the cheesecake pan, and set it in the oven. I shut the oven door.

Nigella shows me how to add a Jackson Pollock–inspired chocolate drizzle when the cake has cooled. "A thing of beauty is a joy forever I'm told," she says.

I stare through the oven door feeling hopeful. At least if the party is a failure, I'll have the joy of a cheesecake.

"Chantal. What is going on?" My mother stands next to the refrigerator. Drenched in sweat and breathing hard, she clenches her jaw.

"You look hot. Are you okay?"

"I came back for water."

I reach into the cupboard, take out a glass, and hold it out to her. She doesn't take it, only stands and stares at the mess on the counters, the licked-clean spoon, the baking cheesecake. She doesn't see joy in this kitchen.

"I'll clean it all up. And I paid for all the ingredients myself. And I'm going to bike. An hour a day. Minimum."

"Who is going to eat that?"

"What?" I wish my dad were here to talk some sense into her.

"You can't use my kitchen to make desserts."

"Fine."

• • •

I carry the cheesecake as if I'm bearing the ring pillow up the aisle of a church. Jillian meets me when I'm a block from Mia's house. She points to my chocolate joy. "You didn't make that, did you?"

"What?" I spent all afternoon on this and suffered my mother's weirdness for nothing?

"We're going low-key here, Chantal."

I guess now that Parker's hot for her she's the authority on teen-specific social faux pas. "It's a cake, not a molecular model of caffeine."

"It's like this, Chantal. When we are ourselves in dork mode, they translate that as we are trying too hard for them to like us. They think that we want them to think we're cool." Clearly she's done her research.

"But we don't care if they think we're cool, do we?"

"Not really. No."

"But we're going to the party."

"Exactly. So we need to blend in." Even with her firmness, she is still being my friend. I can respect that. Still . . . there's another side to this argument.

"You don't think that they might enjoy spending time with two people who aren't exactly like them? And for the record, the cake is a charity buy. From the Girl Scouts."

"It's about balance. We want to fit in. Mostly fit in. And bringing a Girl Scout cake is okay. Just smush up the middle a bit. So it's not perfect." She puts her arm around me. I hope she can't tell that I'm disappointed. I wanted people to know I baked it. That's something special about me that people should know. That I am just learning about myself.

"I comprehend."

• • •

The partygoers are hungry. They gather in clusters of hair extensions and drugstore cologne and they feast on (I can't put it any less bluntly) Jillian and me. Evidently, the best dessert is watching Jillian and me play Cranium. They underestimated our ability to kick Parker's and Will's butts to the couch, and they howl and hoot at our every right answer.

Me as a star performer: I mime putting on my big shoes, fixing my bow between my big ears, holding my long tail.

Horton the Elephant, Will yells.

Lady Gaga! That from Parker.

Jillian's answer is the only one that counts. Minnie Mouse.

And we're not just great at charades. Jillian can spell words backward—gnilleps. And I know the answer to: The day that Ritchie Valens, Buddy Holly, and the Big Bopper were killed in a plane crash is also referred to as what?

As I say with confidence glowing for the win, "The day the music died," Jillian high-fives me. The girls on the sidelines cheer.

I'm not saying I totally love being under their microscopes . . . but when I excel, I can handle a few spectators. If they'd tried to make us dance, they would have gotten what they really expected, a from-the-box yellow cake.

Will and Parker react as if they're each listening to the same music, but feel the beat differently. Parker occasionally drapes his arm around Jillian. Will punches me in the shoulder with his fist while he holds up his camera phone and takes a picture. So, Parker wants to look adoringly in Jillian's eyes and Will wants to take a picture of me with him as if he was part of team Chantal instead of defeated by us.

Maybe Will has grown since middle school and he regrets the humiliation he dumped on me. Maybe Will sort of likes me and he'll get nicer and everything will be fine.

My cake is relegated to the back of the dessert table, but I can't move it front and center or make a place card with a snazzy name like Chocolate Infusion Craving. It's got to remain a secret, just like my ninth-grade crush.

Jillian

Party Paranoia.

Parker is the most attentive date I could imagine. And in spite of the Cranium geekiness, Chantal is the best friend of my dreams right now, oh, except for the group visit to the bathroom. I think she thought the last pieces of the chocolate cheesecake she snagged for each of us on the way would keep me busy.

I wait for her outside the bathroom door, locked in place by the crush of people in the hallway. The Girl Scouts make a delicious cake, even if it doesn't look so great. It's tart and sweet in perfect proportions. I eat the last bite and wipe away crumbs. As I apply my lip gloss I notice that my hand is shaking. What's taking Chantal so long? I'm not the one who panics in this friendship, but I'm finding it hard to breathe when I'm not next to Parker.

I can't shake the feeling that I'm failing to integrate. I'm the girl Parker brought instead of Annelise, the girl who's never been at their parties, the girl who has only finished half of a vodka cooler while girls all around her are at the stumbling stage. *Culture shock fades*, I try to reassure myself, *they'll get used to Chantal and me and we'll get used to them.*

"That bitch doesn't know who she's messing with." I hear Annelise's voice and I keep my head down. "Board games? That boy needs booty and I'm sure Little Miss Brain can't compete with me."

Oh. My head throbs. What am I doing? What is taking Chantal so long? I tap the bathroom door. *We need to go.* I look down at my jeans from the sale rack, and my secondhand T-shirt that's tight like everyone else's but isn't a great color. I'm pretending I'm ready for the next step, and everyone must see through it.

"Jillian." It's Parker. "I was looking for you." He checks to see if anyone is listening, but they're all shouting over the music at each other. "I . . . um . . . can we go somewhere quiet?"

I can't think straight. I know I'm supposed to stay at the door, but I don't want to hear Annelise again or, worse, run into her. I'm not too sure about going with Parker, either. I allow myself to be led away, through the kitchen, to a doorway. *Oh. Please don't let this be a bedroom.*

Will

......

The Competitive Edge.

I see her standing alone for the first time all night and I plan my final move. I weave through the crowd, my focus on the damsel in distress and the final photo challenge. Hip-hop plays. I am in the flow.

"Chantal." I set my hand in the small of her back. "Looking for Mr. Right?"

She tenses up, moves away. "Have you seen Jillian?"

"No. And it was a joke. The Mr. Right. Never mind." I follow her through the hallway, the living room, and the kitchen. We stop by the food table. She stands on her tiptoes, trying to spot Jillian in the party surf. I suggest maybe Jillian's in the backyard.

"Let's take a cupcake outside and look for her." Cupcake must be the magic word because Chantal heads for the back door. We leave the air-conditioning and the heat makes me sweat instantly. I use the bottom of my T-shirt to wipe off my top lip.

Chantal scans the perimeter and gives up. She leans against the wall, her arms crossed. At least she's not a moving target.

"You kicked ass at Cranium," I say. "A total outwit and outplay performance."

"Thanks." Her arms drop, but she still looks uncomfortable. "It was fun."

"You had fun?" I try my biggest smile on her, tilt my head like she's a puppy.

"Yeah. Mostly." She looks at me and away.

"Oh . . . I didn't really think you were Horton the Elephant. I don't know why I get like that. Embarrassed, I guess. You know what they say. A guy torturing you means he really likes you."

"Yeah?" She's totally not buying it, but at least she's looking at me.

This is as perfect a moment as any. I fumble with one hand to set my phone on the camera function. I'm about to reach for her face, pull her into me.

"What was with your nose picking?"

Can she not let that go? I shrug. The moment is gone. "Immaturity." Now what? "Oh. The cupcake."

I pull the paper wrapper off the cupcake and split the cake in half. Frosting globs all over my fingers. "Open up." I hold the cake up.

Chantal balks.

"It's chocolate. Come on." I shove my half into my mouth and smile. She leans forward, squeezes her eyes shut, and takes what I offer her.

"See, it's good. It's great. Isn't it?" I know I have to make my move. I get the phone ready and my left hand slides along her cheek. Camera ready, I hold her face in my hand, lean closer.

Parker

• • • • • •

The Laundry Room.

"**H**ey, I know it's not a trendy café or anything, but it's quiet." I lift Jillian onto the washing machine and stand in front of her. She giggles, but not in an Annelise flirting way. It's more relief. Or nerves.

All I think about is how much I want to kiss her. And this isn't just about completing a challenge.

I lean in to get closer.

Jillian

. . . . . .

Oh. No.

It's not that I don't want to kiss him. I do. I do. The laundry smells of
clean soap and Parker's man smell—sweat and peppermint breath
mints. It's impossible to resist. But . . .

"Um . . ." I lean to the right, out of the path of his lips. "I . . . just
need to ask you a question."

"A question?" Parker stands straight, runs his hand through his
hair. Oh. That is so hot.

"Are your parties always like this?"

"I'm not sure what you mean." His hands end up at his waist and
my eyes hover. *Oh . . . back to business.*

"Um . . . I'm in the laundry room with you and Chantal is somewhere with Will. I mean, I think she must be with Will. Right?"

Parker shrugs and he's adorable. "I'm not sure where Chantal is,
but I'm here in the laundry room with you right now because I want
to be alone with you. Not in front of everyone else."

"That's it?" He could say anything and I'd melt.

He nods. He leans in again.

I am so ready for this kiss. Except. "I promised Chantal I'd stay
with her . . ."

"She's with Will."

And she'll be okay. She doesn't need me *right* now.

Chantal

· · · · · ·

The Cake.

The cake is dry and the frosting hard. I try to swallow but it coats my teeth and tongue. I don't notice, until it's too late, that Will has slid his hand up to my face. And now he's getting closer and, now, his face is in front of me.

His lips touch mine and I want to pull away, but I don't because I promised to be normal. And a kiss is no reason to freak out. I try to imagine it's someone else's lips against mine, and that works. Mitch, my crush from the ninth grade. My lips tingle and I'm okay with the right hand settling on my waist. But then, he's pressing his mouth hard on mine and his tongue is pushing into my mouth and his tongue has left-over chocolate goo on it and my stomach lurches. I try to twist away and it seems Will thinks this is some kind of great technique because he twists his head back and forth, his tongue goes wild in my mouth. And then he's got his full weight against me, grinding into me. *Ugh.*

I open my eyes and see that he's looking up at something else while he's kissing me.

And now the taste of beer and cupcakes and possibly nacho chips with hot salsa comes through Will's tongue and my nausea rises. I push my hands against his chest and press, hard. He grips tighter. More tongue. My stomach begins its revolt. I can taste vomit in the back of my mouth.

A flash goes off. He's taking a picture! I bring my knee through his legs and he groans. Until I lift it and slam it into his crotch. I let the vomit in my mouth go. In Will's mouth. I run for the back door, but I don't make it. I stop and finish barfing where I'm standing. I hate vomiting. I hate how my eyes feel like they're going to pop out of the sockets and my stomach convulses so hard it burns. In between retches, I yell for help.

"Jillian!"

Jillian

· · · · · ·

Rescue.

As soon as the screaming starts I know; it's Chantal. Parker hovers.

"I have to go help."

"Those are cries of joy."

"Sorry!"

He slips his right hand under my hair, cups the back of my neck, and pulls me close. "Will can help her."

"I can't." I pull away but I don't want to.

"Okay. I'll help." Parker slides his hands under my arms, lifts me from the washing machine, and sets me down. His arms wrap around me again and I wonder if maybe Chantal has solved her own emergency. If staying here isn't the better idea.

"I really have to go." I push back from Parker and leave the laundry room, cross through the kitchen.

I'm at the back door when I hear Chantal again. "Get away from me," she hisses.

She's on her knees, piling paper napkins on top of a circle of puke. She hasn't noticed a few bits clinging to her hair. When I say her name, she doesn't even look up.

Parker helps me drag her to one of the deck chairs. He goes off to talk to Will.

"We have to leave," she says after we clean her up.

"I don't want to go yet."

"Jillian. I have publicly barfed." When I don't rush to sweep her away, she adds, "I put up with Will. And I even let him kiss me."

I didn't kiss Parker because I was worried about you.

"I came here for you."

"I know. I know." It's that moment that shifts your world, where you decide that despite your best friend's dire need for help, you want what you want. Annelise is in that house and if I leave, she'll be the one in the laundry room with Parker. I pull out my finest debating skills. I tell Chantal I'm not ready to leave. How we have to salvage our first double date so it will be memorable in a good way. I explain how running away feeds the nerd girl stereotype. I offer a suggestion, "You could laugh it off, joke about it. They'll think it's funny."

"Like *that's* what I want." She stands. "We have to *go*."

I'm considering what else to say when Parker shows up. He offers to walk us to Chantal's house. *My prince.* Of course Chantal insists we have to walk by ourselves but Will saves the day by saying he needs to apologize to Chantal. She refuses to walk with him for four blocks, but finally gives in when he promises he won't touch her. Ever again. Parker, I decide, is close to perfect.

Parker

· · · · · ·

Now What?

Will doesn't want to walk Chantal home, but he owes me. After all, I was the one who got him a date with Chantal.

It didn't matter that Chantal barfed. On him. That, in fact, made the whole challenge better, even considering his gonad injury. I have to admit it was pretty entertaining. That Chantal lives up to everyone's expectations.

I thought the night was going to go my way, not Will's. Now I've got seventy-two hours to complete the challenge. And if I don't, it will be the first and only challenge I've failed.

"So . . ." I slip my fingers through Jillian's. "I'm thinking we have to salvage this whole thing somehow."

"For sure." Jillian slows her pace and we fall back. Chantal pounds the blacktop with Will struggling to look cool as he tries to keep up with her. I have to come up with a rescue plan for Jillian and me, and Chantal. A triangle I didn't expect to draw. A black Chevy truck inspires me—sleek design, shiny grille—I bet the engine roars. Tailgate. Or barbecue. Jillian hasn't been to my place, but my family might scare her off. Ideal: a group event that ends early and leaves Jillian and me alone.

"How about a barbecue at my place? Monday."

"Another double date?"

We watch Chantal cross from one side of the street to the other.

Will follows, shaking his head. "That's not gonna happen. But . . . we can invite other people. Maybe someone else for Chantal? Got any ideas?"

"I promised I'd never tell anyone so you can't tell Will. She sort of crushed on Mitch in the ninth grade."

"Mitch? I thought he was gay."

She gives me the look that says I've crossed over the line. I remember, now, she won a debate on the right to have a gay support group at the high school. "Not that it matters if he's gay."

"He is shy."

"Okay, Mitch and who else?"

"The physics study group? They're . . . eccentric, but Chantal likes everyone. And . . . I do, too."

I laugh. "Oh, another round of Cranium? Or maybe bridge building with straws?"

"Parker!"

I check to see how mad she is, but she's smiling. "I'm sure they know how to party. In their own way."

"Tell me you're not brainiac prejudiced." She stops and the momentum falters. I stare into her eyes and . . . she's hot . . . and my brain (and other parts of me) are responding to this physical attraction. But there's something else. It's like desire with an edge. An edge of curiosity. I want to know her more. Or it's part of the game. It's hard to know with all this . . . um . . . rising action.

"I'm not prejudiced against brains. Not at all." I pull her into me. It's a great line for revving up to the challenge. I hold her. I am so ready to kiss her.

As I'm about to seal the deal, she stops me. "Um . . . the only thing is, I don't think the people at tonight's party will jell with the physics group. Do you?"

Tonight's party. I'm trying to pinpoint the person or persons she's specifically talking about but I don't have to; she says it. "Like Annelise, for instance, would not have a good time at a party with the brains, unless she was making fun of them."

"No. We won't invite her." Jillian's hands rest at my waist. This is my opportunity, but now I'm thinking about Annelise. I'd tried to avoid her all night, but she caught me when Jillian went to the bathroom. She slid up against me, her cleavage exposed in that hot bra with the black lace. I almost wasn't able to untangle myself. Did Jillian hear about that? Maybe she suspects that Monday will be our third and final date.

"Jillian." Chantal races toward us. "I'm not walking with Will anymore. I'm walking with you." She grabs Jillian's hand and pulls her away.

"Gotta go." Jillian holds an imaginary phone to her ear.

I give her the thumbs-up. Looks like we're on track for Monday whether she heard about Annelise or not.

Chantal

· · · · · ·

Split Ends.

When I come out of the bathroom, Jillian is sitting on the twin bed that is identical to mine, a pair of scissors in her hand. Her eyes cross as she stares at a single strand of hair and cuts the end. I straighten the books, pencil holder, and calendar on my desk. She's still cross-eyed and scissoring.

I open the bottom drawer, lift up the file folders, and extract another cello pack of cupcakes. Only two, I tell myself, to replace the awful taste of Will's cupcakes. And Will. I open the package and offer them to Jillian. She shakes her head, while she continues to scissor.

"What are you doing?"

"Cutting off my split ends." She holds up a magazine article titled "Keep Your Locks in Perfect Shape!" I appreciate perfection, but maybe this is going too far. I eat the first two cupcakes and reach for the third, my last. This one I eat slowly, letting the sugar sink into my tongue. I stash the remaining three back in the drawer.

I pull back the covers on my bed, straightening them into perfect folds, and slide between soft sheets, careful not to damage my construction. It's a tight squeeze in such a narrow bed. My mother has tried to convince me to trade in my two beds for a double, but I can't. Jillian and I redecorated the all-girly pink walls to gray with pink and lime green accents right before high school.

This is our room—the perfect place for a serious talk about Jillian's grooming and . . . everything else that is strange about her now: the bikini, the tight clothing, the hoarding of fashion magazines. Parker. "We have some things to talk to about," I say. I reach for my notebook and pen.

"I know. Parker is having a party on Monday. A barbecue actually."

"I'm not going." I want to remind her that we always get under the covers at the same time, that we like to stare up at the stars while we talk, that I insisted that my mother buy Egyptian cotton, six hundred thread count sheets for her bed, too.

"You haven't heard the details."

I wish all of this was over already. I shouldn't have to remind her that I'm grumpy when I'm tired. I take a deep breath, stare at her squarely. "I vote no. No more humiliation."

She says she doesn't even know if Will's going to the barbeque and adds, "We're inviting the study group. They're people you and I both know."

"If Will is going to be there it won't be better. Except maybe he can laugh at everyone instead of just you and me." I stare. Now they're throwing a barbeque? They've only been on two dates. Two. "Now it's *we*? As in the Parkillian? He's going to grill the burgers and hot dogs and you're going to pick the music?"

"Chantal." She drops the scissors on the floor. Finally something more important than looking good for Parker has her attention. She looks me straight on, but it's impatience. "I know you're hurt."

"Humiliated. Degraded." I detail again Will's disgusting tongue in my mouth. I remind her, again, about grade seven and the fetal pig heart.

"It's over, Chantal. Over." She looks at me like I'm one of her little brothers and I've stubbed my toe. She thinks she can fix anything.

"Parker is Will's best friend." Is she ever going to get this? "As long as you're dating Parker, I can't escape him."

She tells me that Parker and Will are not the same person, that

Will wants attention, any attention. And that I shouldn't take it personally.

"I'm standing up for myself." I didn't do anything wrong. Surely she sees that.

She goes back to her own bed. I resist the urge to tell her to pick up the scissors and put them on my desk. She lies down and stares at the stars on my ceiling, the ones we put up at the end of fifth grade. Her bed is messy and out of order and I wonder how she sleeps like that. She thinks she needs to pull me into her new life and I know that the path she's on is going to lead to misery, a repeat of her mother's past. Somehow I need to convince her to listen to reason.

"You're vulnerable," I say. "And you cannot let a guy get in the way of our future."

I lay back and stare at the stars, too. Sometimes a friend has to tell the hard truth.

Jillian

· · · · · ·

Neurosurgery.

I identify the ceiling constellations while I consider whether to tell Chantal what I'm thinking. "I can't be your social therapist."

"My therapist?"

"You needed me by your side the whole time at the party. You need to get better at being with other people. Socially, you're . . . developmentally delayed."

"You're calling me retarded?"

"Socially retarded."

The pause is long enough that I wonder if she's still awake. "So I'm a social retard," she says quietly. "I can accept that." She tells me that when we're at Harvard we'll be surrounded by social retards. We'll be the leaders. And then we'll go on to being hot neurosurgeons and we'll be in New York and working for the United Nations as consultants for medical practices to developing countries. I've heard it a million times before.

Chantal, queen of the plan. I hate that we've come to this, against each other. "I'm not going to be a neurosurgeon," I say.

"Yes, you are. You picked the city, remember?"

I don't know how to respond. I can't tell her that Harvard and neurosurgery are in the same unlikely but pleasant-to-imagine category as winning the gold medal in the Olympic marathon. If I tell her I don't have the money for Harvard she'll tell me I can get a job. If I tell her I can't leave all my little brothers, she'll say it's my mom's responsibility to raise them. If I say I don't think I want to spend the next eleven years studying, she'll say it'll all be worth it. And she's right. To a point. I can't change what she thinks, but I have to be honest. With Dad 3 moving out and my mother where she is . . . I wish things were different, but they are what they are.

"I'm a realist," I say. "I want to see my brothers grow up, and they're going to need me." My voice cracks. I guess because this is the closest I've come to speaking the misery out loud. I hope that she knows how hard it is for me to say it, how much I wish I had a different choice.

"You're giving up." I hear the sadness and the anger in her voice. She's so afraid of being alone. I hear her arrange her comforter, straighten her sheets, and I know we are both staring up at the same stars glowing on her ceiling. "You're a quitter."

My breath catches. I want to be hurt at what she says, but I know she's right. I made a promise, like all the times my mother has made deals with me, and now I'm backing out. It's not fair. Not for me. And not for her. And, because we have all night and neither of us are sleeping anyway, I compose what I think are words of comfort in my head. I think about how kindness might help here and how it might have helped me dozens of times. I practice my words over and over. And, then, I make sure she's still awake. I tell her I have something to say. It's easier with the lights out.

I tell her she's got the intelligence and the support to be a neurosurgeon or anything else. I tell her I don't know any other person who is as brainy and focused and capable. I say that when I visit her in New York we'll go shopping for hot neurosurgeon fashion: tall black stiletto boots and long gloves and designer dresses. "I will be at all the celebrations of your success," I say. "I'll be cheering the loudest."

I wait forever for her to be the best friend who understands, the best friend who says she will be there for me for whatever I decide to become. Instead, she tells me, "Parker is the easy way out, Jillian."

Chantal

· · · · · ·

$\mathcal{W}$hen I wake in the morning, the scissors remain open-mouthed on the floor. The sheets and blankets twist into a rope that points toward the door. Jillian's gone. The air is dried out and filled with dust. My cell battery is so low I can't make a call. I'm forced to go searching for a cordless phone.

The phone waits for me on the breakfast table, mere inches from my mother's hand. I mumble good morning and reach for it, but it disappears into my mother's lap.

"Chantal. I was hoping you'd be up soon. I've got some great news."

"Can it wait?" I squint at the brightness of her smile. "I need to make a phone call."

"Sweetheart. I've been sitting here waiting for you to get up."

"I understand. Seriously, though, can it wait a few minutes?"

My mother frowns. My dad sets down his cup of coffee hard enough for me to know that my phone call will wait. I slide into the chair opposite my dad to form their preferred triangle, the equilateral.

While my mother begins her monologue on the current status of her job as lab supervisor at the hospital, I nod to indicate interest, but I can only think about how miracles happen. More specifically, how I can make a miracle happen with Jillian. "So," my mother reaches to hold my hand. "You and Dad are going to have a wonderful summer at Lettuce Loaf."

"Lettuce Loaf? You always go by yourself." I stare at my dad. Crud. I missed something serious here. I hope this isn't about to turn into the we-need-our-space talk.

"Chantal, you weren't listening, were you?" he asks.

"I have to make a phone call."

"You know . . ." My mother leans in and my father follows her lead, creating a triangle nearing acute proportions. "Most of the time we are fine with the world revolving around you, but, honestly."

"Your mother has been promoted to hospital administration." Dad repeats that my mother's job as lab supervisor has been changed. Now she'll be dealing with budgets, hiring, and firing (oh . . . those poor slackers won't last long). She'll have an office with a big desk, a view, and an administrative assistant. I act like it matters to me and my dad continues talking. They're sending my mom on a week-long training course in Oregon. She leaves tomorrow. So that means I'm leaving town tomorrow, with Dad, for the next four weeks. He's staying longer than usual, he explains, because it's his year to pitch in on the cottage landscaping and maintenance.

"Well." I push away from the table, forcing an obtuse shape. "I'm really glad you both gave me some advance notice on this one."

"I only found out, for sure, Friday." My mother's bob is perfect. She's probably been up since 5:30 A.M., already gone for her run and read the newspaper.

"Chantal. What is going on?" That's my dad. Intersecting the angle.

"I can't go away. Not right now." I hate that my voice is wobbly. So revealing.

"You have no choice." My mom leans back in her chair, crosses her arms.

"Why do you feel you can't get away for a month? It's the summer. And your cousins would love to see you."

"I know it's going to disappoint you guys, but I have a life. One that's independent from you two."

"Well," Dad says. "There's a lot of power behind that statement."

"I told you we've spoiled her." My mom specializes in discussions about me, right in front of me.

"I'm not spoiled."

"The facts would indicate otherwise." My mom ignores my dad's attempts to interrupt while she lists the ways in which I am spoiled: I don't do any chores, I don't have a job, I don't even have the courtesy to listen to her when she tells me something important about her life.

I push even further away. *Top student isn't enough.* Not for my mother and not for Jillian. But it should be worth something, right? Any molecules of self-confidence that might have been clinging to me have been stripped away. "I am going to die of suffocation."

"Drama." My mother lifts an eyebrow as she looks at Dad. He rubs his chin. This is his I'm-not-sure-how-to-tell-you-I-disagree-with-you gesture. I pick up on it though. All I need to know is that one of them is on my side.

"I'll stay home to do the chores. It'll be a test. You'll only be gone a week. If I pass, you can let me stay home while you're working this summer. And if I fail, I can take the bus out to Lettuce Loaf."

My mother's response is swift but expected: all the reasons I can't stay home after she returns from her training. She'll be working long hours at her new job, she won't have time to cook for me, and she can't be responsible for what happens during my days.

"Seriously? I need you to watch me at all times?" I remind her that next year I'll be off to college where she won't be able to protect me. "You only think you know where I am anyway." She needs to know I'm serious. "I could be anywhere when I answer my phone." My dad's eyebrows indicate I've gone too far so I shut up and let him talk. Our triangle refigures, becomes more of a right angle, with my mother at 90 degrees.

The negotiations consume four hours of my life. They involve grilling me about what to do in an emergency (no matter that tornadoes are unlikely in the mountains), and the essential vitamins and nutrients (not found in cakes or cookies, even if they're homemade, my mother stresses). By the time my parents have gone out for coffee so my mother can decompress, it's late afternoon. The phone at Jillian's house rings but doesn't get picked up.

Three lonely cupcakes call out to me from my bottom dresser drawer. I cradle their package in my arms to the living room, remove a paper wrapper from the chocolate cake with the pink fluffy frosting and tiny pale green sprinkles.

I stare at the television screen wondering if this will be my summer occupation. Without my parents or Jillian, my active brain will disintegrate from lack of motivation. I wonder if a summer of under-stimulation could jeopardize my chances for top student next year. I wonder if it's going to matter. If Jillian and I can't get past this, I'll probably home-school my final year. I couldn't face going to school alone. Not my senior year. Not after it, either. I try Jillian's phone again. And her cell. Four more times each. She's avoiding me.

The second cupcake seems a bit off, the frosting grainy and, actually, unlikable. And the cake is dry. I shut the lid on the half-eaten second cake and the untouched third one. Really. Unless I'm totally desperate, I'm not going to eat any more of those things. It's probably the preservatives that make them taste strange.

Nigella comes to the rescue. I calm as she cooks. She's setting out to make her late-night dessert, Caramel Croissant Pudding. The gas stove clicks as she sets a wide pan on the burner. She adds a small pour of water and a third of a cup of sugar while she talks. "I don't like to do this in a kind of sensible, quiet way."

Me, neither. I replay what I said to Jillian last night. I know I can't take it back now. Like the only precalculus test I didn't ace, I've got to live with the consequences.

Nigella adds double cream, whole milk, bourbon, and eggs to the boiling sugar. "What I want, what anyone wants, is a luscious, smooth, flowing caramel." She pours her caramel over croissant chunks in an iron skillet and slides the dessert onto the middle oven rack. The camera stays at the oven door until Nigella's hands reach out to open it again, and now she's wearing black silk pajamas. She plunges her fork into the center of the pan, feeds her open mouth, and moans. Fade to black.

I click the TV off. I wonder if it's strange to read messages into Nigella's TV shows, as if she talks to me. Nigella said what anyone wants is smooth, flowing caramel and I agree. Caramel is divine. Isn't caramel exactly what you need when you're wondering what you've said?

I will prove to Jillian that I am not a social retard. I'll bake the most luscious cake anyone has tasted. And deliver it. On Monday night. To the barbecue.

A cake between friends can only be a good thing.

Jillian

· · · · · ·

Alone.

The walk home from Chantal's house takes me over an hour in my party heels. An RV driver slows and stops to ask me for directions to see the bears. I tell the bald guy and his small wife how to get to the bear statues downtown but they insist they want to see the real bears. We're a small resort town, I tell them, we don't have a zoo, but I suggest that they might see some at the dump right outside town.

"No. We want to see them in the wild," they complain.

I point out that the dump is the fast-food restaurant for bears around here. Guaranteed sightings. When I pass the Information Center twenty minutes later, the RV is parked at the booth and the bald guy is leaning out the window, shouting questions. I'm beginning to think the world is full of people who don't give up until they get the answer they want.

It's only 8:27 A.M. when I walk in the front door and the first thing I see is my mother. Awake. Folding laundry.

"Hey," I say carefully. "Is everything okay?"

"Oh, you're home early. I thought you'd sleep in after your party. How did it go?"

We have a conversation that lasts ten minutes but doesn't include the details of Chantal's puking or the reason I'm home early. I focus on the stellar bits: the Cranium game and a little about Parker.

The boys must have had a late bedtime last night because they are all still asleep. Mom and I hardly spend ten minutes a week alone together so I sit back and relax as if things are right in the world. She appears to be in redemption mode—her hair is freshly washed, she's got on mom jeans and a clean T-shirt; she might even make pancakes. The sun catches her skin and I get a vision of her when she was younger, freckles and an easy laugh and no bra. She is still so proud of her body, still willing to dance on the edge of anything. I remember once a weather balloon was flying over the house on Columbia Street and she told Dad 2 that we were going to track it down. She had on her hippy skirt and hiking boots and we got into Dad 2's truck and followed it for ten minutes until it dropped near Mount Begbie Falls. We never found it, but we looked for an hour and I collected moss and rocks and sticks while she told me about the time her parents drove her out east and she saw a hot air balloon take off. "I've always wanted to float in a hot air balloon," she told me. "Imagine the freedom."

My mom talks about the nursing home, mentions that she's got a few days off in a row, as she folds T-shirts and underwear. And then I realize a pattern. A laundry pattern. Those are *her* T-shirts and underwear. And her socks. And her jeans.

Before I ask her what's going on, she tells me, "Dad Three left for Vancouver last night to meet up with his brother and look at this house they're talking about flipping."

"Yeah . . ."

"And he's coming back in a few days to get the rest of his stuff. And I thought it would be good for me to get away. You know, clear my head before I see him again."

"So you're meeting up with someone else . . ." I shake my head. Take a deep breath and hold it.

"Jesus, Jillian, you do not have to give me that attitude."

I don't even ask her what attitude she's referring to.

"I'm not sitting around feeling lousy. That's not me. I know women who obsess over being left and you know what? They're not happy. Me? I'm going to be happy."

There's no use talking to her when she gets like this. I'm supposed to tell her now that she deserves whatever it is her heart desires, but I'm not going to do it. Not this time. My mother is an only child. Just like Chantal.

"So . . . who have you got lined up for day care?" I ask.

She drops the black lace underwear she's holding. "I told you I didn't need your attitude. You know I need you to help me. And I'll pay you."

Right. I'll put it on her tab.

"What if something goes wrong?"

"Jesus, Jillian, nothing is going to go wrong." But she's never left them with me alone overnight.

She carries her clean clothes out of the room, singing a country music song about a woman going after what she wants. I want to stop her and tell her to get out. Before the boys get up. I also want her to know that when she leaves I'll stay in my bedroom because the worst part is watching her shut the door behind her. What my mother will never understand is that, like the boys, I have separation anxiety, too.

She's gone within thirty-five minutes. The last I see of her she's concentrating on getting her lipstick on straight. She promises she'll be home by Monday at 4 P.M. since I've got a party to go to.

Chantal

••••••

A Social Retard Cake.

My mother's crystal bowls cradle flour, cocoa powder, baking powder, baking soda, salt, unsalted butter (2 sticks), sugar, eggs, egg yolks, vanilla, buttermilk, and bittersweet chocolate (melted and cooled). I am surrounded by sparkle in the kitchen spotlight. I am a cake princess.

What makes me a top student also makes a confident baker. It's all about precision and focus. As I take on the first step, buttering the cake pans, dusting the insides with flour, tapping out the excess, and lining the bottoms with wax paper, guilt begins to creep in. My parents left this morning, but it's as if my mother is still here, trying to protect me from the evils of sugar.

On Sunday afternoon Mom and Dad returned from the coffee shop as I finished my shopping list. I sat on the ottoman to hear their final statement. "Your father has convinced me that giving you responsibility in stages is a good thing. This next week will be a trial period. We can revoke your privileges at any time."

I nodded, though I had no choice.

"And. This is a request." She looked at my dad for approval. He shrugged. "No junk food. It's only a week."

"Request heard," I answered. I don't even ask her anymore why she's so freaked about sweets and cookies and cakes. It's one of those off-limits topics. I don't want to endure her lectures about sexual abstinence and she doesn't want to discuss dessert with me. The deal works.

I whisk together the flour, cocoa powder, baking powder, baking soda, and salt.

The stand mixer I borrowed from Mrs. Ellis next door (my mother-in-case-of-an-emergency) is a beautiful machine. Pale yellow with silver bling, it sparks sunshine.

I slide the slab of butter into the mixer bowl and beat on medium speed until soft and creamy. Sugar falls in. More beating. A yellow color forms; a color that is difficult to describe as anything but hopeful. Next come the eggs, one at a time, then the yolks. I beat in the vanilla.

"One could be no more happy if one had won the lottery," I say to my invisible television audience.

I turn the mixer down to low and add the dry ingredients alternately with the buttermilk, mixing sparingly.

Socially delayed individuals would probably eat the cake with their mouths open, crumbs spilling out. Or take the last piece instead of cutting it in half and offering someone else the rest. Or taste the cake and announce that it tastes disgusting. Or worse, spit it out. If I am a social retard, then this cake will redeem me. I may be different from the rest of the crowd but that doesn't have to be a bad thing.

I divide the batter between the two cake pans and it nearly doesn't fit. There's only a quarter inch of space left at the top. I read the recipe over and over to make sure I measured correctly and I do what I have to do—slide the pans into the oven and hope for the best. I set the timer.

The ganache part of the instructions for the Double Layer Chocolate Buttermilk Decadence with Chocolate Caramel Ganache and Toffee Accessories is six paragraphs long. I stir sugar, water, and a cinnamon stick in a saucepan on medium-low heat until the sugar dissolves. (As a chemistry princess I have mastered the dissolving of a solid into liquid.) Now I increase the heat, and boil, without stirring. The mixture bubbles out of control. I poise my spatula over it. Lift the pan, observe the color. I'm supposed to cook it until it turns a deep amber color. What is the color, exactly, of deep amber, I wonder? More boiling bubbles. And more again. I consult my rec-ipe. It's supposed to take from five to seven minutes. I don't know how many minutes it's been and I think maybe I should have ad-justed all the cooking times for a higher altitude. The bubbles are definitely brown though so I move on to the next step: adding cold cream to hot sugar.

I am caught in the crossfire. The mixture bubbles, scalding cream splatters violently, the dark sugar seizes into a ball of goo. "This is not the moment to panic." I try to channel Nigella. "Baking chemistry re-quires trust on the part of the baker."

I whisk and heat and whisk more. Finally the thick gooey stuff looks mostly like caramel sauce. I pour it over the bowl of twelve ounces of chocolate I have set aside. I stir, the chocolate melts, and, eventually, smoothes to a glassy lake of loveliness. I think I've sur-vived baking disaster, but then, the timer beeps and I look through the oven door.

My cake batter has overflowed the pans and pools of cake smoke on the oven floor. The cakes themselves are domed but col-lapse into a well of boggy batter.

This is what happens when you break the rules, my conscience speaks to me in a small squeaky voice that's a mash up of my mother and Jiminy Cricket. I ignore it. I tell myself any independent choice will result in an infraction of some sort. And for every misstep a solution exists. I babysat Jillian's six little brothers and I survived. Heck. I did better than survival—I was an optimized thinker. This cake baking di-lemma is another opportunity to prove myself. And after cake baking, maybe on to Jillian and our knotted-up friendship.

I consult my recipe, Google my problem. I turn to Nigella's Web site and on a forum I discover a solution. Though my cake will not be as pretty, it will still be edible, the writer assures me.

I test the center of the cakes for doneness every two minutes, until, twelve minutes later, I pull them from the oven, the edges dried and nearly burned. Failure has never looked this bad. I feel my eyes sting and I recite the elements of the periodic table, starting with hydrogen, the element with the lowest atomic number and, arguably, the greatest potential for everyday explosions.

Jillian
· · · · · ·
Call Waiting.

She could have called. *She,* of course, is my mother, but I'm not calling her my mother right now because that would suggest respect.

I had to tell Parker I was sick. He said he understood, but I *felt* the pause. The pause that says what you really want to say before you say what you think you should say. Pause = How could you let me down?

I called the physics group and told them Chantal wasn't going to the party and neither was I. I didn't have to tell them not to go. Without us they wouldn't feel comfortable. And honestly, I was having nightmares about them all together in the same room with Parker. Chantal might have enjoyed having them around, but I know I'd have been on high-alert to stop Gavin's Darth Vader impression or Brenan's plot analysis of *Simpsons'* episodes or Callie's insistence on Dance, Dance Revolution. All party killers. Maybe even boyfriend killers.

Even though I'm relieved the party won't wreck my chances with Parker, I still wonder what he's thinking now. I wonder how much girl drama a guy can take before he walks away. I wonder how much mom drama I can take. I lock myself in my bedroom, ignore the screams of the twins as they pretend, for the 127th day in a row, that they are knights slaying a dragon.

I know what's coming; the boys will realize their dragon is invisible but they can slay each other instead. It will be up to me to limit the damage. I've tried to stop them in mid-battle, to take away their swords, to distract them, but the slaying is part of the game. I can't change their knight and dragon story any more than I can interrupt whatever story my mother tells herself when she's drinking.

She's probably totally shitfaced in the hotel room doing some-thing with the-guy-without-a-name that's disgusting. Justifications like "I deserve to have fun," "I've had a hard life," "Jillian's brothers love her," cancel out the one thought she should have: I promised I'd be home by 4 P.M. When she shows up she will tell me one of her lies: the traffic was awful, the clock didn't work in the hotel room, the car broke down, or I got a phone call from a friend and had to go help.

And then, like now, and like always, I won't know how to respond. Nothing prepares you for having a lousy mother, just like you can't really be ready for an earthquake. It's all about minimizing the harm. I know it's easy to imagine that you wouldn't stick around after the first natural disaster—you'd move to a safer building or transfer to higher ground. But, listen to me: it's not easy to admit you're living on a fault line.

I don't call Chantal because I don't feel like dealing with anyone else right now. I sit on the floor, my back against the metal bed frame that collapses if I sit on the right corner. It's 5:45 and I know from experience that if Mom's not home before happy hour, she won't be home until the bar closes. Self-pity itches at the back of my throat, but I pull my headphones from my pocket, ready to extend my break from responsibility. Four small fingers and a thumb stop me.

Baby Ollie's chubby fist wiggles under my bedroom door, his fin-gers stretch, and then retreat. A few sticky "O" cereal pieces are left behind. It happens again. I hear him digging deep into the cereal box, gathering another handful. He crunches a few with his four teeth and adds the rest to the pile he's creating for me. Again. I smile. My brothers do this, thing, to me. The moment I decide I hate them, they show me their sweet side, like Ollie with his O's message. The next time his hand slides under, I tickle his fingers. I hear him giggle.

But the cuteness wears off when I realize what's really happening— Ollie's feeding me O's because he wants to take care of me. If I'd been drinking I'd probably have laughed the way my mother does, giggled and blathered about how Ollie entertains himself so easily and I wouldn't have made the connection that *he's* trying to take care of *me*. I can't let this happen. I can't.

My brothers will tell my mother that they didn't even miss her while she was gone. Josh and Stevie will rush to explain the rules of the best-ever game of dragons and knights (make that one mother dragon and six brave knights). Travis, Thomas, and Trevor will remember that I told ghost stories with a flashlight under my chin. Baby Ollie will beg for nacho chips and cheese with pickles on the side for dinner. And me? I will find a way to help myself.

Chantal

. . . . . .

Shrunken Diameter.

$\mathcal{T}$he SRC^2 (Social Retard Cake squared) is a cool, sophisticated quadrate. Caramel Chocolate Ganache fills and envelops two layers of the insides of my formerly round cake, precisely reconfigured at right angles. The toffee accessories pebble a horizontal line a third from the top edge of the cake. The SRC^2 is more a mistake of genius than a planned treat, but either way, I think Nigella would be patting me on the back. *That's a girl,* she'd say. *You fall off the pony and you get right back on.*

Getting back on the pony was not easy, and it was not quick. It was dark by the time I had a cake carrier fixed to the front of my bike and I had to ride in my lowest gear up the steep climb from downtown to the suburb, my tires grinding slower and slower in the gravel shoulder.

Now, the ground is level and I glide under streetlamps, alternately feeling like a star (lights on) and wondering what crisis will befall me next (lights off). When I arrive at Parker's house, the shade-drawn windows suggest the party is in the backyard, though I don't hear any party noise. My cell phone shows that it's after 10 P.M. I wonder how late these sorts of parties go. I remove the cake from the basket, careful that it doesn't slide off the aluminum foil–covered cardboard platter.

I step past the partially open gate and stop. I could be holding the cake that will seal my fate as the nerdiest girl ever. Cool kids bring bags of chips to parties. But I am not one of them and I never will be. I don't want to be. If I did, I wouldn't have spent hours baking a cake. I wouldn't be standing here, about to give them another chance to like me for me.

The slate path leads to the center of the yard and an outdoor dining table, a fire pit with Adirondack chairs, and a gazebo hung with gauzy netting. The perfect party location. Like a TV family, but without the obvious dysfunction, Parker's parents have money and good taste, and they pull both things together. I set my cake on the dark wood table, slide into a contemporary polished wood chair. Abandoned coals in the fire pit glow a faint red. *Crud. The party is over.*

The longer I sit in the chair the greater my regrets grow. I'm sorry that Jillian didn't witness my attempt to sweeten our soured relationship.

Even though I know I'll have to listen to the details of a party I failed to get to, I reach for my cell phone to text Jillian an invitation to my empty house.

The patio door swings open. Two people. And Jillian isn't one of them. My hand, gripped around the cell phone, is trapped in my pocket as I dive for the ground. My shoulder hits but I recover and shuffle on my hands and knees to the gazebo. Through the slats, I watch Parker and Will settle into the Adirondack chairs, beer bottles in hand.

"Dude. I guess no party was better than a nerdfest." Will leans his head back and chugs.

"Maybe it would have been okay."

"Dude. All they'd want to do is sit in the basement and play video games."

"It would have been different if Jillian was here . . ."

"And what's with that? She didn't show. She didn't freakin' show. So that means, my friend, that you have forfeited the man challenge."

Man challenge?

In between long swigs of beer Will talks about how great he is and details the terms of his winning. "And this is the shot of the party girl." He holds up his phone to Parker as proof. "The kiss that wins the big prize."

"Let me see that!"

Will hands the phone to Parker. He laughs so hard he nearly spews beer from his nose.

"Dude. It's perfect. Isn't it?"

What sort of prize, I wonder, and who is the subject? Then he talks about kissing *her* and having *her* puke in his mouth.

I am the subject. *Her* is me.

No.

Oh God.

• • •

In my mind I'm back in time: seventh grade, in the hallway outside science class. Valentine's Day.

Will held a box wrapped in red with a pink velvet bow. I blushed. My heart beat hopefully. Will had fallen for me. His lopsided smile grew. He handed me the box and I was sure it was chocolates— heavy truffles. As I pulled away the bow, he mumbled something like, I hope you like it. I stared into his eyes, trying to memorize the look of someone crushing on me. It took me nearly a minute to fig- ure out what was in the box. I couldn't imagine why the chocolate would be gray. Then, why it was so squishy. And then I smelled the formaldehyde.

He laughed. That's when I knew for sure.

• • •

Once again I am the subject of his ridicule. I imagined that I'd become slightly hot. Cute. Smart. Fun. Turns out I am, still, not normal.

I mean, I hated the kiss, but I . . . damn . . . I liked that I had to fight him off. Didn't that prove that I was something?

Nothing more than how stupid I am.

Will
......

Geniustastic.

We chill in Parker's backyard. The beer and the man challenge that I, alone, completed make the nerdfest night celebratory. Though every time I look at Parker, I get this vibe that he's pouting. Tonight was his last chance and Jillian called in sick. He doesn't lose well. Not enough practice.

Parker is part of the mad money clan. They've got the cash all right. He's the fourth boy in an all-guy lineup who rep Mr. Big Cheese, Accountant: Parker's dad. They drive great cars, they date hot girls, and they have, like, two houses each. Parker's mother does not rearrange her furniture twice a year to "freshen the place up" like they do in my mom's reality shows. She buys a new couch. And Parker has never borrowed money for lunch. He's the bank.

You might think Parker is given everything, but he isn't. He saved up his allowance to buy half of that car. I respect Parker for earning his own wage. I wouldn't hang with him if I didn't.

Sure, I've been jealous of him—with an old man like mine, you don't get help with anything. And it's normal to want what the next guy has, especially if he lucked out with the family he grew up in. In that family you get to be part of a whole group of people, all going for the same thing—even if it is a weird-ass team of bean counters.

Except for Brad, he's a bean counter turned manager—my dad's boss.

Seriously. One night I'm at their house having dinner over the Christmas break and Parker's brothers are talking about accrual accounting. One of them must have made a joke because they all laughed and of course I chuckled along but, dude, what was so freakin' funny?

I turned to Parker, thinking I'd give him the Halo signal but he was all-in with them, talking about how important accruals are for understanding the revenues and expenses for each month. The brothers clapped. Howled with laughter. Frick. I really needed a Halo break. I jabbed Parker with my elbow.

He startled when he looked my way, having apparently net-zeroed me out of his family accounting love-in. He shrugged. Shrugged like an apology. And I got it, right in my gut. He was sorry he'd shown how smart he was in front of me. Sorry because he sort of knew that, even at number four in the class, I'd never be at his level.

It's one of those times that'll stick with me for life. Like when your head's on the lino next to the toilet and you're vowing to never drink another vodka and Kool-Aid? Parker shrugged. I told myself, I want his life.

And this is where it starts. Beating him on the man challenge was a bonus. What I really want is the girl. Annelise. Since Parker's dumped her she's available.

As I drain the last of my beer, I notice Parker hasn't even finished his first one. Frick. The pouting vibe is serious enough that it's got me worried. I'm about to suggest a new man challenge when I see he's got a picture of Jillian on his phone and he's frickin' staring at it.

"She's sort of hot." I nod at the phone. "I mean, for a challenge."

"I was this close, man. I almost kissed her. But I wanted it to be for real." He doesn't delete the picture before he slides the phone back in his pocket.

"So you're saying you forfeited? Dude, c'mon."

"No. You won. I'm just saying . . ." He grins.

"Dude, that girl is under your skin." I slide my sunglasses down over my eyes to hide my brilliance. It's so obvious. I get Parker to dump his girlfriend and then, it turns out he likes Jillian? Genius. Nothing can stand in my way to getting Annelise. Nothing.

Chantal

· · · · · ·

Revenge.

The challenge was supposed to end with Jillian and me jilted. Destroyed. It is half-successful.

I'm trapped in the gazebo, waiting for a chance to escape. I learn that humiliation grows when you can't leave the scene. I suffer again and again, telling myself I should have known better.

I cut my hair when I was in the third grade. I used safety scissors and I didn't look in the mirror. I'd met Jillian by then, but we couldn't spend every day with each other, which made the days I wasn't with her longer and lonelier. I loved everything about her, especially the way her hair floated wild and free under bands of daisies her mother taught her how to weave. I'd begged my mother to let me wear my hair loose.

"You're cursed with frizzy hair," she said. "Ponytails. One? Or two?"

I cut it so short she couldn't tie it back.

I piled all the long curls up in the top drawer of my desk, and went to the bathroom to check out my hair. I was shocked. Yaks had better hairstyles than mine. I tried to tame the wildness with water and a glob of every hair product I could find.

I knew my mother would be upset when she saw it, but I hoped she would laugh, like the mothers on those religious commercials you see on TV. Where the kid does something wrong and the mother smiles. My mother was enraged.

"You look like a boy," she said, her voice full of rage. "A fat little boy."

"I'm not a boy."

"Everyone's going to think you're a boy."

"You'll tell them I'm not."

"I will do no such thing."

It doesn't matter that my mother took me to the hairdresser to try to fix it or that it grew back and I've worn my hair in one ponytail or two ever since. I haven't forgotten the moment I didn't feel love. Love expected me to look a certain way and to follow the rules even if I didn't understand them.

And now, here I am again. If I had known the rules. If Jillian had been more clear. If I had worn my hair differently, or said less, or gotten some questions wrong, even on purpose, or let Will kiss me because that's what he wanted. If I could do it all over I would be someone different. More like Jillian.

Even if Jillian had come to the party tonight, Parker wouldn't have followed through on the challenge. She has a certain something that commands respect. And I have a certain nothing.

And now as I'm thinking that the torture of hiding here in Parker's gazebo can't get any worse, I watch him stand up and walk toward the table. And . . . the cake, my cake.

He dips his finger through chocolate and toffee bits and tastes my delectable ganache.

"God, this is so good."

He likes it. I can claim some part of myself as worthwhile. My cake.

"It must be from Jillian," he says. "She said she was planning on bringing something. She must have had her mom drop it off."

He doesn't know Jillian very well. She doesn't have time to bake a cake like that and if she did, it wouldn't look like the cake he's destroying, one finger of frosting at a time.

"Hey, how do you know it's for you?" Will stands near the table. "That cake is definitely for me."

"Who would send you a cake?" Parker asks.

Will takes Parker's beer from his hand and chugs it. If he dips his finger in the cake, I'm going after him. "There's a girl who's got me in her sights."

If I had him in my sights, I'd have put laxative in the melted chocolate.

"I know who it isn't. Not only is Chantal so not into you, she's the last person who would bake a cake. Man, tying her shoes stresses her out."

"You got that right. Like kissing a plastic goldfish. Dude. Let's eat a piece of cake and speculatize on the girl who is after me."

Parker drops his finger, mid-lick. He picks up the cake. They turn their backs to me.

Finally, I'm free. I can go home. I can go to bed crying. I can bike off the edge of a cliff. Or I can plan my sweet revenge. Will is not going to get away with humiliating me. These two aren't the only ones who appreciate a challenge. And when Jillian dumps Parker, he'll turn on Will. We'll see how he likes it.

Will

. . . . . .

The New Deal.

$\mathcal{M}$y mouth is still rocking the chocolate cake as I exit Parker's house. I ate three pieces, but left the rest for Parker's family. I don't want to have to explain a cake to my mother. She'll ask questions and I'll have to lie because telling my mother something means my dad finds out.

I drive two blocks in the Green Machine, pull over to the curb, turn down the radio, and dial Annelise's number.

It's busy. She's got to be on the phone with one of her friends because Parker told me he hasn't talked to her since they broke up. He said it was over, and now he's gone for Jillian. That dude has it all wrong, but it's going right for me.

Annelise turned me down a few years ago, but things are different now. She must be feeling a guy with a little danger on his side is where she's at—otherwise she wouldn't have left a cake for me. A cake. Only Annelise would think of doing that. When I talked to her last night I told her that Parker was digging Jillian but I was available.

Then, she asks, get this, "Are you trying to hook up with me, Will?"

I played it cool. I said there was no sense in us both being lonely.

She giggled. An invitation.

Maybe she's leaving that cake to make Parker jealous, but how I end up with her doesn't matter. It's the keeping her part that shows I am the man. With a girlfriend like Annelise, people are going to look at me differently—the way they look at Parker.

Chantal

······

Vampire Vanilla.

In Nigella's world the mere smell of comfort can provide solace. Somehow, I don't think sniffing vanilla is going to solve this problem. I cream a cup of butter with one and a half cups of sugar and add in a full tablespoon of vanilla.

I crack six eggs, separating the slippery whites from yolks.

I'm baking. It's not too stressful. And neither is tying my shoes; it hasn't been for years. And I'm sure if I *wanted* to kiss someone I would be less like a plastic goldfish. I try not to dwell on the insults Parker and Will threw out and that's why I'm baking. We task-oriented girls find solace in tasks. Each time I picture sitting down across from Will, with my cupcakes in hand, swear words rise. I baked these BEEP cupcakes. I am not goldfish-lipped, you BEEP. You obviously need more practice at making out with plastic, cold-blooded, aquatic vertebrates, you BEEP.

I add the egg whites into the butter and sugar.

Visions of Will laughing at me make me cough, as if I'm allergic to mere thoughts of him. I cough harder. I have to turn the mixer off because my coughing fit is becoming a panic attack.

I can't catch my breath. Past my kitchen windows is the darkest night and I'm under the lights. The shark is out there. I fly through the house pulling down blinds, shutting curtains, turning off lights, until it's only me again, in the kitchen, leaning against the counter. How could I have been so exposed?

I'm so desperate I consider calling my mother to ask for her advice. She'll say, with friends like that you don't need enemies. Next year, I'll be homeschooled.

The recipe tells me I need to finely chop some almonds. The knife slips on the first almond, nearly cuts the end of my finger off. Wait. I retrieve my dad's hammer from his toolbox in the garage. I smash an almond. That's Will's pathetic face. Will's parts zip across the counters and the floor in smithereens. When I've gone through the entire bag of almonds, I gather enough shards from the counter to make the cup that I need. My feet crunch the floor. If my mother were here, she'd be the one having the panic attack now.

As I dump the almond bits in with the flour and baking powder, I remember what Nigella said in her chocolate croissant episode. "If you make these, you can get your way at any meeting." As I pour the sparkling batter into the liners I decide I'll get on with it, as Nigella says. My enemy will suffer his own humiliation.

I swirl the cooled cupcakes with a velvety cream-cheese frosting. I'll call them Vampire Vanilla Cupcakes, because now, I am the predator. And these morsels will be irresistible to my prey.

Parker

· · · · · ·

Shoe Gazing.

I wake up to knocking on my bedroom door. "Hey, get up. I need a golfing partner." It's my brother, Brad.

I shove my headphones into my ears and turn the volume to high. My Bloody Valentine plays. Noise. That's what I need. A distraction from what I don't want to do.

I drift in between asleep and awake, surfing on the music and seeing Jillian, mud flying off her heels as she runs past me at Twelve Mile Flats. She's got great calves. And other great parts. Really. Great. Parts. And she laughs like she's having fun. Like she's real. The lead guitarist slips in a riff that explodes in noise. My Bloody Valentine has a surprising sound, you think they're all pop and then this riff shows you they're totally serious. Jillian surprises me like that.

I keep my hands on top of the blankets. I have to keep my head straight about all of this.

The door opens, daylight forces me to squint at Brad. "Mom's making breakfast. And then we're leaving. Get up." He shuts the door.

My thoughts fizzle out. I remove my headphones.

The three of them are waiting for me in the kitchen: my mom at the kitchen sink, Brad at the espresso machine, Dad at the marble island, memorizing the financial news.

"Oh, hey, Parker. Tee time in thirty minutes." Brad steams the milk for his latte.

"Sorry, man. Prior commitment." I pour a glass of milk.

"You gotta come, man. I like outshooting you."

"Sorry. You'll have to get your ego boost elsewhere." I pick up the plate of scrambled eggs, hash browns, and bacon my mom has set aside for me and take my seat at the kitchen table. Brad says his life is perfect because his wife lets him golf twice each weekend. She doesn't want to go with him.

"Your girlfriend is making cake for you?" Brad holds a piece of the chocolate cake. From the looks of what's left on the plate, it's not his first taste. "It's frickin' great cake, but, that, little bro, is dangerous . . ."

"Brad, stop with that. Annelise is a sweet girl," Mom says.

"And she's from a good family." Dad's idea of what's important.

I'm really wishing I hadn't talked to Mom last night. When she asked me who made the cake I told her I thought it was Annelise. I didn't mention Will figured she'd left the cake for him. My parents don't know I broke up with Annelise. They don't know about Jillian. And I'm not going to tell them, at least not until I'm sure.

"Mom." Brad wraps his arm around our mom's shoulder. "Parker's going into senior year. You have to be unattached. That's the rule."

"The rule." I slide two pieces of bread into the toaster. Hell is three older brothers who constantly preach the rules.

"I think your brother's got something there." Dad's arms cross over his chest and he's got this voice that's loud, clear, commanding. This is his authority pose, the way he stands when he fires people. "Girls in high school are . . . practice . . . for real life. You'll meet the girl for you in university."

While my brother and Dad give myriad examples of how right they are, I watch my mom. She's buffing the top of our stainless steel stove, which is already spotless. She hasn't had a job since my oldest brother Ellis was born. I wonder what she thinks of what they say about women. Finally Dad finishes his speech on the merits of finding a smart girl who is willing to quit work and look after all the kids and me, too.

"Got it." I take my plate to the dishwasher but before I can open the door my mother takes it from me. I turn toward my bedroom. I think I've heard enough.

"Hey. How about that golf game?"

"Uh. I'm meeting up with Will."

"His dad is the pain-in-my-ass employee who's always complaining." Brad hasn't ever liked Will and now that he has to deal with Will's dad being the union rep, he likes Will even less. "You know what kind of hell he's putting my office through? I told Cindy this morning that I needed golf for stress relief. I got all the departments breathing down my neck."

"Man, sorry to hear that." What diversion would get me out of golf and get him off my back about Will? "We're planning my campaign. Class president. You set the bar high, bro, everyone expects something big."

"Class president?" My mom turns toward me. "I hoped you'd change your mind and run. It's so important to keep up the family tradition." She hugs me and I smell her perfume, something French and expensive Dad bought her on his last business trip to Europe. "Brad and your dad can go golfing. Your dad can mow the lawn later."

"Now that's a deal." My dad claps his hand on my shoulder. Brad is loading his clubs into the X5 before I get back to my bedroom.

I sit on the edge of my bed and slide the music into my ears. I should have said I was too sick to get out of bed.

My brothers don't get me. They think I'm like them, that I have some master plan for my life. I'm happy to hang out. That's safest. Just be around, to like everyone. When Will was into watching the old mob movies last year, he kept saying my dad was like the head of our mob family. And, actually, he was kind of right. I mean my dad sees it as his job to keep all of the boys in line. Not to be criminals, but to be accountants and married, with nice cars and a summer cottage each. The answer to all problems, my dad seems to think, is to work harder.

My Bloody Valentine soothes out the rough spots again. I lie back on my bed, inertia claiming me, Kevin Shields's riffs entertaining me. I saw this video of Kevin playing and he never looked up. They call it shoe gazing because the guy has so many noise pedals he's always looking down to see what he can do with them.

You have to respect a guy like Shields for doing exactly what he wants and keeping at it. And my dad, too, he's successful. Even my brother Brad's working his ass off to be good at his job. But they chose what they wanted to do. I haven't chosen. In fact, I am in total avoidance-mode. Last month the career and life management teacher told me to write down my career goal. When I wrote the truth, *I don't know,* she told me to erase it and write something else. The teachers are all worried that next week we're going to be doing drugs or painting graffiti or listening to explicit music. This is the number one thing Will and I agree on—most of the world doesn't want to get who we are.

Right now I'm texting Will even though I feel like I've just run twenty kilometers. Class president? That's in what-am-I-thinking territory. And Jillian—I know because I'm lying to my mother about her—is a train wreck about to happen. I can't stop myself and I'm halfway there.

Jillian
· · · · · ·
Lightning Strike.

I'm barely awake on Wednesday morning when Dad 3 buzzes into the kitchen, his electric razor grating the remains of his moustache and beard from his face. Irony unplugged had Mom and Dad 3 showing up on Tuesday night within thirty minutes of each other. My mother and I were just starting our fight when the door slammed shut and Dad 3 shouted, "I'm home."

"You've got the wrong address." I knew it would be the last time Dad 3 would be walking through that door without knocking. She wants everyone to believe that she kicked him out; not that he left us.

I expected to find him asleep on the couch when I got up with baby Ollie. Instead, I found a discarded crocheted afghan, two fingerprint-covered scotch glasses, and an empty bottle of Dad 3's favorite brand. Yes, my mother is inconsistent.

Dad 3 leans over baby Ollie's breakfast tray to kiss his forehead, showering the bowl of oatmeal chunks with dark hairs. I don't tell him I think he's disgusting; it's a bit late for hygiene lessons. Instead I dump the oatmeal into the garbage, reach for a box of Cheerios. I wipe down the tray and pour a pile of O's in the middle.

"Oh! Oh! Oh!" Ollie holds one in the air, showing his four tiny teeth. I'm the only one who knows that he wants Dad 3 to notice.

Dad 3 is busy chugging a cup of coffee. The Hat Trick and Double Minor are too sleepy-eyed to look up.

"Hey. Jillian." Dad 3 sets his cup down, reaches into his back pocket for his wallet. "I . . . uh . . . want to give you some money for . . . ice cream. Take the boys out a couple times until I can take 'em out myself." He pulls a hundred-dollar bill from the wallet, holds it out for me.

Whatever bad things we could say about Dad 3, we couldn't say he was cheap. From the first night we met him, he's tried to win us over with trips for ice cream or to the convenience store for slushies and candy. I wonder if the Dairy Barn will give change for a hundred.

A horn sounds in the driveway.

"That's my ride." Dad 3 doesn't turn around to Ollie or me. He slams the door behind him.

"Is that it?" Travis asks. "Doesn't he have some stuff?" Mom must have told them Dad 3 was leaving.

"He'll be back. He'll say good-bye."

"Or not . . ." My mother shuffles into the kitchen in a pale blue bathrobe that is shapeless, stained, and ugly. Smeared mascara bruises her eyes. She pulls her favorite pottery coffee cup from the dirty dishwater, rinses it, and reaches for the coffeepot. "And he drank the last damn cup of coffee." She melts down against the counter. This is not a woman who is bouncing back from rejection.

Out of habit I rescue her. "Boys, we're going out to play."

"We just got up," they complain.

"I'll take you for ice cream." Maybe I can text Parker, see if he wants to meet us there. He called me three times yesterday to ask how I was doing. I told him we could meet up today, that I thought I'd be feeling better.

"Ice C-eam? For b-ek-fest?" Stevie jumps up, bounces like he's being bonked on top of the head with a rubber mallet, runs a circuit around the table, his eyes wide, his sleeper pajama feet slipping. It's his best cartoon imitation. Usually we all laugh.

Mom doesn't respond.

I'm in my room changing into shorts and a T-shirt when I hear my mother screaming.

"You bastard! You bastard!"

Feet fly across the hardwood floors.

My mother is beating Dad 3's chest, he stands just inside the door. He grabs her arms, holds her wrists between them. She struggles. "How could you? How old is she? Eighteen? Twenty?"

Behind them a girl with a brown ponytail holds a box labeled RECORDS. A pile of stereo equipment rests by Dad 3's feet.

"There's nothing going on," Dad 3 says. "She's Bernie's sister. She's helping me move."

"You think I'm stupid! I watched you kissing her outside in the driveway."

Bernie's sister, if that's who she is, turns red. *So . . . Dad 3's moved on to another woman . . . uh . . . girl.* I want to vomit.

Their argument continues. Bernie's sister is stupid enough to stand and listen. And, I'm stupid, too, because I need to hear it all, understand how my mom drives away one dad after another. "I told you, I'm dying here," Dad 3 says. "There's nothing for me in this town." The Hat Trick whisper among themselves and they run for their bedrooms. Stevie and Josh make a break after them. Baby Ollie shouts from his playpen in the living room. The energy changes from fight to acceptance as Mom stops struggling and Dad 3 lets go of her arms. They move outside to the driveway. I follow. We are between the front door and a beaten-down truck.

"She . . ." Mom points at Bernie's sister. "She walks through my door one more time and I'm calling the police."

Suddenly, the air is filled with little boy testosterone. The Hat Trick, with the Double Minor behind them, rush out, hockey sticks and plastic swords raised, screaming as if they are actors in a gladiator movie. They fly at Dad 3 and Bernie's sister, smash hockey sticks against their arms, legs. At first Dad 3 laughs as if this is some game he always plays with them.

Bernie's sister dumps the box she's holding and gets into her truck. Slams the door. The boys all gang up on Dad 3. He tries reasoning, "I never hit no one, not one of you, now get off of that."

Mom doesn't try to stop the boys and I don't, either. For me, it's like watching an explosion in slow motion. Mom screams, "Get out! Get out!" Dad 3 surrenders. The boys chase him to the passenger's side, but back away when Dad 3 slams the door. The truck jerks as the girl shifts into reverse.

And now, as if this is some ninja/hockey/vigilante movie, Travis smashes the side mirror with a hockey stick before they get out of the driveway. The boys punch fists in victory. The truck backs away, leaving shards of silver mirror but Dad 3 doesn't look back.

The boys wave their hockey sticks in the air. They are the winners. "Let's get ice cream. We need ice cream," they chant. My mother turns away, hides her eyes behind her hands, the bottom of her robe drags on the walkway to the front door. I could strangle her, her and her self-pity; she's walking away just like Dad 3. She should be consoling the boys, thinking about the consequences of her choices.

I shake in my flip-flops.

And then, I see what can only make this the worst day of my entire life. Parker. He's at the bottom of the driveway. He waves. I wave. Awkward. We both know that he was a witness. Now, what little we have between us is reduced to nothing. I turn to go inside, knowing that he'll head back home. I'm choking on a lump in my throat.

"Jillian. Wait up. Jillian." He still wants to talk to me?

Chantal

• • • • • •

Diva Encounter.

I carry two of my vanilla cupcakes in my backpack. My plan is to give him one first, and after he's experienced the sweet power of cake I'll say, "And I make chocolate, too. With toffee bits. That was one square cake. Baked by one square girl. Quite an extraordinary feat for a plastic cold-blooded fish." I'll watch as the recognition seeps into his thick brain. I will own the moment when he realizes that I know all about the man challenge and I'm about to blow the whole thing wide open. The. Sweetest. Revenge.

I've turned away from downtown onto Will's street, bungalow central, cheap and cheerful. I can't wait to see the embarrassment on his face. Cake is power.

And then I see Annelise. Coming toward me, driving a brand new car. You know how some girls shine such a bright light that squinting and feeling at your ugliest is inevitable?

Annelise is one of the red carpet high school divas and today she's in a canary yellow convertible something-or-other. She's wearing all white, even her sunglasses—the old movie star look, complete with a scarf around her neck. She sees me and slows down, makes a U-turn in the middle of the street for a 360 view. It's sort of wasted on me.

I usually don't pay much attention to cars. If you don't have a driver's license it seems an inefficient use of time.

"Chantal." Annelise stops the car. She turns her top 40 beat down. "Nice wheels. Don'tcha think?"

I nod, but go back to my thoughts. I wonder if the heat is going to melt my cupcake frosting.

"I'm taking it for a test drive."

I move under a shade tree. Not just because of my skin cancer fears. I can't let Annelise watch me walking up to Will's door. She's the kind of girl who'd invite herself along.

"Did you hear me?" Annelise's voice takes on that little girl whiney sound.

"What?"

"Get in."

"I can't. I've got an appointment."

She frowns. Motions me over. I move to the curb only because I want this finished, I need to get on with my life. "I had to, like, do some things, and I needed a car." She tells me how she hates walking so she told the dealership guy that her dad wanted her to test drive some cars to pick one out for grad next year. Of course the sales guy was, like, all over it, she says, knowing, after all, that Annelise's dad is the rich tourism guy. "Don't I look hot?"

I can't stop myself. "You can get some shade if you put the top up." I say this with a straight face and, of course, because Annelise is a bit dim, she thinks I'm serious.

"I don't mean that kind of hot."

I shrug my shoulders and start walking back the way I came from, to knock her off my trail.

"Wait. Wait." She beckons me with her Hollywood wave. "Hey, I have this problem that I wouldn't even have if it weren't for your best friend Jillian." When she leans forward her cleavage mocks me. "Doesn't she know that Parker is totally out of her league?"

I wonder if I could be any more disconnected than I feel right now; like there's a new set of rules that I wasn't smart enough to study up on. "And that's your problem because?"

"I've got Will after me. Will. He thinks I left him a cake at that stupid party that I wasn't even invited to! I need Jillian to let go of Parker. I want my boyfriend back. We're perfect for each other."

She's watching my face so I try to make it frozen like hers. I'm sure my smile isn't nearly as cute. I don't even wear lip gloss. So Parker is in her league and Will isn't, but he'd like to be.

It pisses me off that Will thinks Annelise made him that cake; she's maybe a nail-painting master, but not a cake baker. At least not a cake like that. But of course its specialness was lost on Will. "What did he say about the cake? What flavor was it? Was it anything special?"

"I don't know what kind of cake it was! That doesn't even matter. It was chocolate, I think."

"Did you tell him you didn't bake it?"

"He didn't believe me! He thinks I'm playing hard to get. Not that me baking a cake is impossible! I bake cakes all the time. I get the box of Supermoist Triple Chocolate, that's the best. And the Whipped Fluffy White frosting in the little tub. But why would I bake Will a cake? Honestly, he's delusioned."

"Delusional."

"Whatev."

She's right. He has a hard time seeing reality. Which means that even when he tastes my Vampire Vanilla Cupcakes, he might not believe I made that chocolate cake. He might not care that I know about the man challenge. My revenge might not be sweet. It will simply be another embarrassment. Unless . . .

"So I think I get it. You don't want Will after you?"

"OMG no!" She digs in her purse for lip gloss. "Will over Parker? That's like a fake Chanel classic flap bag over the real thing."

"An imposter." Like processed instead of homemade.

"Exactly."

"And you want me to help you get Parker back."

"Yes! Geez, Chantal, for the smartest girl in the class, you are pretty dense. You know what I'm saying? Get in my car. We need to talk."

I hesitate. Maybe Annelise can help me get my revenge on Will. But my plan could work too well. She might end up on Parker's front line again and Jillian would be benched. But who could blame me? I just want Will to know the wounds of rejection.

I cross in front of the car, open the passenger's door and slide onto the leather seat. The door closes, solid, behind me. "I have an idea," I say. "You can make Parker jealous . . ." I wait for her to catch on, "by . . ."

"By what?"

"By flirting with Will. Let Will think you're all into him."

I lean back against the seat, and catch myself in the side mirror. I look cool. The bright pink headband and my light pink T-shirt are happy against the background of the yellow convertible with white interior, Audrey Hepburn with a few more pounds and a whole lot more hair. I've never felt cool before and I always thought I wasn't missing out. Maybe a girl with brains exudes more cool when she develops a talent for the art of baking.

Annelise's smile has faded. "Why are you helping me?"

I am not stupid. I can't tell Annelise that she's part of my plan to set Will up. She's only in this for herself. Better to give her a simple reason. "I want my best friend back."

"I totally get that." Annelise reaches over to me and puts her hand on my arm. "I always thought you were a stuck-up snob. But actually, you know how to keep it real."

I am charmed by her sudden . . . genuineness. At least for a few seconds. Before I can get too comfortable she shatters my illusions.

"But . . . uh . . . maybe you should get out of my car before someone, like, figures out we're teaming up. I'm not gonna tell anyone about this conversation, you know."

"Right." I'm reluctant to get out of the car because my practiced politeness is pushing me to thank Annelise for this encounter, to tell her that my whole day has just gone from bright to brighter. I end up saying, "Have a nice day," as I wave to her from my spot on the sidewalk.

Now that Annelise has gotten what she wants from me she reaches for the radio and turns it on. Pink sings, Annelise presses the gas pedal. The car moves forward half a block before it lurches to a stop. She turns around and shouts back at me. "Chantal. You've got to ditch those capri pants—they cut you off in the middle of the calf. Wrong, girl, wrong. And the shoes, go for sleek and sporty. Those shoes are for running. Only. They were never intended as streetwear."

"Uh . . . thanks." I wave weakly at her.

"Style is for everyone!" She drives far enough away that I know she won't be stopping to insult my hair or my skin. I can't believe I didn't say anything back. Nerdy *is* a style category. They don't make capri pants for short legs.

Cars pass. RVs follow. And dogs go by. And people at the end of dogs' leashes. And kids on bikes. And skateboards. And the ice cream truck. And I stand, my cream cheese frosting melting. This is my last chance to back out. If I don't go to Will's house, I can hope that Annelise leads him on and his heart is broken. If I go to Will's house I can make sure the job is done right.

I read that Nigella was often nervous about filming her TV show. "I need to be frightened of things," she said. "I hate it, but I must need it, because it's what I do."

Thank you Nigella, you're brilliant. I'm meant to be the girl who moves bravely forward despite the threat of panic attacks. It may not be the first cake or the second, but for sure by the third my plan will have Will cradled in its sugar-coated claws.

Will thinks Annelise baked him a cake? Well, she's about to bake him some more. That's what he'll think anyway, with cards saying, *From your secret admirer.*

As their deliciousness grows, so, too, will his expectations. When the secret admirer cakes no longer arrive and he realizes that he has been publicly dumped by a secret admirer—who by the way, is definitely not Annelise—his humiliation will be more acute than a burst appendix.

This is the easy part of the plan. The hard part: I have to go to Will's house to create a distraction. Right back where we started: a summer project.

Will
• • • • • •
This Charming Man.

The Smiths. Snap. Johnny Marr's guitar and Steven Morrissey's vocals on "This Charming Man" find the sweet spot on my playlist. The guitar forces me to sit back from the screen and stop. My brain connects with sound. Parker calls The Smiths intellectual pop. For shizzle. I know it works. Especially today. At this moment.

I am This Charming Man. Annelise is making my world glow all kinds of groovy-ass colors. The girl is all in. She left me a cake. A cake! And it even tasted great. Okay, so she tried to deny it. That's just one of those girl games. Parker has told me all about how Annelise brings you close and pushes you away until you can't stand it anymore. And I intend to play the game right back at her. The how of this hasn't come to me yet, but it will. I am the master planner.

I lean back in my chair, let the music flood my veins. This is where it's at. It's all good.

I'm interrupted by a knock on my door. Must be my mother. The Ogre never knocks.

"Will. Turn that down. Please." Another knock. "I need to talk to you."

I start out polite with my mother. I try hard to like her, even when I think she's weak and I wish she'd get a new haircut and wear something other than those hideous mom jeans and track pants. She sits in my desk chair and I shift to my bed. When she says, "Your dad's been talking to me," I know I want the conversation to end. "He says you need to get a job. And, before you interrupt me, I don't think it's a bad idea." She reaches out to pat my leg and I push farther away. "What about the hardware store? Maybe they'd take you back on for a few weeks?"

"I don't want to work for them." She doesn't know that Del's Hardware is the reason I won't be getting a job. Anywhere. Last summer the guys at Del's treated me like I was a dumb kid moving lumber from one place to another. I guess that's why I started sticky fingering things. I kept the stash under my bed, tools mostly—a cordless drill, a set of wrenches, screwdrivers, some knives. After a few weeks, I was shopping for the future and I yanked a coffeemaker. The boss called me into his office three days later and I left my nerd apron behind. I told my mom they laid me off.

"Mom. I can't get a job, not this summer. You said it yourself, high school is the best time of your life and it's almost over. Remember, you met Dad in the summer and if he'd been working and you'd been working, well . . ." I would never have been born.

"He wanted to work, though, Will. But his father made him stay home to take care of his brother." And that didn't work out too well; Uncle Bob ended up in jail for armed robbery—holding up tourists at the KOA campsite. "He wants you to stay out of trouble."

"This is my last summer. Everyone is at the lake, every day, and I want to be there, too." I know it's bullshit, and probably lame, but I say it anyway. "I deserve what you and Dad had, at least." It could work. It's got potential.

"Will. Honey." She's got those pity eyes like I'm a UNICEF commercial kid. "You have to get a job if you're going to take girls out on dates."

"Mom. We're not having this conversation." Before I can tell her my personal life is just that, personal, the doorbell interrupts us.

I'm chewing at the dead skin at the edges of my thumb nail, having bitten all of my nails down to the quick, when my mother appears at my door again. "You've got company." My mother's wearing her fancy apron. Bad sign. She couldn't say no to whoever came to the door.

Now, she'll want me to get rid of the intruder. "Mom. I'll give you ten dollars to buy the Girl Scout cookies or make a donation to the bible pushers. I'm busy." I reach for my headphones.

"It's Chantal," Mom whispers. She smiles.

"Chantal?" I stand up too fast, knock the keyboard off my desk. What the hell? I check my look in the mirror. Out of habit. That's all.

"Why didn't you tell me? You know, her dad is the nicest man. And she's sweet."

"Mom. Stop. This isn't what you think it is."

The smile on her face caves. I hate like hell that I'm as much a disappointment as my dad. I wish I could tell her that I am reaching beyond my potential and Annelise, not Chantal, is part of that. Instead, I wrap my arm around my mother's shoulder, squish her in toward me, and her head lays soft against my shoulder. "I wanted to tell you, Mom. I didn't know she was coming over."

Stunned. If I looked into the mirror I'd see a stupid grin plastered on my face. Only my mom would believe I'm happy to be seeing the girl who puked in my mouth.

"Big summer plans, Mom." I know this is what my mother has wanted all along, for me to meet her expectations of a limited life. A girl like Chantal. A job. This town. Grandkids. Money has never been as important to her as family. "Chantal and me, we've been hanging out."

Chantal

· · · · · ·

Blindness.

If you walked into my house, you would find rooms that adhered to these rules of successful decorating: furniture placed in conversational groupings, a selection of black-and-white photographs, and shelves with height-diverse objects in odd numbered clumps. If a person's surroundings say a lot about them, you could say my family is cool and calculating, or cautious and orderly. Jillian's house, with its last-chance-before-the-trash-bin furniture, chaotic patterned curtains made from Indian saris, and wall colors at the extreme ends of the spectrum, could reveal the disorganized and impulsive or represent spontaneity and a love for the quirky.

I expected Will's house to echo his stubbornness, his disregard for social conventions. From outside appearances, it's the last stop before assisted living, a plain bungalow with an arthritic foundation. Inside, I expected overstuffed and floral, a chaotic combination of spoon collections, beer cans, and sticky flypaper strips hanging from the ceiling.

When Mrs. Donovan opened the door and hurried me inside, I stopped and stared at the coordinating fabrics without a rose or hydrangea in sight. The walls with chocolate brown and quiet blue accents whispered sophistication. I wondered if Will's mom watched the same decorating shows that I did. And the smell of vanilla and sugar! Maybe she had a chef-crush on Nigella, too. Sure a pile of supermarket magazines staggered across the sofa, and under the coffee table a stack of high-cleavage romance novels stumbled, but those details were small leaks from Mrs. Donovan's personality, as if she couldn't be completely confined by the rules.

"Chantal." She offered me a chair. "I'm taking some scones out of the oven. You'd like some tea, then?" We knew each other from volunteering at the food bank, one of those social responsibility things my dad insisted on. I'd never seen Will there, though. "I've got a lovely Earl Grey with lavender."

"Great. Great." Now I was going to eat her baking while perpetrating my fraud? I wondered if my guilt was flushing red on my cheeks. "Lovely."

While I waited for her to return I recalculated my assumptions. Mrs. Donovan, from lonely and forlorn to lovely and happy. Will, from sullen and callous to . . . Honestly, I was stuck.

Scones arrived on a delicate plate, and a teacup on a saucer. As we talked I thought about how Mrs. Donovan resembled Nigella. She had dark hair that with a little product could end up in waves.

I sipped my tea and answered her questions about school and my summer and my parents, almost embarrassed at how much she seemed to like me. And how she wanted me to like her.

Mrs. Donovan had returned from the kitchen wearing a black-and-white paisley apron over her faded jeans and stretched sweat-shirt. And she'd combed her hair, slipped on some lipstick in a too-pink color . . . still, her smile was real.

She didn't know that her son was out to get me. Love is blind.

She finished the last bite of her scone. "So . . . you have some plans with Will then?"

I proceeded with caution. "Will's friend Parker and my best friend Jillian are dating, so we've ended up . . . uh . . . spending time together."

Her delight nearly broke my heart.

"I guess I should tell Will you're here, then, shouldn't I?" She got up from her chair and set her empty teacup aside.

"Um . . . sure. Thanks, Mrs. Donovan."

• • •

Like the ingredients of a cake set out on my counter, I have to believe that I have the necessary ingredients to become a convincing imposter. I can think fast, I'm motivated, and I'm not willing to accept defeat.

"Uh . . . Chantal . . . uh . . . great to see you." Will walks into the living room, his hands in his jean pockets and shoulders slouched. If this is great to see you I wonder what the opposite would be.

"Was I early?" I say. "Didn't you say ten thirty?" I can't keep the shaking out of my voice. Lies do not come easy for me.

Will looks uneasily at me and then at his mom. "Oh . . . um . . . I was listening to music. And I lost track of time. No. This is perfect." He sits in the nearest chair to mine. "Perfect." Will, though, is smooth and clearly practiced at lying.

We smile at each other and take turns looking toward the doorway at his mother. When she senses the awkwardness she retreats. "Oh . . . I'm going to do the dishes in the kitchen. Just holler if you need anything. Tea. Scones. Lunch."

Will waits until she's gone. He smiles. "You want to tell me what's going on?"

And in that second, or maybe half-second, the way it happens in books and movies, I know the color drains from my face. *I can't do this.* I want to come out with a quick response, something clever, but I don't. *Didn't I have a plan? What was it again? Crud.*

"Seriously, Chantal." Will's intensity unsettles me further. "Not that I'm complaining or anything. It's just . . ." Will listens for kitchen noise, reassurance that his mother is occupied. "Why are you here?"

"I . . . um . . . want . . ." It's action time. Action. Action. "I want to do a summer project."

"A what?"

I explain how Jillian and I have always had a summer project and how, now that she's with Parker, there's a good chance that there won't be one. "I like to have a purpose for the summer."

"So you want me to hang out with you all summer and, like, bake cookies for the day-camp kids?"

"What?" Bake cookies? Uh-oh.

"Well, isn't that a summer project?"

"Oh. Yeah. No. I didn't mean that just you and me would do the summer project. I meant that *we* could do a summer project. You and me and Parker and Jillian."

"O-kay . . ."

He is not making this easy. "I need your help. Okay?"

He sits back in his chair, nods.

"Our best friends are dating and if I'm not friends with you then I'll be the third point in a triangle and that's always . . . awkward. But if it's the four of us, I'll get to hang out with Jillian and we can do a summer project."

He says nothing, but his face says he's skeptical.

The panic feeling comes in a rush. My hands shake. I wonder if I'm hypoglycemic, if I should risk pulling a cupcake from my bag. I could tell him it's my emergency low-sugar stash. I press into the back of my chair. I can almost hear the squished cupcakes cry in protest.

"Well, I do want to do a summer project because it . . . gives structure . . . to the summer." Even though I'm breathing hard between each sentence, I am communicating. Will is listening. "But I miss Jillian, too." That is not a lie. Even though it's not the entire truth.

Will strokes the patches of stubble on his chin. "I could be down with that. As long as I get something out of it." He leans in so close that when he talks I see three silver fillings in his bottom molars. "I need a girlfriend. And you can help me out there."

"Um . . . um . . ." This is too strange. I've got Annelise convinced to flirt with Will to make Parker jealous and I'm planning to send him cakes that I'm sure he'll believe are from Annelise and now he wants me to help him find a girlfriend? Some other girl could wreck everything. I think fast and, hopefully, smart. "My only real friend is Jillian, and she's, like, taken. I'd help you if I could."

"You can." He stares at me. Really stares at me.

My eyes must go wide as the panic sets in again. He wants me to be his girlfriend?

"Relax." He laughs, then, whispers, "You're just for show." He motions his head toward the kitchen.

Oh I get it. The classic villain move—make friends with the good guys to convince people that you're good. He needs me to keep his mother happy.

"So . . . you'll help me with getting the four of us to do a summer project if I pretend to be your girlfriend." I cross my arms and sit back. I thought the summer project would keep Will busy and, more importantly, away from me. He could be in charge of one thing, me of another, and then I'd have lots of space to bake and deliver the cakes. And now he wants me to pretend to be his girlfriend? Doesn't that imply time spent together, just the two of us? "Well, it could work, but we have to have rules."

"Rules?" He clenches his jaw.

"Relax." I smile. "I have rules for everything. It makes things easier, not harder."

"It's not a problem. I can come up with rules, too."

"That's fair, I guess." I take a deep breath. This is not easy. "Um . . . first . . . you and me . . . we are friends. Only friends. No physical contact. It's . . . I don't really need the complication."

"Agreed." He nods. "Except. Around my mom, we definitely need to make it look like we could be more than friends, okay?" He waits for my agreement. "And around everyone else at the lake, we're just friends."

I nod and keep my face neutral. They don't need to know about this. He wants to make sure Annelise thinks he's available. Yes. This works. I try to ignore the disappointment that twists in my stomach. I know I'm not what he, or any other guy wants. I try to imagine myself as fifteen or twenty pounds lighter. Would that make me better looking?

"This is a deal breaker." He interrupts my self-flogging. "You're going to have to trust me. Like if I hold your hand or something it's only a part of our image. Okay? You can't, like, debate with me in front of people."

I nod. We go through some more rules: no dating other people because that could wreck our "image," no showing up at each other's house unannounced, but no refusing to come over when invited. Suddenly Will asks, "How do I know you're not playing me after what happened at the party?"

"I have never been a vengeful person." I say that straight up. I don't think I have ever wanted to hurt someone, even if they've hurt me. Until now.

"Everyone wants revenge, Chantal. You just hide it." I hate his smugness and, interestingly, anger fuels my ability to think.

"Trust me," I say. "Like you said."

Parker

. . . . . .

Not a Masked Man.

$\mathcal{I}$ really wasn't out to rescue her. I walked to her house as a test. See, if I could pass her house without knocking on the door, I knew she was a temporary date, not the kind of girl I wanted to date-date.

But, of course, it got complicated. My mother would have called the cops. I saw the swarm of boys wailing on that guy and his girl-friend's truck with their hockey sticks and I was, like, holy crap, this is unbelievable. Jillian's mom was screaming. The two littlest kids, and they were in diapers or those pull-up pants, they were calling him a bastard. By the time the truck tires screeched out of the cul-de-sac, the mom was gone and the boys surrounded Jillian. She covered her face with her hands, and I almost turned around to leave, but I was hooked, like watching some YouTube viral thing you know is too raw. It was, as Will would say, White Trash Central.

And this was the girl who beat me in a foot race, the girl who was number two in our class, the girl who didn't sleep around, with any-one. She wasn't white trash, no matter how much it looked like it from the outside.

I cheer for the underdog: the Edmonton Oilers, the Cleveland Browns, the Baltimore Orioles. I like Will even though he's a scrapper. From where I live, it's easy to succeed. For people like Will and Jillian, it's not.

I walked up the driveway carrying one of the abandoned hockey sticks.

"Parker. It's not a good time." Jillian picked up both of the little boys, one on each side. They gripped her sweatshirt, strangely contorting her shape, and buried their runny noses in her neck. She didn't seem to notice that she looked like hell; her hair was back in a greasy ponytail, her eyes ringed in yesterday's makeup. I'd never seen Annelise that rough; even the times we'd fallen asleep watching a movie at her place she woke up near perfect.

"I . . . uh . . ." I searched Jillian's face for what she wanted to hear. She chewed the flaky skin on her bottom lip. The boys seemed to be waiting to find out what I was going to say, because none of them moved. "Um . . . I just came by to see how you were doing."

"It's embarrassing." Jillian stared at the ground, like the shoe gazer, trying to figure out which pedal to play next.

"It's life." I shrugged. Man, I was dying, like playing a show and realizing the crowd had drifted away. And then, channeling a geek philosopher/health teacher, I added, "Anyway. It's not your fault."

One of the three boys sniffled behind me. His brother punched him in the arm. "Quit cryin', ya baby, or I'll give you somethin' to cry about."

I laughed. I couldn't help myself. Will used to punch me all the time to toughen me up. Just like us, these kids did stupid, brave shit like attack a grown man and his truck with hockey sticks. I pointed at the slivers of mirror spiking the driveway. I laughed. The three boys with the hockey sticks sort of came around.

"Hey, you got any nets?" I asked the crier. He looked up at me through his flop of brown hair. He frowned but I figured I had him. When I was his age and all my brothers were too busy to hang, sometimes a miracle happened and one of them would take me out to throw the ball. The three boys whooped to the backyard to get the nets and goalie pads.

"Thanks." Jillian, I could tell, was more relieved than enthusiastic. "I'll . . . um . . . get the Double Minor in some clothes."

"Double Minor?"

"You know, two penalties at the same time. Hockey?"

"I know. It's just . . . funny. Really funny."

"You think so?"

I nodded.

"Well, if you're still up for it, I guess we can go for ice cream."

"Sure." I wanted to reach out and kiss her. I wanted her to know that I wasn't looking for the emergency exit.

Jillian

· · · · · ·

Not Cinderella.

It's happening . . .

No. No. No. Not *it*.

Parker and me. Dating. Girlfriend and boyfriend. The Parkillian, Chantal says.

Parker laughs; he laughs at things Chantal says and he laughs at things the boys say. He laughs. We laugh together. All that laughing is good. It's all good. Maybe this is how it's supposed to happen when you have a boyfriend: you become happier.

But I worry. I worry that I'm a pity girlfriend. What he saw would make anyone pity me. It's not like he can relate to my life. He has had the same dad his whole life. And his mom was head classroom mom every year of elementary school, in charge of bulletin boards and parties. My mom dropped off a bag of chips at Halloween. I would date me—that's how sorry I feel for me.

The boys *love* him. He plays hockey, he wrestles, and he listens to their detailed stories of television show plots. He reads bedtime stories, with funny voices. And my mom likes him. She's always leaning over and whispering to me, "He's a real keeper." But look at all the fish she's thrown out.

The worst and weirdest thing is that before Parker was at my house all I dreamed about was kissing him and . . . (You know what those sorts of dreams can be like.) Now, sometimes when he stops me in the laundry room or in the kitchen and he leans in to kiss me, I am strangely reluctant.

I wonder how you get rid of a curse against men in a house.

Chantal

· · · · · ·

A Planning Princess.

As a straight-A student I appear to be capable of many things. And I am—but not quickly or without the proper research. Example: when I was in the sixth grade my teacher said I took too long solving math word problems. This was inexplicable, she told my mother, because everyone knew I was smart. So I went into training: train A left the station at 1 P.M. traveling at 40 mph, train B left at 4 P.M. traveling at 60 mph . . . you get the idea. A month later the teacher was asking me to solve problems at the board, claiming she knew all along that I would "just get it." It was more about not giving up than it was about a sudden magical insight.

It isn't surprising, then, that when I left Will's house I went directly to the library where I spent the next three hours poring over cookbooks. I needed to be sure that I could create one beautiful, delicious, scrumptious cake after another. Let's face it, the cheesecake tasted good but it looked sad. The SRC^2 was an unlikely-to-be-repeated miracle save. And the Vampire Vanilla Cupcakes were delicious (though I never shared them with Will)—but you repeat vanilla/vanilla too many times and your audience is going to get bored. I had to be sure that I was up to the task.

I started with Nigella's *How to Be a Domestic Goddess*. It isn't so much about being a domestic goddess, but *feeling* like a domestic goddess. You don't see too many domestic goddesses my age around, but not many girls know how useful it can be.

"Everyone seems to think it's hard to make a cake (and no need to disillusion them)," Nigella writes, "but it doesn't take more than twenty-five minutes to make and bake a tray of muffins or a sponge layer cake, and the returns are high: you feel disproportionately good about yourself afterwards. This is what baking, what all of this book, is about: feeling good, wafting along in the warm, sweet-smelling air, unwinding . . ."

Yes. I devoured her recipes. Her burnt-brown sugar cupcakes, her almond cake, and her dozen variations on chocolate layers captivated me. Her book alone was enough, but the Dewey decimal system is such a hook: 641 is now my favorite subdivision of the preferred 640 class, Home Economics and Family Living. I found *The Art & Soul of Baking* by Cindy Mushet, *Baking, From My Home to Yours* by Dorie Greenspan, Pierre Herme's *Desserts by Pierre Herme,* oh, and cookbooks by Anna Olson, Alice Medrich, and Rose Levy Beranbaum. I studied their formulations. I realized that I'm no longer baking to eat cake—I'm in love with creating cake. And with the message I'm sending out. The sweet revenge is always there.

I should have slouched all the way home, with the three thickest books in my arms and the additional weight of a bag of baking supplies, but I walked with a new confidence.

When I open the front door, I'm startled the radio is playing until I remember that I left it on, a strategy my mother insisted would keep the burglars away. Michael Bublé serenades me, inspiring me with his "Lost" lyrics. "You are not alone," I sing with him. "I'm always there with you." The crescendo to the final chorus is coming and I grab the cordless to serve as my microphone.

I stop singing. As if someone has just walked into the room. And, really, she has.

The flashing light on the phone tells me someone's left a message.

Crud. I was supposed to phone my mother three hours ago. I listen to her message. She'd already texted me her hotel phone number and room number and if I don't want her to call me every hour for the next twenty-four hours I'd better text her back. I find my phone and text. *I am fine. Love you.* I try to recover that feeling of . . . freedom . . . again, but it's covered, as if a blob of black ick has dripped on my sweet, buttery yellow day.

I need to forget that I only have unencumbered use of the kitchen until my mom comes home on Saturday; that's three nights. I pile my groceries in a pyramid on one counter, the cookbooks in a stack on the table. You can handle Mom, I repeat three times. I have to banish worry and doubt so I can bake.

Suddenly, I realize that I'm hungry. Starving. Twelve splendid cupcakes sit on the counter next to my bricks of unsalted butter. I take one and cut it in half, one half for now and the other for five minutes from now. But after the first bite, I pause. Do I want a cupcake? My brain spins. I sort of feel like something healthy. An apple. A peanut butter and jelly sandwich. Maybe a glass of ice water. I'm so thirsty. After I feast on solid brain food, I stare at my cupcakes. *Is it fair if I no longer want to eat you? Can I love you enough by looking at you?*

The radio plays a summer song, Sheryl Crow singing "All I Wanna Do." I dance around the kitchen. Who knew that living in my house alone would be so much fun? And that I would be smarter than ever? And that I am such. A fantastic. Singer. And dancer. I dance and let my brain cells go to work for me. My invisible audience cheers.

The solution is easy. I'll give the cupcakes away. But . . . the obvious recipients, Jillian and her brothers, won't work. It's not that I have to keep my cake baking a secret from Jillian. It's that I want to. It's sort of like those makeover shows on TV, where the girl goes shopping in New York with thousands of dollars and she gets her hair and her makeup done and then when she goes home, everyone throws a party for her and she walks in and it's a big ta da? I want to be that girl. I want my moment. When I surprise them with my baking expertise. I know Jillian will understand.

Before the cupcakes leave my home, I will treat them to a photo shoot. Then I'll parade them over to Mrs. Ellis next door. After I explain the art and soul of my newly renamed Very Vanilla Cupcakes, I'll ask her if I can keep her beautiful mixer for a few more days. Problem solved. Next!

The rest of the evening is faultless.

I cream six ounces of unsalted butter with three quarters of a cup of sugar, beating them until very light—almost white—in color. I add three healthy large eggs, warmed to room temperature, mixing completely between each one and, finally, I trickle in heavenly scented vanilla. Honestly, if I was only allowed to smell one thing for the rest of my life I might choose vanilla.

The dry ingredients of sifted cake flour, baking soda, and salt go into a bowl and I whisk them together before I add them, alternately, with the sour cream to the egg batter. I'm careful not to under-or over-mix. I pour the batter into the prepared pan (that's baking speak for buttered and floured) and let it bake in the 350-degree oven for thirty minutes. My joy is irrepressible as I retrieve the exquisitely domed, light, and evenly colored layer from the oven. Success! Again! If only everything were so predictable.

With some of Nigella's ease, I create the same frosting I made the night before, only this time with a little cherry extract and several drops of red food coloring. It takes away the emptiness of a long night alone. Pink pizazz for a girl who is hopeful that life is on an upswing.

Jillian

······

The Unexpected and Unexplained.

I lost the debate with my mother.

I have won every debate I've prepared for, except for the ones that matter the most.

It started when she announced that with Dad 3 leaving town she couldn't afford to put Ollie in day care for the next two months. I'd known this was coming; I'd listened on the other side of her bedroom door as she talked to a girlfriend on the phone.

Ollie was down for a nap and the Hat Trick and Double Minor were playing video games. I knew I'd have about thirty minutes before a fight broke out. I found my mother sitting in one of our plastic lawn chairs in the backyard. She appeared to be half-ready for work wearing her nursing-home scrub top and her denim cutoff short shorts. She rested her feet in the plastic kiddie pool. She was smoking again? Her right hand held a cigarette to her lips and she inhaled, held the smoke in her lungs, rested her head against the back of the lawn chair and exhaled, a thin, toxic, sighing stream. A lighter and a pack of Marlboro Lights lay in the grass.

I wasn't sure I could cover each of my debate points, wasn't sure that she'd let me talk until I was done. I handed her my list of arguments, printed from the laptop Dad 2 gave me before he moved out.

"I don't think it's appropriate for me to babysit Ollie while you're at work this summer," I began. "Developmentally he needs more stimulation than I can provide while I'm trying to take care of the other boys."

My mother smiled as she looked over the paper. "Those boys have each other, that's the good part of having them in sets."

Her smile encouraged me. Maybe we could talk about this. "But they fight, too, and they get into trouble. They tore the fence down, twice, last summer. And I wasn't watching Ollie then."

"Take away their video games if they do anything bad. They love shooting bad guys on the screen. That's what they're doing now, isn't it? And we're sitting out here, relaxing in the sun." She closed her eyes.

"This is about Ollie. He needs to be with someone who can help him grow intellectually."

She laughed. "Jillian, you'll be perfect for that."

"But . . . a professional will have a plan for talking to him about cause and effect relationships, sharing picture books and crafts and . . ." That was point five; I'd just skipped three and four.

"Get Chantal over here. That girl loves a freaking plan."

I swallowed. I'd practiced this in my head. I was just going to say it. Say it. "You need to get someone else."

"You act, Jillian, like there is an option here. There's not. And all this high and mighty stuff . . ." She read from the top of the paper. " 'Developmental Stages and Intellectual and Emotional Needs of a One-Year-Old.' Shit, girl. You're ready to go. If I could pay you, I'd give you a raise."

My stomach twisted at how foolish my words sounded when she read them back. "I don't want to do this." My voice shrank to a small dismal sound. I knew my stand against babysitting Ollie didn't have to do with not being confident or capable, at least not very much. I couldn't take care of all the boys and be Parker's girlfriend.

And more than anything else, I wanted to be able to have him look into my eyes and not see the panicked me—worrying about breaking up fights, or how I'd handle the next temper tantrum.

"Don't be a victim, Jillian. It's embarrassing." She let the paper fall from her hands, into the kiddie pool. The black ink became more visible as the paper soaked up water. Words don't mean anything to my mother.

She lit a second cigarette, her lips pinching together, the wrinkles defying her attempts to look young and hot with her carefree hair, her bralessness. She was only fooling herself. "You're embarrassing." I wished I hadn't said it the second that it came out of my mouth.

Her reaction was shock, but that didn't last long. Not long enough to give me real satisfaction. She laughed. Snorted. "I am doing you a favor and you're not even grateful. Those boys are the only way you're going to keep that boyfriend of yours. Men want to rescue girls. They want to be the prince on the white horse." She pulled her feet out of the water and pushed herself up from her lawn chair, the skin ripping against the plastic. As she bent down to retrieve her cigarettes and lighter, the cellulite on the back of her red-streaked thighs jiggled.

"Just be careful," she said as she turned toward me, waving her cigarette in the air. "Once you graduate you can get yourself pregnant and hold on to any man you want, but you're going to graduate first. You need to have an education to fall back on."

She took one last long drag, the cigarette paper curling into ash as she sucked on the filter, then she dropped it in the grass. I wanted to warn her about the fire danger. Instead I watched the smoke trail up.

• • •

Just as I'm almost ready to take the boys to the library for a couple of hours (it's self-contained and they expect children), Chantal calls, excited about another summer project. We haven't talked in nearly a week and she's still on about the summer project?

I cut her off before she can get too far. "I've got all the boys this summer. Even if I wanted to, I can't do a summer project."

"But you have to." Chantal has that only-child whine in her voice. Being her best friend doesn't mean agreeing to everything she wants. "I think we already went through this. My brothers come first right now."

"But . . ."

"No." Before I can press pause, I say everything. "You do not need me this summer. Because I can't be needed by you. Do you understand?" I don't even stop to hear her feeble protest. "You know what you need? You need to loosen up. You need to have more fun. You need to stop thinking everything through and deciding the most efficient, less painful, less potentially embarrassing path. You need to let yourself be unorganized. You need to let yourself be wrong."

"Jillian, what's going on?"

"You need to know."

"Know what?"

"Know what you're missing. Where you *ought* to draw the line, instead of where you're drawing the line because you're afraid." I hold the phone away from my mouth so she can't hear my rapid breathing. I don't know how to stop.

"Ouch. I didn't know you felt so strongly," she says. "I'm working on it. I took care of your brothers, all by myself, even in a flood. And I'm . . . biking . . . I've been doing a lot of biking. And I love it. I mean, it's so . . . creative . . ."

Creative biking? Tell me this isn't the summer project she wants me to do. Now I'm beginning to feel sorry for her.

"And I feel like I'm growing into someone who is . . . better." After a week? I wait for the crying to start. I wonder why she hasn't insisted on coming over here to talk this out face-to-face. I wonder why she isn't at least sighing heavily into the phone. I wonder if she's still on the line.

"Chantal? Are you there?"

"I thought we'd do the summer project with Parker . . . and Will."

Huh? "You don't want to do a summer project with Parker, and definitely not with Will. Please."

"Remember last summer? Remember you called me and you said that three times that morning you nearly got in the car to drive away? You said you just wanted a break from the drudgery."

"I think I said prison duty." But, I get it. She's desperate. And if she's willing to accept Parker, well, things could be very different. "What about my being too vulnerable to be around Parker? What about throwing my life away?"

"I went too far." In the silence that follows, I hear a whirring noise in the background; it must be the dishwasher. "Can I have a second chance?"

We're even. We both said things we shouldn't have, and now we can break up. I can tell her that we're not a good match and we've grown apart. I can say I'm sorry for what happened. I can tell her it's not her fault. I can tell her we need time apart. I can cut this complication out of my life. Instead I say, "We need to have some rules."

"I love rules."

"We're not creative biking."

"What?"

"Everyone gets to decide and I'm saying right now I veto creative biking."

"Strike creative biking from the list."

"You can't roll your eyes."

"What?"

"You're not allowed to roll your eyes when Parker or Will talks— it's not polite."

"Jillian. I don't roll my eyes," Chantal starts. "Okay, I just did. And I won't."

"And you can't make that big sighing noise if they say something that you think is stupid."

"I don't—okay, I won't. Any more conditions of engagement?"

"Yes. We need to say we're sorry . . ." Though my words stop, the communication doesn't end. Sometimes silence says more.

"You know I'm sorry." Chantal has that choked-up sound in her voice. "You're my best friend . . ."

"And I'm sorry for not listening to you before I started my verbal—"

"—Assault."

"I was going to say punishment."

I hear her stifle a sigh. "And I'm sorry for . . ." Chantal breathes into the phone. "For the night of the party. I'm going to respect your right to run your own life. I won't say another disparaging thing about Parker. And I love your brothers, almost as much as you do."

"Okay." It comes out choked, as if gratitude were the wishbone of a chicken stuck in my throat. If only my mother could listen and understand me like Chantal does. I have given my mother a thousand chances. "Apology accepted. But we do have an issue. I have to take care of all the boys this summer."

"Even Ollie? Why?"

It's like I didn't say this at the beginning of the call. "It doesn't matter why. And don't bother telling me it's not fair."

"I wasn't going to say that . . ."

I don't fill in her pause.

"Okay, I was. But, we can work it out. We *need* to have a summer project. It's our last project before we graduate."

"*You* need to have a summer project," I correct her. "And I *would like* to have a summer project that's fun, if everyone is included."

"Don't worry about the boys. We'll all pitch in."

"I don't know. If Will gets ahold of them, they'll be little slang masters. Yo, so snap, dude." We laugh. "And what's up with Will? You don't even like him, do you?"

"Not like, like." Chantal stutters. "Um . . . well, we've come to a truce. An understanding."

"Okay . . . but are you sure you want to try to do a summer project with him?"

"Oh, it'll be fine. I'm the master planner you know . . ."

"And that's your favorite part, second only to the performance," I add.

"Performance? Oh . . . maybe we don't need a performance this year. Or . . . maybe there could be something. Maybe a little less nerdy than last year. But fun. Still fun."

I stand in front of my mirror as I talk. I look pretty good today. Pretty good. My hair has just enough body. My T-shirt curves in all the right places. My legs are just enough tan. I think I can see why Parker is attracted to me. Maybe my mom is trying to keep me away from him. Maybe she's jealous that she's not young anymore or that she can't have a summer. Sad.

"So you'll meet me at the lake tomorrow morning?"

"Definitely," I say. "We shouldn't let anything stop us."

Chantal

· · · · · ·

Crushing.

I click the phone off, clutch it against my chest, and collapse against the wall. That was close. Crud. I was ready to tell her everything about the revenge plan and my secret cake baking, but what she wanted was an apology.

Jillian's always been the one who talked me down from the ledge of this-is-going-to-be-a-disaster. But, this summer, I'm going to prove that I can do things differently. Not only will I participate in the world's most unlikely summer project, but I can handle Will and the problems that he's dishing out—all on my own. Jillian will be shocked. First her best friend babysits her six brothers, deals with a flood and a blackout, and then she successfully avenges the guy who threatened her reputation. And they all lived happily ever after.

The cake is gorgeous. Cherry pink swirls flirt over the top and down the sides of my vanilla-scented Crush On You creation. Named and baked by me, it will be the star of a show-stopping performance. The note made with cut-out letters from my stack of old magazines spells out the instructions.

I set the cake in my bike basket, pull on my all-black shirt, shorts, and biking gloves, snap the strap on my helmet. I don't want to get caught during my first delivery.

Jillian

· · · · · ·

A Charming Morning.

This morning, despite my saying three times, "This is really insane, Parker. Five little boys and a one-year-old at the lake will be our last date," we load my brothers into the van with towels, sand toys, and a picnic lunch. I drive while he reads *Sesame Street* stories from the front seat. Ollie giggles at the Oscar the Grouch growls. As we pull into the parking lot Parker retrieves his phone from the van console and starts texting. Within minutes a crew of four girls arrives at the van; one is our physics teacher's daughter, Chloe. She introduces her friends and makes a rush for Ollie.

"Oh, I'll take him," Chloe coos. (I'm not kidding, she coos.) She scoops him out of my arms. "I love babies."

"Um . . ." I'm used to people wanting to hold Ollie, he is that cute, but Chloe is sort of *taking* him. Before I can object, Parker steps in.

"Okay, boys." He gathers the Hat Trick and Double Minor into a sports huddle. "We've got a camp all planned out for you this summer."

"We? Who are we?" My stomach cramps. He's taking over? I don't need this. Do I? He leans out of the huddle.

"Well, I guess it's me. Me and the babysitters." He outlines the schedule: the girls will supervise the six boys for two hours in the morning at the playground. Parker and I take over for swimming time and lunch. After lunch it's either naptime if you're little or you're hanging out with Chloe and her friends for two hours. We end the day with more swim time and we all go home together. He is enthusiastic and precise, a male version of Chantal minus the anxiety.

"Parker?" I wave him over. He grins and moves close to me. Very close. I smile through clenched teeth. "How are they getting paid?"

"The girls?"

I nod.

He avoids direct eye contact with me. "I'm paying them."

"No."

"It's a gift. Chantal called last night. She explained that we're going to do some sort of project—the four of us. I thought you'd want to have fun without the kids sometimes." He doesn't hide the mix of confusion and annoyance in his voice.

"The boys are my responsibility." I'm not going to waver.

He takes a deep breath. Stands up straight. Stares out at the lake and back to the boys. Finally, he speaks. "You are a sister. Not a mother. We will be here if they need us."

Even though I want to say something back right away, something like you hardly even know me, I'm smart enough to squash that impulse. Instead I consider what he's said. I am a sister. Most sisters would take help.

Rocks ping off of trees. Boy-generated entertainment. I watch. Chloe dives in to rescue Ollie from the firing range. Now Travis is trying to convince Stevie to run through the woods so they have a target. "We'll aim for your legs," Travis says. One of the other girls grabs Stevie's hand to stop him. If I'm in charge alone, we'll probably come to the lake once a week if we're lucky. That means we're stuck with the backyard and the kiddie pool. "If I agree, I'll give you an IOU. And I'll pay you back."

"If you want to." Parker shrugs.

"Of course I want to. You act like money doesn't matter. It's going to be expensive. Four girls every day for the summer. And . . . that's a lot of money." I bet he's never had to cut the mold off the bread. They probably throw their old bread out at his house.

"Think of it like this. You're my girlfriend. Instead of taking you to the movies and going out for dinner and I don't know, bowling, our dates are at the lake."

I'm his girlfriend. I weaken. "But what if someone gets hurt? Someone always gets hurt."

"The girls have first aid training. I taught the class. I was a day-camp counselor four summers in a row. And Chloe is the perfect age, fourteen. In another year she'll probably be into boys but we've got her for this summer anyway." Implying there could be another one.

"And if it rains?"

"We all go home. Together."

I can't agree. I can't say yes. I can't commit to this just because I want some time off.

Parker's hand is at my elbow and then the other one. And we're in that let's dance position. I look up at him. God, he's so gorgeous. "We're good then?"

"Parker." I stare at him. I want him to see that taking charity isn't easy. That I don't expect it. That I am not my mother. He leans forward, kisses me and, finally, I feel like I don't want him to stop. Maybe the curse against him is only at our house.

"Gross!" Trevor yells. "Can we go now? This is boring."

Everyone deserves to have fun. Especially us.

Chantal

· · · · · ·

Circle Perfection.

I understand the problem with perfection. I am, after all, the daughter of a mother who believes that if I eat healthy enough, sleep eight hours a night, exercise no less than thirty minutes each day, study a minimum of thirty minutes for each subject every school night, limit my exposure to TV and the Internet, stay away from drugs and alcohol, and floss my teeth after every meal, I will be the model of a perfect daughter. But would a perfect daughter be baking cakes when her mother told her not to? Would she wish her mother would stay away for a little longer?

My mother wasn't here, but I was still arguing with her in my mind. So . . . I talked to Nigella. Virtually. (That sounds better than I was hearing her voice in my head. Right?)

You are two things, a baker and a daughter. Like a yolk from the white, you've got to separate the two. Both are useful. Both are good. Yes, that's well put. Both are good.

I'm not saying virtual Nigella told me what to do, but she reassured me. And my mom? I don't have to do anything about her for another two nights. Today, I'm at the lake amid the circles of umbrellas and the towel rectangles to plan a summer project and watch my cake's debut.

· · ·

I hike up the hill to our tree, hoping I'm not the first person to arrive. It's okay if I'm only meeting Jillian, she doesn't think prompt arrival is dork[2], but Will probably does. He wouldn't say it now, would he? Now that we're sort of on a team. I wish I didn't care what he thinks. I trip over a sippy cup that's rolled away from a little kid. I grab it before it rolls too much farther and return it to the girl. The mom thanks me.

See? I'm a kind dork. A mess of panic under pale skin. I ignore the trembling in my legs. I see our tree, and people under it. This is a sign, clearly, that the day is going to go my way. The next sign is that Jillian and Parker are there, and Will isn't.

So little space separates Parker and Jillian that I wonder how close they've gotten, off the hill. Still, I smile wide and drop my backpack across from them.

"Hey."

Parker shifts away from Jillian, his hand trailing along her back and Jillian looks down, awkward that I see this closeness. Before it can get any weirder than that, we hear Will's voice.

"Amigos!"

He fist punches Parker, says hi to Jillian, and then it's my turn. His voice is softer than usual, and he looks me over before he meets my eyes. "How's it goin'?" His head nods almost imperceptibly and he smiles with half his mouth. I wait to feel something other than anxiety fuelling my pounding heart and my sweaty palms, but it just gets worse. Crud. I want to hit him. I need to sit down. But he's still staring, waiting for a response.

"Um . . . the weather station says the warm front is going to be with us for a few days. I sort of saw it coming, you know the stratiform clouds the day before yesterday, but we didn't get any rain, usually you get rain before a warm front. But . . . no rain. Not a drop. Dry as a . . ." My voice trails off. Clearly my dad's advice—you can always talk about the weather when you don't know what to say— is making this whole thing worse.

"Do you watch the Weather Channel?" Will asks.

"Not much," I say.

"Great memory," Jillian says. "Nearly photographic. One of her many gifts."

"Really?" Will unrolls his towel. "So you'll never forget my face, even when you're ancient."

I shake my head. And now, because I'm still in panic mode, I speak without thinking through the consequences. "That would be a disadvantage of having a great memory."

Parker laughs first and Jillian joins in. Even Will halfway laughs along. I laugh last, when I realize it might be safe.

"You're funny," Will says.

I pull my towel from my backpack, lay it out, and sit. I smile. And I feel good, more than good. Great. I'm funny. I am. Funny. I notice that our rectangle towels are laid in a circle. Through long breaths in and out, the panic begins to subside.

Will

......

Stoked on the Bridge.

It's like we're two punks and two folkies trying to write a song. Me, I'm stoked on the bridge, that long instrumental solo that's like an explosion of complicated sound that kicks you right in the gut. I want the big show. Parker, he's playing the transitions. Dude, I want to shout at him, just 'cause Jillian's your girlfriend, doesn't mean you need to freakin' lose your mind and stop being you. First the rug rats, now he can't make a decision? Jillian's all about the chorus, let's all get on the same page, let's all sing together. And Chantal, oh my freakin' boxer shorts, her mind noise volume is maxed out.

Jillian looks up from her spiral notebook. "Okay, so we know we want something that will benefit the community, something that's fun, something that involves everyone's skill set, a big show of some sort, a way to keep the boys interested, and we want to make some money for charity."

"That's closer," Chantal says. I watch her spread sunscreen along her arms for the third time. I consider grabbing the tube and firing it into the lake.

"Can we move on? Forty-five minutes on goals and objectives?" I lie back on my towel. "The summer will be over before we finish planning." Maybe working at a job I hate would be killer over this.

"Hey, stay with the brain trust, man." Parker grabs a can from the cooler and tosses it to me.

"Now, we're ready for popcorn." Chantal slathers her lips with some SPF 75 lip balm.

"Popcorn? What the hell?"

"You throw out ideas, whatever pops in your brain."

"What have we been doing for the last hour?"

"Well . . . this is like popcorn extreme. Badass, if you will. Kernels straight up, no chaser." She laughs at her joke and everyone else laughs along with her. What the hell?

"Funny." I say. "Funny." Who is this girl? Until yesterday, I'd pretty much only witnessed her spewing factual information at any given point—even Cranium is about showing off what you know—and now she wants to be funny? What gives? Is she trying to impress me? I tune out of their conversation and I watch. Chantal.

In a plain T-shirt and long shorts, her dark hair pulled back by a stretchy hair band, she is the sort of girl a guy marries, not the kind he dates. The girl I'm going to marry has to be more hipster than mess of the moment. I don't want a girl I have to rescue every other day or call every hour while I'm out with my friends. And I want a girl who can think on her own. And she should like my kind of music. And it would be cool if she played kick-ass Halo. Chantal laughs with her mouth wide open, like a chimp. I don't know if I can get used to that. I wonder what she'd say to one of my favorite lines—if you could get a tattoo what would it be and where? She'd probably say the chemicals in the ink haven't been approved for use in the body. Does she know the awesomeness of Dinosaur Jr.'s lyrics? Could she learn to love them?

Now, she's furiously writing on her clipboard, focused and sort of, I almost hate to say it, looking fine. She'll be someone's girlfriend one day. Married. With a couple kids. A top corporate something.

A lawyer. An ambassador. Living anywhere but in this small town with its limited jobs and/or small-minded failure to appreciate most things hip and cool. Maybe we're sort of the same in a weird way, at two ends of the same spectrum, running parallel. In some other dimension, we might be the perfect couple. I think Dinosaur Jr. has a song about people like us.

Just as I'm trying to remember the song that could be our song, I'm stunned.

It's Annelise. The bikini that's two strings away from illegal catches my attention first. And I'm not alone. Heads swivel and stay with her as she passes them; everything sways in the right proportion; her long hair is the harmony. As she gets closer I see her model-wide smile, notice how she doesn't look around to see who is looking at her. No, she is marching almost directly at me. I sit up straight. Glance over at Chantal who is writing something on her clipboard, oblivious to what is about to happen. This is a different Annelise from the one who always makes it clear that we will only ever be friends. And I'm not sure. I swallow, like I'm eleven and on the playground and the girls have just told me they want me to play CCK—chase them, catch them, and kiss them. This new Annelise could be after me. And . . . she's carrying a cake. The song in my head crashes to an end. The cake is all pink and swirly. A final bass beat sounds, out of time. What the hell?

Jillian

· · · · · ·

A Complicated Morning.

So I'm at the lake suffering from attention deficit disorder caused by incredible kissing flashbacks and the ex-girlfriend shows up. She hoofs up the hill as if she's Tyra Banks on the Victoria's Secret runway. But she's got a cake in her hands. The way she's carrying it, you'd think she'd made it herself. Long legs, tanning-bed-even-skin tone, and all the confidence of a supermodel, she's at the edge of my towel, her right butt cheek planted in my general direction. I shift closer to Parker.

"Will," she says.

"Annelise." He nearly chokes on her name, his eyes undecided on the view above or below the cake.

"I'm the delivery girl." She giggles.

Her butt cheek shakes. Why does she have to be here, with her so . . . perfect body? I look over at Chantal. She's furiously writing something on her clipboard. I'm not going to get any help from her.

"Will's birthday is in November," Parker says. "I don't understand why you're here." Did he read my mind?

"Oh . . . you think it's for Will?" She turns and tilts her head at Parker. Ugh. She's such an obvious flirt. I thought guys hated obvious.

I answer before Parker can, "You're standing right in front of him."

She startles at my voice, but recovers quickly. "Yeah, yeah. Okay. It's for Will. From a secret admirer."

"A secret admirer?" Parker and I ask at the same time. Chantal looks up as if her geek nerves are buzzing. It's the same expression she had when I reeled off the first ten digits of pi in the eighth grade. (Even though she was impressed, she'd already memorized the first twenty-five.) But it's Will's reaction that grabs me.

"And the secret admirer's name begins with an A?" Will smiles his foxy smile. Now it's his turn to be obvious. He must think Annelise is in love with him now. "Oh . . . let me have a lick." He slides closer to her long, waxed leg and tiny triangle bottoms and sticks out his tongue. I can't watch. Instead, I see Chantal's face has gone white. We both know disgusting when we see it. It's like witnessing one of my mother's dating games. No wonder I feel sick to my stomach.

"It says 'from your secret admirer' on the card. No first initial." Now Annelise sets the cake down and reaches into her bathing suit top. Will's eyes stay with her hand, and her cleavage. She removes a folded piece of paper. Ew. "Here's the note." She tosses it at Will. "It was at my front door this morning. I'm just the delivery girl. Not that I mind that, Will." She zeroes in on Parker as she says that last part, adding the giggle and the butt cheek. Ugh.

I look around for the lifeguard who sometimes has to tell the European tourists that this is a family-oriented beach and we don't do the topless bathing thing. Annelise is as close to topless as I've ever seen her. Chantal's whole form-follows-function speech would be well placed, but Chantal is obviously so flustered by Annelise and her lack of clothing that her eyes are on clipboard lockdown.

"Some girl left a cake for me on your doorstep and asked you to deliver it." Will holds out the secret admirer note. It's retro—cutout letters from a magazine. "It's not poison, is it?"

"Nope. I had a little piece, on the side here." She points to a chunk of missing cake. "It's too pretty to be poison."

I don't point out that Snow White ate the poison apple because it looked delicious.

"Maybe you should sit down," I say. *Your butt is making me nauseous.* "Next to Will. I'll get a picture of you two."

"Oh sure." Annelise bends over to sit down and I turn my head. She settles next to Will. I don't get it; I know she's pretending something but I'm not sure what it is. Is she trying to make Parker jealous by throwing herself at Will? If she's doing that why wouldn't she say the cake was from her? Does she really like Will and she's making up the secret admirer thing? Or, maybe she's trying to add herself to our group. Anything's possible with Annelise, especially the things that don't make sense.

When she poses, she flashes her white teeth, and half of her right boob, but the cake steals the photo. It really is something amazing, two circled tiers of pink swirls (minus a chunk from one side) and a dash of sprinkles that flash in the sunlight. No way Annelise made that cake, or bought it at a bakery in town; that sort of cake is homemade, by a mom who's been baking for years. It wasn't Will's mother, was it? She used to send the best chocolate chip cookies. Would she think Will was so hard up she's pretending to be his secret admirer?

Chantal

· · · · · ·

Secret Keeping.

No one suspects. No one has looked my way, except Jillian, once, but I tried to act mildly interested and I think she bought it.

Annelise hands the first slice to Parker. Light yellow vanilla love sweetened by delicate pink air kisses. Parker lifts the cake to his open mouth. As the frosting and fine textured crumb touch his tongue, he smiles. Moans his delight. Maybe he's an okay guy.

Annelise serves Will, and he holds his cake uneasily, perhaps waiting to see if Parker's going to drop dead first. I'm the next person and I wait, too, because watching them taste my cake is most thrilling. Annelise shaves a sliver for herself and holds it up to her mouth.

"What about Jillian?" I ask.

"I'll take care of Jillian." Parker holds his cake wedge near her lips. She hesitates, looks at me. I can't help but smile, even though my uncertainty about Parker should be getting the best of me right now. This is about the cake. "You're gonna love it," Parker says. Jillian accepts the cake love. Her eyes close, I'm guessing involuntarily, at the complexity of delicious tastes. If I was all panic before, I am all glowing now from a bright ball of happy light that spins inside me. Nigella was right. Cake is magic.

"Oh it's so good." She takes three more bites, each bigger than the last. Jillian is back to her old self, laughing, knowing that Parker has chosen her over Annelise.

"Jeez, Jillian, if I ate like that, I'd never fit into this bikini." Annelise smoothes her hands over her impossibly flat stomach.

Quiet descends. In my brain I'm composing things to say: if you ate like that, you'd have more to love than your body. You'd understand the difference between real and fake. You'd . . .

"About that bikini." Parker clears his throat. "Did you bring a shirt? Will's probably got an extra one. Jillian's little brothers are too young for the *Sports Illustrated* version of you. Uh, no offense."

Jillian and I stare open-mouthed at each other. We might both be thinking the same thing, that it's likely Parker has seen much more than her fabric covered parts and he's turning it down, publicly. Ouch.

"No offense taken, Parker." Annelise grins. Grins. I guess her primary goal was to be noticed. "Will. Darling. Please hand me your shirt."

Parker rubs Jillian's shoulder. For the first time I think that maybe they make a cute couple. Maybe he's a good guy with a friend who is a bad influence.

After Annelise pulls Will's band T-shirt over her head, she cuts another tiny sliver of cake, while we are all on our second "real" slice. She can't take more than a bite though, before she's looking uneasy. Her smile falters for the first time since she came prancing up the hill. She's watching Parker and Jillian, their shoulders touching, his index finger tracing a pattern on the inside of Jillian's wrist. Annelise must feel my eyes on her because she catches my gaze and clenches her jaw. Puts on a happy face again. Is she, like me, wondering if a guy will ever want her like that?

"Will," she says. She holds up her piece and he takes all of it in one bite. He growls. He considers the cake he's holding, and turns toward me, lifts the cake to my mouth.

I open my mouth, close my eyes, and bite. I imagine that it's not Will who is holding the cake, but the mystery guy. Someone who is more like me.

Parker

· · · · ·

Acoustic.

Annelise is whispering in Will's ear and, now, he turns to her, grinning. She bites her bottom lip. I can imagine what she said.

You're the hottest guy here. You know that, right? And you're with the hottest girl.

Annelise's game is to always make you feel like being with her is something special. She tells you her secrets. She wants to know yours. And she likes contact. You know what I mean? Lots of contact. Will, man, he's eating it up. I thought he and Chantal had declared a truce (he fed her cake!), and now he's playing ear tag with Annelise. Chantal is so busy writing bullet points on her clipboard, she doesn't even notice. Not that Annelise is competing with Chantal; no, her target is Jillian. Annelise was my girlfriend for long enough that I know (a) that she has no interest in Will, and (b) that she wants me back.

She's whispering, or tonguing, his ear again.

· · ·

Jillian's got her own clipboard and she's writing, too. I rub Jillian's shoulder. She leans in to me, her smooth skin against my chest. I close my eyes and breathe; I get morning shampoo and French toast with a touch of sunscreen, not "musky woods with distinct notes of apple martini," the scent of Annelise's perfume. I run my thumb along Jillian's jaw, the skin here is damp from the heat, not powdery. When she speaks her voice resonates in my chest, a deeper, more even tone, devoid of whine. Jillian is, I decide, an acoustic girl, an echo of sweet melodies around a campfire. Annelise is electric, always igniting the fuse. As she reaches for Will's ear again, she drags her fingers down his arm.

I thought her whispering was "our" thing. And if Will wanted her you'd think he'd have cleared it with me first. And he's got Chantal on the line, too. That's not cool. I want to get up and leave. Clear my head. Hit some pucks.

"Parker. Dude." It's Will. "So what do you think we should do?"

"Do?"

"The project. You know charity-slash-fun for all?" He actually takes in my disgusted stare and he understands that I am peeved. He moves away from Annelise and closer to Chantal, scoping out her notes.

"Hockey." I don't even care at this point about the summer project. I've got enough going on with Jillian and her brothers, but hockey is my primary sport, and I like to do things I'm good at.

"But it's the summer," Annelise says.

I frown. If I told her that her split ends were showing she might leave.

"Street hockey." Jillian's wit clearly outweighs the ex-girlfriend's.

"It's, like, too hot." Annelise picks a stray leaf from Will's hair, hoping that he'll take her side on this one.

I look Will square in the eyes. "Hockey should be our summer project."

"Dude, I'm with you." Will holds up his fist.

I celebrate my victory, Annelise turns to her phone for comfort, and Chantal screws it all up.

"Wait a minute," she says. "The objective here is not to reach consensus on the first idea and I don't think we have that, anyway, because two people haven't voted."

I argue my point as long as I have to that Jillian's brothers have to be included and hockey is their favorite sport. What if we run a two-week hockey camp for all the little kids at the lake? I can see that I'm winning Will and Jillian over and I keep throwing out more details; I love the chase of getting what I want, especially when it's so close.

When Chantal protests that hockey is a guys' thing, Jillian reminds her that the boys were left out of synchronized swimming, except for the final performance. That must be an inside joke because the two of them melt into a private laugh fest. I watch them: heads down, hands over their mouths, ponytails shaking. Did they become blood sisters when they were in elementary? Did they have challenges? Are Will and me just part of their plan? Annelise sighs and thumb types on her phone.

Who is in control of what, I wonder.

"Okay, if we've got to compete with synchronized swimming or whatev, let's do a final performance for the hockey camp." Will, trying to one-up me as a man-with-a-plan, forces the girls to give up their giggling. "We can have mixed-age teams, sell tickets, and donate the proceeds to a charity." He begs a high-five from Chantal and she gives in.

Now that Chantal has caved to our supreme ideas she moves on to assigning roles. She agrees to handle publicity. Will will organize the tournament. Jillian and I will run the hockey camp. And Annelise, well, I expected her to drift away, feeling left out, but she stayed. Finally, Chantal turns to her.

"Um . . . so, Annelise. You would be good at . . ."

I can't believe Chantal doesn't tell Annelise there's no room at the party. Annelise would have told Chantal to take a hike if things were reversed. Maybe Chantal doesn't think Jillian cares, but I felt her tense up when she realized that Chantal was inviting Annelise to join. The tension rises as we wait for Annelise to consider her skills. Finally, she speaks.

"Texting. I'll text everyone I know. They'll help. They'll come to the game. How's that? I can be your assistant, Chantal." Jillian laughs at the hilariousness of Annelise and the tension fades.

"We can share you as an assistant." Will gropes her shoulder. She smiles. Truly disturbing.

We agree to meet every day before the camp to keep our planning on track. While Chantal reviews the details, I watch Annelise and Will trading whispers. I tell myself that she doesn't matter, that this summer project will be the best because I'll make it the best. I trip my fingers up Jillian's arm and tangle them in the hair at the back of her neck. As hockey coaches, Jillian and I will make a great team.

Chantal

· · · · · ·

Cake Deux.

$\mathcal{I}$ consult each of my cookbooks' recipes for chocolate cake and
I watch Nigella on YouTube making her Old-Fashioned Chocolate
Cake. "The fact that this is scarcely any harder than a cake-mix cake
to make, makes it a joy," she says. She wears a pink sweater and I
wonder, is pink always an over-the-top Annelise color or can it belong to a quieter celebrity? Or a secret celebrity. Like me.

Nigella stacks a layer of cake on chocolate–sour cream filling and
spreads the frosting over the top and sides of the cake. She adds
sugared violets as decoration.

"I can't think of a more welcome sight in the kitchen than this,"
she says.

*My decision is made. Bring chocolate cake. Be welcomed. If I'd
known it was this easy I'd have started baking years ago.*

Darling . . . Nigella's throaty laugh tingles my spine . . . *all things
happen in their right time.*

I remind myself that I will have to edit my story, when I tell it to Jillian, of Nigella's influence on my life. If I told her that I create Nigella's
voice when I need encouragement, she might think more psycho-
logical help than my dad can offer is in order.

Another thirty minutes of research and I decide on a combination cake: Dorie Greenspan's chocolate cake with Nigella's chocolate–sour cream frosting. Mix and match.

I whisk together the flour, baking powder, and salt. The dry ingredients shimmer.

This is joy, darling.

Working with the stand mixer and the paddle attachment, I beat the butter and sugar together until glistening and smooth, adding just enough air and sweetness. I know I've reached the optimum mixing when a sliver of gold shines.

In goes the egg and vanilla. I set the mixer on low. I observe. I panic. I've got . . . a mess. Curdled butter bits in goop. The colors have evaporated.

Nigella! Help! When she doesn't answer, I consult my laptop. There—in black and white—is my answer: don't fret if the mixture looks curdled, it will smooth out soon.

I add half the flour mixture, half the milk, the remaining flour, and the final splash of milk. The batter flutters in dove-wing white. *Ahh. It's all good again.*

Now chocolate. Seven ounces of pure refinement, melted and cooled. I add, then blend until mixed. *Oh, Nigella, it's perfect.*

I knew you could do it.

I half-fill my two layer pans evenly. Sparks of copper strike as I strew a mixture of dark chocolate chips, cinnamon, and five-spice powder on each layer. The rest of the batter covers the sleeping chocolate chunks.

I sit on the kitchen floor, staring through the rectangle at the two layer pans snuggled up on the oven's middle rack.

The radio plays in red and blue tones as Lady Gaga finishes singing about boys, boys, boys. *Who needs them?* I roll my eyes.

"And now for something retro, but totally on the pulse of today's generation. I was out at Williamson's Lake today sharing . . . uh . . . cake. No, really, cake. Pink cake. To be exact."

What? That's Mitch. I pull the radio from the table and hold it in front of me. He must have been at the lake today. I was so busy worrying about Will I didn't even notice.

Mitch. The Mitch from my class. The Mitch from the ninth-grade dance. The Mitch who is the son of the dad who runs the radio station.

"It's a favorite of mine. From the Archie cartoons. And it goes out to the secret admirer who is not named . . . yet." A guitar starts strumming and then four voices begin in harmony:

You are my candy girl
And you've got me wanting you.

Mitch. He's playing a song for me. Even if he doesn't know it's for me. I wonder if he remembers the hour we spent at the ninth-grade dance talking about the laws of matter. I thought it was the beginning of *something*. But *nothing* happened. He didn't ask me to dance or accidentally on purpose run into me in the halls or sit next to me in French class. By the end of the year I'd forced myself to stop thinking about him while hugging my pillow. Still, he lives in my subconscious. Could it be that I live in his?

The telephone rings. The song ends, but another starts up again instead of Mitch's voice. My mother's militaristic tone, over the answering machine, commands my attention.

"Okay. I guess you're not home and it's almost midnight your time. That makes my decision simple. I'm coming home first thing tomorrow morning. I was going to stay until Saturday, but I haven't heard from you and your dad hasn't either and . . ." She's got the panic sound in her voice.

I rush to the phone. "Mom. Mom. I had the radio on and I was . . . falling asleep. But I heard your voice on the machine." It takes me twenty-three minutes to convince her not to come home until

Saturday. I promise, not for the first time, that I will have my cell phone on twenty-four/seven and that I will charge it at night. I'm looking forward to seeing you, she says. Yeah, me, too, I answer.

I hang up the phone and the timer beeps.

The cakes are magnificent. This is the second-to-last cake. My mom is home on Saturday. Will gets one more cake, one more day to be the star and then his misery begins. A boy dumped publicly by a secret admirer. And my life goes back to the way it used to be. Only—maybe—better.

• • •

It's 1 A.M.

I am in black, with my latest cake—titled the Epitome of Refinement Chocolate Cake—riding shotgun in my bike basket. I've got fifteen blocks to cycle before I reach my destination. This is worth it, I remind myself. Everything that matters takes effort.

My route takes me downtown; Third Street is the most direct, and the safest for secrecy. Third Street is mainly houses with offices in them. I pass the house where my dad has his office. He told me patients feel more comfortable in a familiar environment. And it must be true because doctors, lawyers, and accountants all have houses along this street, but no one works at an office 1:07 A.M. Friday morning.

Except. I see a kid in jeans walking down the sidewalk and I know from the sort of hunched-in shoulder sway and the hair that flies out from underneath a ball cap, it's Mitch. He must have just finished at the radio station. He's walking toward a car parked six feet away from me. He doesn't look up as he fishes in his pocket for his key fob. I turn my front wheel sharply right and narrowly pass through two bushes alongside the dentist's office. I stop to steady my cake and get my panic under control. The key fob beeps.

"Hello?" *Crud.* It's Mitch's voice. It's calling in my direction.

I crouch over my handlebars. If he searches the bushes, the first thing he'll spot is my butt in black spandex. And if he ever thought I was hot, he'd change his mind forever. I hold my breath and wait for doom. Instead I hear a car door open and slam. The car starts up and music drifts through an open window. I wonder if maybe it's a good thing my whole secret identity is going to be temporary. One more night. One more delivery. And then it's back to safe Chantal. I don't know how long I can take this.

I ride forward, in the dark.

Will
. . . . . .
Mr. Chrome.

It's all over Facebook. And apparently Mitch talked about it on the radio. He only has that job because his dad owns the station. So what? So now everyone knows that I have a secret admirer. And it sucks.

I hear my bedroom door open. The sound of the light switch clicks. The funnel of light from my ceiling fixture competes with the glow of my computer screen. My dad, a man forever in striped train-men's overalls, moves to the spotlight. He doesn't recognize that it's nearly 1 A.M. or that he hasn't knocked on my door or that I might not want to talk to him. I call him the Ogre for a reason.

"Will. I've . . . We've . . . The company is . . . uh . . . having a . . . a party next week. They're giving me an award for service. And your mother wants us all to be there." He pulls his bandana from his back pocket, wipes his forehead. I love it when the Ogre needs me.

I click from one profile to another. I've got 327 friends, some of them I don't even know. "Uh . . . next week? What day? I've got a lot on my plate . . ."

He clenches his jaw. Finally he speaks, "Your mother wants you to be there."

"But you . . ."

"I don't want your piss-ass attitude. What's your excuse now, Will? If you had a job to go to that would be one thing . . ."

He's baiting me. I'm usually the stray that goes for the bait and gets a kick to the ribs, but not this time.

"Yeah, I'll come. I'm going to bring a friend, too. A date."

His forehead wrinkles up and he considers me for a few seconds. I think maybe he's formulating a father/son conversation, but the only thing he leaves behind is the glow of the light. "I'll tell her you'll go," he mumbles as he closes the door.

I wonder if I did the right thing, caving into him this time, but my defenses are down with this whole secret admirer gig. I mean—I don't want Annelise playing me like this, in public. I so want her, I'd be crazy not to, but without the frickin' parade. Parker loves a parade. Me, I like to drive the float.

• • •

The whole summer project is problematized, that's what I'm thinking as I stand under the tree watching how things play out. First you got your Parker and Jillian do-gooders with the rug rats. Now that is some annoying crap. Those kids are all running around like it's Christmas and Parker is Santa Claus. He hands out the plastic hockey sticks and then he transforms into Super Coach, giving them the rules of engagement. When I agreed to this with Chantal, I didn't think I was going to waste my summer on inspiration. And then there's Chantal; the girl carries that damn clipboard around as if it was gold-plated. And don't get me started on Annelise. The texting genius has got a crowd gathered. Around her. I am supposed to be the one organizing this hockey tournament. People should be consulting me. The expert.

And then if things don't get worse than having a rusty nail shoved under and through my eyelids, Annelise's friend Danielle is walking up the frickin' hill with a frickin' cake on a frickin' plate.

"Hey, hey," Annelise shouts. "Everyone. Hey. Will's secret admirer is back!" Danielle, dressed for the occasion in the shortest cutoffs and a bikini top, stops in front of me, pulls a card from her back pocket, and hands it over. It's the same retro cutout letters.

The Epitome of Refinement Chocolate Cake. XXOO, Your Secret Admirer.

Epitome. Annelise must be hiring someone to help her.

"Oh, Will." She stands so close to me I can smell her cinnamon gum. "This looks even better than yesterday's."

I nod.

"Okay everyone. I brought plates and forks today. Line up. Line up." Annelise glows in the spotlight. "But Will gets the first piece."

As she cuts into the cake she whispers that Danielle texted her when she found the cake on her doorstep. That's how she knew to bring the plates. I want to tell Annelise that stating the obvious is stupiculous, but she probably wouldn't get it.

"This is so cool, isn't it? Getting cakes from a secret admirer. Like, this only happens in, like, movies."

She holds a piece of cake to my lips and I take a bite. Chocolate and spice with thick fudgey frosting. It's good but I want to spit it out. I don't want to be played by some girl, even if it's Annelise. And yet, consider my circumstances. Parker is off to the side with the baby posse. A hot girl is close enough that the air between us sizzles. Fans await. All over a cake. *This is easy. Easy. I am chrome. High polish, unbelievably resistant. This is easy.*

I smile. Take another bite. Give the thumbs-up. The crowd cheers.

Jillian

 . . . . . .

Role Model.

If only she'd left for work or been too self-absorbed to notice Parker's car out front. If only she'd applied her third coat of mascara instead of looking out at the driveway to see me at the driver's side door of the minivan, about to get in, and Parker helping the boys into their car seats.

"Parker!" She comes out in her nursing-home scrubs, her arms wide open for a hug. Parker finishes buckling Ollie into his car seat and he startles when he turns to face her. I read the what-the-hell on his face. I close my eyes.

"Mrs. Uh . . ." He has no clue what to call her. Her name changes faster than the boys can register for the next school year.

"Call me Mom."

Oh. God. I open my eyes to see Parker ease away from her and close the van door. "Well," he says. "We've got to get going. Big day. Hockey camp." He pulls the door shut. Maybe he thinks he'll avoid a conversation, but I know that is impossible.

"So Parker. I just want you to know that what you're doing for Jillian and her brothers. Such a gentleman." Her voice has a tight sound. I recognize it as the voice she uses with my teachers when she tells them how she's so grateful that they're giving me A's. It's the suck-up voice. Please, no tears. Please.

"Uh . . . thanks." Parker shifts uneasily.

"And . . . you know . . . I wish I could pitch in with some money. Jillian tells me that other kids are donating cash for the hockey camp and all that, but things are tight right now. You know we're just in, transition, I guess you'd call it. And . . . uh . . ."

She stares at the ground. "It's through the kindness of others that we'll get through . . ." Her voice trails off. I close my eyes again. Why does she have to be a train wreck? No one says anything, not even the boys. Time waits for my mother's dramatic pauses.

"Anyway, I just want you to know how grateful all of us are to have you as part of our family."

I groan.

"Jillian!" She snaps and turns away.

I follow her to the front door to make her face me before she goes inside. "You can thank *me* later," I say. She doesn't respond.

I leave her, mouth wide open.

• • •

She's all I can think about while I stand on the sidelines of the hockey field Parker and I have created by the park. We've got fourteen boys and girls today and three mothers have already found me and signed up their kids for tomorrow. I'm the overall supervisor and snack provider while Parker and three other volunteers that Annelise text-recruited run the kids through the drills. The Hat Trick and the Double Minor are both on the field right now and it's like they're playing the game all on their own. The other kids are just running around them, trying to get into the action.

"This is so great." Mrs. Gibson, one of our neighbors when we lived over by Chantal, joins me on the sidelines. "A hockey camp. Just wonderful. You kids are such great role models."

Role models. Mrs. Gibson knows my mother and I'm sure she's thinking I turned out amazingly well despite the circumstances. If my mother were here she'd say she models independence, freedom, self-expression. I sigh. Try to let go of my anger. It doesn't do me any good.

Ollie makes a break from Chloe and dashes onto the field. His chubby face jiggles with the rhythm of his stride, stiff on those new running legs. He aims for the center of the action, looking for a ball to kick. The players seem oblivious to his little body. Just as Mrs. Gibson and I are ready to rush out to save him, Parker blows his whistle.

"Time out. Caution. Baby on the Field." Time out. Time out. The volunteers echo. The players stop their drills. Parker runs through them to grab Ollie, scoop him up, and airplane him back to Chloe. Ollie's giggles cascade the music scale; he and Parker turn heads. Parker seems to notice envious moms and kids watching him and he airplanes Ollie around the playground. Twice. When he sets him down he acknowledges his audience with a shrug. He runs back to the field, his shoulders squared, I hate to say it, prince-like.

"Wow. He's great with kids," Mrs. Gibson says. Her eyes hold mine. "He's a good catch, Jillian. All the mothers think so . . ." She laughs as she walks away.

I watch Parker for the next hour and I can't find any fault in him. He loves the boys. And he's good at what he does. A natural leader from a family of leaders. Every male in his household has been class president. And he will be next year, too. My currency in the high school will increase exponentially. I'll be invited to A-list parties, I'll be at the center of the action of any school event. I'll be happy. I think I'll be happy.

Parker

······

Magnanimous.

It's an out of the park, great day. The weather. The drills. The kids. Jillian's brothers. Man. Oh, man.

I've got the speakers faded to the back of the van so I can talk to Jillian without the boys hearing us. I tell her what I suspect; her brothers could become hockey stars. They listened to the instructions, they stopped at the whistle, and they outperformed everyone else. "You know what this means, don't you?"

"They're good at hockey?"

"No. They're exceptional at hockey." I study her profile. She's got this elegance about her, so different from her mother. It's incredible, really, what she puts up with. "You know, hockey could be the way out for them."

"A way out?" She gives me a quick look that I can't analyze, because it's gone in the time it takes her to make a left turn. We're headed for a slushie celebration at the convenience store. The one near my house is the best, seven flavors. No drive-thru. I promised we could go into the store for once.

"They'll have something that they can be proud of, something no one can take away. Man, it's so . . . phenomenal." I am almost, literally, buzzing. This must be how Glen Sather thought about the Boys on the Bus. I watch the Hat Trick and Double Minor in the visor mirror. They're talking hockey. Jillian pulls into the parking lot of the convenience store. She turns to me.

"Just so you know, you are about to experience a nightmare. They will whine. They will beg. And then they'll get mad. They will lie flat out on the floor and hammer their fists until they are bloody to get what they want. And Josh will scream over and over. You. Are. Not. The. Boss. Of. Me." Her face transforms into Josh's scrunched-up eyes, pouty lips.

"But what do they want?"

"Two things, but my rule is one thing only."

"Because . . ."

"It's the rule. My mother has no rules. I have rules."

"And if your rule was two things, they'd want three."

She smiles and I want to kiss her, but I know the boys are watching us.

"Okay . . ." If I were a kid again, how would I want this to go? "Okay . . . here's a solution. Each boy gets one thing. If he behaves with good manners, he gets twenty-five cents in his account. Four times to the convenience store where he behaves and he has an extra dollar to spend."

Jillian shakes her head. "Bribing them to be good? No immediate payoff?"

"Come on, Jillian. Let me try it. If it fails, it's my rule that fails. Please. I'm getting carried away after our day at camp."

"Alright." She opens the door. "I'll wait for the meltdown."

I gather the boys in a huddle. I explain the deal as simply as I can and the Hat Trick are the first boys to go into the store. It takes me a long time to convince the Double Minor that twenty-five cents over four times is better than throwing a fit. Josh drags his feet as he walks away. Baby Ollie can't be reasoned with, I decide. I tell him we're going to shop together, we'll each get one thing and I'll share mine. I give the Hat Trick and the Double Minor five minutes before I walk in with Ollie, enough time (I hope) to successfully choose without my supervision.

I see the five boys lined up at the cash register, each with a slushie. Jillian's eyes are wide. Ollie and I give each one of them a high-five and I turn to take him to the back where the slushie machine waits. That's when I see my mother. She looks at me. Then Ollie. Then Jillian. Then the five boys in the lineup. That's why Jillian's eyes were wide—she was trying to warn me. Everyone in school knows my mom from elementary school. She was the mom who couldn't pass a kid in the hallway without telling him to tie his shoes, put on his mittens, and wear a hat. Everyone avoided her.

"Hi, Mom." I wave. Ollie waves, too. Five steps closer and Ollie hugs me tight. Usually I'm okay with this sort of public display of affection from him. Now, I wince. I hope Jillian didn't just see that.

"Parker. To whom does that baby belong?" If I could make anything happen right then, it would be to change my mother into someone else. The disgust in her voice, the distaste on her face, the way her eyes shift from Jillian to me as if she's accusing us of something. It's wrong. I want to tell her she's wrecking one of the most perfect days ever. I want to tell her that I have found what it is to be magnanimous. Noble in mind and heart.

"Mom. Can we talk about this later?" I move close enough to her that Ollie reaches for the gold chain that hangs from her reading glasses. I grab his hand. I lower my voice, make sure that my back faces Jillian. "It's not what you think. I'm doing some babysitting, that's all."

She looks up at me. "I'm glad to hear it's temporary," she whispers back and I know that she knows I am lying and that we are now both pretending, for Jillian's sake. How noble is this. If I were a samurai I'd be reaching for my sword. "He's a cute baby," my mother says loud enough for Jillian to hear. "And those are well-behaved young boys." She nods at me and at Jillian before she walks out. I have no idea what she'd planned to buy, but she's not carrying a bag out the door.

I help Ollie with a slushie and we find a chocolate bar to share. The boys, Jillian, and I are back in the van without a whine or a scream. I can't look at Jillian. I kill off my half of the chocolate bar in one bite. "Great job following the rules, boys," she says. "And Parker, I guess you schooled me."

I allow myself a quick look in the mirror to see the boys high-fiving each other. Jillian starts the engine. With the music on in the back, she can talk to me. Just what I don't need. "Well, that was awkward," she says. "I don't think your mother likes the idea of you with me and my brothers."

"Oh, she'll come around," I say. I'm glad Jillian's watching the road so she can't see how I'm trying to avoid this. "Anyway, she's not the boss of me."

Jillian laughs and I hope that we can get back to normal. Soon.

Chantal

· · · · · ·

Friday Night Cake.

In our small town, just like all the kids go to the lake every day of the summer, Friday night is for hanging out with your friends. At least this is what I've pieced together from my research. If you're old enough to drive and you have your own car—or your parent's car isn't too geriatric—you and preferably more than one friend drive from Pizza Shack at one end of town to the Dairy Barn at the other. You drive slowly, with the radio cranked, windows down, and sunroof open. Most Friday nights of my teenage life, Jillian and I babysat, watched movies, made caramel popcorn, and studied. We talked about how lame it was to cruise on Friday night, but I know she secretly wanted to be part of the crowd. She's probably cruising in Parker's car right now. Not that I have a problem with that. I'm sort of over it. I've got my own thing going on, after all.

This being my last cake, I am looking to exceed expectations. And that always means research. I pass up anything that is chocolate, anything with nuts (it's too late to shop), and anything that looks too complicated. My final cake must be perfect.

I find inspiration in Nigella's Forever Summer/White 1.

In a seaside house, Nigella's children race ahead of her through the dining room to the kitchen where a close-up shows her in a sea-sky blue silk robe. She combines ricotta cheese, milk, and two eggs that she separates by hand (not even wincing at the white goo-ing between her fingers). She adds flour and baking powder and mixes slightly.

When Nigella asks her children, Bruno and Mimi, to help her, the back of my throat begins to ache. Bruno whisks the egg whites while Mimi stirs the batter. And Nigella doesn't stop them six times to tell them how to hold the whisk or ask them to stop being so loud or scold them for dipping their fingers in the batter.

Nigella. What makes it so easy for you to cook with your children?

Nigella would never understand a mother like mine; one who thinks that a clean kitchen is a happy kitchen. I think my mother would develop a heart condition if I suggested she make pancakes for breakfast instead of a bowl of fibre-added cereal.

The next scene shows Nigella in her silk robe with her hair wrapped in a white towel turban. "Cooking while I'm on a week-end away kind of reminds me of what it's all about; having friends over, cooking with them, and eating with them," she says.

I turn away from her. *I get it, Nigella, I'm just not there yet.*

Two cookbooks later, I find what I believe will make my final offering the *pièce de résistance*: Perfect Party Cake. One of my favorite words is in the title. Not party, of course. Perfect.

I assemble the ingredients for a cool white four-layer cake with a tart-sweet raspberry filling and a decadent lemon meringue butter-cream: the usual flour, baking powder, sugar, eggs, and vanilla, but I add lemons to the table and raspberry preserves and buttermilk instead of milk. I realize that the refrigerator is abundant in unsalted butter and buttermilk. I'll have to get rid of the evidence tonight before my mother returns. And also the bars of fine chocolate in the cupboard, the extra-large bottle of vanilla extract, the cake and pastry flour, the large bags of sugars. I stack it all in the corner of the kitchen. Where it will go later is unknown. I'd hide it in my closet, but my mother has been known to go on cleaning sprees that don't stop at my bedroom door.

I wonder if Will is going to grieve the loss of his secret admirer—especially when he realizes she wasn't Annelise—the way I'll miss my cake baking. I hope it's worse for him. Pure misery. I will be breaking my own heart while at the same time embarrassing Will's—the irony is not lost on me.

As Julia Roberts said in one of Hollywood's best chick flicks, "I would rather have thirty minutes of wonderful than a lifetime of nothing special." Of course, I'm not about to die from kidney failure so that is a bit melodramatic.

I sift the flour, baking powder, and salt into one bowl. In the second, I whisk together the milk and egg whites. I put the sugar and lemon zest in the mixer bowl and add the butter. I'm beating it at medium speed, reaching to turn up the radio (I think Mitch is going to be on again tonight) when the phone rings. I turn everything off. Wait for the call display to flash the number.

It's Jillian. This can only be bad news. She's supposed to be out with Parker.

"Hello. Jillian? What's wrong?"

"Wrong?"

"Why are you calling me?"

"We're friends?"

"But . . . it's Friday night. And . . ." And what? I'm busy?

"Do you think a guy's mother not liking the girl he's dating means the relationship is doomed?"

Life goes from strange to stranger; Jillian's calling me for guy advice. And I'm such a pro. My response? "You can't break up with Parker." That would wreck everything. The story of Will being dumped by his secret admirer will be old news far too quickly.

"But maybe Parker will break up with me." Her voice sounds rainy-day lonely. I know how she feels, in a way.

"He's not going to break up with you!" I say. "This hockey camp is his passion, other than you. And he loves hanging out with your brothers. Tell me he doesn't."

"He does, but . . ." She tells me about his mother. The way she was glaring at them over the top of her reading glasses. It was clear that this girl and her six brothers was not what she had in mind for her son.

"Jillian." I reach for her rational center. "Parker's going to say the right things to his mother to avoid the confrontation. And he's still going to go out with you."

"And what makes you the expert on parental deception?"

"You master the skills you have to master," I say blankly. If she only knew what skills I'm developing. We talk long enough that she's calm and then she tells me Parker's coming over after the boys are asleep.

"See? He is so into you." Our conversation ends. It's incredible how easy it is to hang up with Jillian when I have a cake to make. I read the recipe over again. Twice.

I turn the mixer back on and turn the radio up. A classic Journey song is playing and I'm pretty sure Mitch is behind the mic at the radio station. Once the butter and sugar are very light, I add in the vanilla extract, a third of the flour mixture, and then alternate the milk-egg mixture with the remaining dry ingredients. After a couple of final stirs, I divide the batter between the two pans and put them in the preheated oven. I set the timer.

You and me.
And me and you.

I recognize the lyrics of "Happy Together." Another classic. It's the best summer anthem, a whole song of hopeful notes. I daydream about a guy who laughs at my jokes and makes jokes that I think are funny. Like Jillian. But, I need something more, too. Not better, just different. Someone who wants to make the rules together, not change them on me. Mitch is the kind of guy who is smart but doesn't have to prove it. And he can talk about important things without debating them until I agree with him. He's the kind of guy who listens. And I'm listening to him, through his song choices. I stop making lists in my head of pros and cons and I let myself feel hope tingling. Mitch could be more than my radio friend.

I ignore the dishes that need washing. I fight for happiness in the right here and now with my back against the oven, the fan blowing in my face. I imagine that Mitch is thinking about me, too.

Will

· · · · · ·

One.

e drink at the deserted tennis courts. Parker convinced Coach Fenton to give him the key for our Friday night tournaments last year, before the turn-the-lights-out initiative killed late-night tennis. You can't play tennis with battery-operated lanterns. Which sucks. Because I kick ass at tennis. Instead, we sit in the backcourt on camp chairs and drink beer. And, tonight, talk about what the hell I'm going to do about these cakes. It's ridiculudicrous, even if Parker doesn't agree.

"Whoa. Whoa. Whoa." Parker holds up his hand. "It's cake, not hate mail. Chocolate and . . . pink . . . whatever flavor it was, it was damn good. Anyway, it's just a challenge." Parker tips back in his camp chair.

"As in you issued this challenge?" Why would he be going against me?

"No, man. It's a challenge for the person baking them."

"And that is . . ."

"Annelise." He drains the rest of his beer in one go. "It's so obvious. She's trying to get me back."

"I'm the one getting the cakes, not you." I stare him down. Does he really believe the crap that's coming out of his mouth?

"Doesn't matter. What she wants is attention. And once everyone is paying attention to her, she's going to start texting me and calling me and she's gonna try to sneak her way back into my life."

"But you're not interested. In Annelise." I've got to know for sure.

"Exactly. I've got Jillian and the boys. Something important." He pulls the label from his beer without ripping it.

"I don't know. It's gotta snow reindeers in the summertime before I'll believe that Annelise baked even one of those cakes."

"She's paying someone."

"I guess that could be true." Annelise has unlimited funds, but I doubt she'd come up with such a complicated plan. To use me to get Parker back. Am I the ass under Don Quixote's butt? "You know what, I'm not going to be the ass end of this joke."

"Challenge."

"I'm going to talk to her. I'll be straight up—she doesn't have a chance with you so she can stop playing sugar fairy with me."

"No . . . man . . . no. You don't get it." Parker cracks his second beer as he winds up his lecture voice. He starts in on how we can use this to our advantage.

"Wait," I interrupt. "Maybe you didn't hear me. I'm stopping this thing. I've got junior high girls taking pictures of me with the cake. They want to know what's on my iPod. It's like they finished their vampire books and they see me as their new Edward. Dude. They made a Facebook page. They're posting photos of me on it. And there's like two hundred and twenty-seven fans."

"Even better. One thousand, one hundred and thirty-five more dollars." Parker tells me that is what 227 fans at five dollars per fan will add to our fund-raising efforts via the hockey tournament. "I never thought I'd hear you complain about too much action."

"Frick. Dude. This is over." I chuck my beer bottle into the pine trees and stand up. I can't reason with him. He's turned into one of them. A guy with a cause.

"Sit. There's something in this for you."

"And for you, I'm sure." I take my third beer from the zip-up cooler bag. He refuses the one I offer him. Parker is almost always a beer behind, as if he's better than me.

"Hey, we're a team, right?" He holds his beer up to toast. I ignore it and look out into the dark.

"Maybe."

"Look. I know you want Annelise." I don't respond. I've never told him. But I've never really gone out with a girl for more than a week of text messaging. And the deal with Chantal is only for my mom's benefit. "And I know a way for you to get her."

Swarms of kids will pay to get into the hockey tournament, he explains, if we convince the secret admirer to reveal her true identity between the second and third periods. And with the stands full of the student electorate, and all the attention focused on me, the secretly admired, it will be the perfect time.

"For what?"

"For you to announce your candidacy for class president."

"Class president?" Do I look, I want to ask him, like a pig wearing a blindfold on the way to the barbeque spit? "You want to be class president."

"My mother wants me to be class president. I want to be . . . something else."

It occurs to me that he's been thinking about this for a long time, judging from the smoothness of the details, and he hasn't talked to me about it. Not at all. Is this like one of those double-cross things? Maybe I am the pig who doesn't know he's about to be skewered and bathed in barbeque sauce. Is Parker in on the cake baking with Annelise? "What if the secret admirer refuses to show?"

"Moot point. It'd be like the icing on the cake. Ha. People will still give the money. They'll have a good time. And they will associate you with the good time. Voters vote for charisma. And you'll have it on that night. Man, this is brilliant."

I sink half my beer. "So what do you get out of it?"

"I want to be vice president. In charge of fund-raising and special projects. You'll be class pres. And Annelise wants to date the guy at the top. We all get what we want."

Uh . . . problem. "The vice president doesn't do fund-raising and special projects."

"Yet." Parker reaches in for his third beer. "What we're talking about is the making of a legacy." He stares up at the stars and makes me wait while he composes and delivers a soliloquy. "Only once in every few generations comes a thinker who changes a system so dramatically that his innovation is remembered for decades afterward. My contribution to the bureaucracy of class office will be to forever alter the mandate to serve not only the senior class, but the community. And not just through bikini car washes, bake sales, and cheesy Halloween haunted houses. From now on, students will seek to give to greater causes than themselves. I'll be like Bill Gates. Warren Buffett."

"Parker . . ." Like a stray dog staring at a bologna sandwich, I want to put an end to my misery. "Parker . . ." But he continues. And I drink my beer in silence. Really, I guess I get to be class president. And get the hot girl. That's all I ever wanted, isn't it? It's another two beers down before Parker winds up his plans to show his mother who he really is, save Jillian and her brothers from a life of certain poverty, and build a school in Africa with bricks we'll make by hand from the abundant red clay.

"We'll be revolutionaries, man." He fist-punches me and fixes his glassy-eyed stare, finally, at something other than his imagination. "You and me."

Revolutionaries. Frick. What a guy. "Che Guevara." I hold out my hand. I remember why I love hanging out with Parker. He can be just as stupid as me and no one else knows but us. I hope he remembers all this in the morning.

"Mahatma Gandhi."

"The greatest man challenge yet."

"Man."

"Dude."

We shake our secret handshake. "Stealth."

Chantal

· · · · · ·

Fraud.

Alone with my yellow mixer and pink spatulas, I rest my head on the table in the fan's cool breeze. I daydream about a bike ride that weaves through wildflowers. In my bike basket, a few cupcakes, carefully wrapped to protect their delicate buttercream swirls. In Mitch's, a picnic blanket, an iPod of oldies, and a thermos of lemonade. "Sugar, Sugar," the song Mitch has played again tonight in honor of Cake Girl plays first. (I really have to do something about that name, it sounds like Cat Girl who dressed like a cat. I'm not a walking cake.) His smiling face comes closer and closer to mine.

The phone rings. I race to pick it up without even looking at the call display; I am that sure that Mitch is on the other end.

"Chantal?" It's a girl's voice.

At least it's not my mother. "Annelise?"

"We have a problem."

"A problem?" How could Annelise and I have a problem? We've had fewer than five conversations.

"We've got a copycat baker. Someone just left a cake on my doorstep. And it's definitely not from the Cake Girl."

"Annelise." I slip to the floor, lean against the wall. I don't need this complication. "I don't mean to . . . like . . . not support you in this crisis, but why are you calling me? I don't know anything about cake." Oh please, please believe that I am not lying.

"You do! Remember when you sat in my car? I told you that Will thought that I was the one who left him that chocolate cake. And then you told me that if I flirted with Will, then Parker would get jealous. So I just let Will think the cake might have been baked by me. The next thing I know, there's a cake on my doorstep. For Will. From a secret admirer. Ta da. Parker is getting more jealous with every bite!"

"The details are a bit hazy."

"Doesn't matter. The point is that someone has left a cake. Again. For Will. But . . . it's not the same baker girl. This cake is disgusting. It tastes like sugar and cardboard."

"What? Wait a minute. What are you saying?" As Annelise repeats herself, the pounding begins at the back of my head. I only had to get through one more cake delivery and I was set to watch Will's misery in motion. If someone else sends him cakes his plunge from fame will not happen.

"Chantal. Are you there? I don't think you understand how serious this is. Parker is not going to be jealous of Will if the cakes taste like caca!"

"Right. You're absolutely right." There's this: in Annelise's mind this whole cake-baking thing is about getting Parker back. And this: some silly girl could be making substandard cakes for Will to get attention for herself. "Um . . . um . . . I've got an idea."

I tell Annelise that if this copycat baker wants Will, maybe we could scare her off. Maybe we throw the copycat cake away. Maybe someone starts a rumor that Will has figured out who the secret admirer is, and that she is totally hot and that no girl in her right mind would try to compete with her.

"Oh . . . I get it. So . . . we don't tell anyone about the copycat cake, we just make it clear that the real Cake Girl . . ."

Here's my chance. "Annelise. Don't you think Cake Girl is an unre-markable moniker?"

"A what?"

"A dumb name. How about . . . uh . . ." I try to sound spontane-ous. "The Cake Princess."

"Oh . . . nice . . . the Cake Princess. Okay, tiara and lots of pink. That works. So she's hot and no one can compete. Hey, can you hold on a second? I got another call."

"Sure." I think it's a solid plan. I think it is. I crawl on my knees to the living room window. What if the copycat baker is out to get me? What if she or he is watching me? On my hands and knees, I stop at every window on the main floor. When I reach the back of the house, I telescope my neck around the edge of the patio door. No spies with floured hands. Finally, I can return to my princess quarters, the kitchen, and lean against a cupboard door. I breathe deep.

"Okay, I'm back." Annelise is breathless again. "I got the rumor started on Facebook."

"On Facebook?"

"Yeah, on the Cake Girl, correction, the Cake Princess fanpage. It has two hundred and twenty-seven members. No . . . wait, two thirty-one."

"A fanpage?"

"Du-uh. The Cake Princess is the most popular girl at the lake. Okay, the rumor is: Will knows who the Cake Princess is and he said that she is totally hot and in charge and a girl going up against her would be a fool."

"It's only been two days." Two hundred and thirty-one people are following my cake exploits? My mouth goes dry. Annelise re-minds me that two days is all you need to make a trend happen. As proof she points out that last March she wore pink leg warmers to school and the next day seventeen other girls wore leg warmers, too. Like, OMG. I was not one of those seventeen girls.

"I'm famous for being a trendsetter," she adds. "Chantal. You need to friend me on Facebook. And join the fanpage, too. Okay?"

"Sure." I don't tell her I'm not on Facebook, because, honestly, when she said friend, I sort of liked it. I think I want to know what everyone else is doing. Especially if it involves my secret identity.

"And Chantal, thanks. People say you're stuck up, but I don't think so. You're actually easy to talk to. Well, you are very smart. But like, you're nice."

"Oh. Um . . . you're welcome." Maybe it would be nicer for me to tell her what I know—Parker dumped her to compete in a man challenge. Doing that might compromise my secret identity.

"Okay, one cake in the garbage. Friend, I've got to go. Wait—

"You gotta hear this. Danielle says she just saw Parker and Will walking away from the high school. Without Jillian. And she thinks they're drunk. Chantal, this Cake Princess is so getting to Parker. By the end of the summer he'll be mine again."

Not if Parker turns out to be Jillian's real Prince Charming.

Jillian

• • • • • •

Waiting for Parker.

I saved our two allotted pieces of the Epitome of Refinement Chocolate Cake for my after-hours date with Parker. We were supposed to meet in the backyard. I lit candles and draped blankets over our plastic lawn chairs. In the dark, it whispers romance. The two cake slices hug each other on the one unchipped plate we own, to make the sharing obvious, intimate. It's after after-hours, though, and I haven't heard from Parker. I'm not going to call him because that's something my mother would do. Me? I take a fork from the drawer, poise it over the top of the deep chocolate cake that everyone said was "to die for," then pause at the last second.

If I take a bite, I know I won't stop at one. Should Parker show up, we wouldn't have cake to share. Worse, he'd either think I was a pig or he'd know that I gave up on him and ate it solo. But I'm pretty sure if he was going to knock on my door he would have been here by 12:02 A.M. I stare at my fork.

I could call Chantal.

Are you sure he said he was going to come over? She'd ask.

I'd answer, Well, he either said he might come over or he would come over.

Hmm . . . she'd say . . . do you think he's been in a car accident?

Unlikely, I'd say. He was going to walk over to Will's house and then walk here.

He probably doesn't intend to disappoint you, she'd say.

And I'd say, Yeah, you're right. He's such a good guy. With the boys, especially. Thanks. See you tomorrow.

I wouldn't tell her that I'm thinking my mother has put a curse against men in this house. I wouldn't ask her to come over here and watch the boys while I go out looking for Parker and proof that he's ditched me.

She probably wouldn't tell me that she's sort of suspicious of him, but I can tell that she watches him and she wonders the same things I wonder. Why is he so interested in hanging out with my brothers? Why doesn't he seem to notice when I'm wearing certain clothes that make me look really good? Why does each conversation he initiates start with a story about hanging out with the boys? Why are Parker and my brothers the lead actors and I'm the supporting cast?

I pick up my fork. One bite. My lips drag along the fork tines, making sure to pull every chocolate molecule onto my tongue. It's fireworks in my mouth, a continuous burst of chocolate, spice, and sugar dancing with butter. This is not my only bite. My fork dives.

Sometimes I get tired of being vigilant. I want to stop looking at each situation in my life as a complex puzzle that I can rework, solve, and erase. Sometimes I get this sharp pain in my brain that makes me say, Hello. It's like the knock at the front door that I don't expect. I hear it no matter where I am in the house and I run to answer it. Always. I run to the door and then I stop, right as I'm reaching for the handle, and I wish, the same silent wish that hovers over my birthday candles, that my dad was on the other side. *I'm sorry I didn't come sooner.*

My fork slides effortlessly through the chocolate cake. Each bite takes me deeper.

Sometimes I don't want to wake up in the morning, reminding

myself that my most important job is being a good sister, that doing the right thing will make me feel right inside. Sometimes, I just feel taken advantage of, used.

I scrape the last bit of cake from our one unchipped plate.

Sometimes I want to ask for help. Salvation. I slide my index finger over the remains of the chocolate frosting, lick the sweetness from my finger.

But I know the only thing that will make me truly happy is to save myself.

I open the dishwasher. Slide the plate in the bottom rack.

Will

• • • • • •

Disappointment.

"**S**o . . . me and you in Africa building schools, brick by frickin' brick." Parker sways as he stands, misses the first time he reaches for his camp chair. It's been another hour and I've lost count of how many beers. I'm doing a little better than him, more practice and good genes, I guess.

"What about Jillian?" I lock our camp chairs in the shed. We start walking toward my house.

"Jillian? Jillian will probably be, I don't know, teaching kids how to read under the shade of a boaboa tree. They have boaboa trees there, don't they? Or maybe it's Joshua trees. Or maybe, like, both. Making bricks is man work."

"Dude. I was talking about tonight. You said you were going to her house."

"Tonight?" Parker stops. He stares at the bottle in his hand. "I can't go over there tonight. I'm drunk. Bad role modeling."

"You're not gonna call her, are you? She'll know you're drunk and you know what that means . . ."

"In the doghouse." He has to stop to whiz in the bushes. "Man. What am I gonna tell her?"

"You fell asleep."

"That's pretty good."

"You're the one who told me every guy gets one get-out-of-jail-free card."

"Yeah." He nods. "I'll play the sleep card. So let's go to your house and play Halo."

"My house? Nah . . ."

"We can't show up at mine. Relatives in town."

As we walk Parker starts in on his new favorite topic, his legacy, and by the time we get to my garage, I'm thinking I've listened long enough. We shake hands and I watch him weave down the sidewalk like a squirrel following a nut on a string.

I don't know that my mother is in the living room when I open the door or when I close it as quietly as I can or when I slip off my shoes to carry them in my hands. It's the Ogre that's got me acting all burglar in my own house; still, I freeze when I hear her voice from the dark corner.

"Will," she says. "I've been waiting up for you."

"Mom. Why are you in the dark?"

"I have a headache."

"Oh." I set my shoes down and move to the living room, shuffle to the couch. I can make out her outline in the chair opposite me. The orange light from the heating pad she puts at the base of her neck glows. "Is he gone?"

"To work."

"Oh." We've been waiting for him to leave for seven years. I was ten when I walked in on them fighting. I'd been at Parker's house for dinner and I heard the Ogre yelling at her as I walked up the front steps. He didn't stop when I slammed the door or when I stood in the kitchen doorway. *We don't need a goddamn new couch or a new color on the walls.* My mother wiped her eyes with the kitchen towel. I'd heard him yelling at her before and I'd decided weeks before that the next time I would do something. *Bullying is wrong, I told him, I learned about it in school. And you have to stop.* I remember that pounding feeling in my chest. It felt great. Warriors must have felt just like this, I thought. The Ogre moved a step closer to me. My mother told me to go to my room, but I stood my ground in the kitchen. I pulled the biggest knife we had from the wooden block on the countertop. For five seconds or so I was in power, the kid with the weapon, and then, the Ogre changed his battle strategy. He turned on my mother. *You trapped me. You got yourself pregnant. Now you've turned my own son against me.* Put that knife down (my mother's voice had never been so angry), and go to your room. Hours later, in the middle of the night, she told me that I needed to be good, that if I was bad and acted up again my father would leave us. I was never sure why that would be such a problem.

"Tuesday," she says. "Your dad's party is on Tuesday. You need to bring that nice girl, Chantal. And you need to wear a tie."

"I might be coming down with the flu."

"You're going."

I play over in my head what I think about whenever my mother wants me to do something to make the Ogre happy: the Ogre missed my hockey games so I quit the team. He never went to a parent-teacher conference so I slipped up and got C's in the ninth grade. Sometimes when I'm drunk, I just don't care. "Why are you sitting here in the dark?"

"To make a point."

"And that is?"

"You complain about your dad and the ways he's failed you." Her words are scripted, but her voice is weak and wavering. I want to tell her I know she's trying to make me respect him but it's way too late. "Your dad points out everything that's wrong with you, not to mention the shortcomings he sees in me. Not once do you stop to consider that you are just like your dad. Both of you are letting me down."

I open my mouth. I'm going to say, he's the adult, but I stop. It's one night. In a year, I'll be graduating and move away. The Ogre is worth less to me than a lightbulb is to a bat. When I get elected class president my mother will realize she's chosen the wrong side. That I am the smart one, the one with charisma. I'm the star to hang onto.

"Okay. I'll be there." I put my shoes back on. Make a big show of walking to the front door, opening it up, and slamming it behind me. She doesn't try to stop me from leaving.

Chantal

· · · · · ·

Surprise Visit.

$\mathcal{I}$ am finishing the final secret admirer note for the I Like Him, I Like Him A Lot, Cake—a splendid white meringue frosting decorated with thin-piped daisy petals and a center of highlighter yellow nonpareils—when the doorbell rings.

I look at the oven clock. It's well after midnight. No one rings our doorbell at midnight unless it's an emergency, or my mother. The pile of evidence still sits in the corner. I open the linen drawer in the buffet and pull out our Thanksgiving tablecloth, drape it over the KitchenAid and ingredients. I'll tell my mother there's a surprise under there if she asks. And . . . the cake . . . well . . . I'll tell her that someone dropped it off for me, but I refused to eat it.

Now she's knocking at the door. She must have her keys in her luggage or she wants to surprise me. But she'll think I've been asleep. I tangle up my hair, yawn to get that sleep look going, and shuffle to the front door. I don't look through the window at the top, I want to avoid that first look where she'll figure out I'm pretending. Head down, I open the door.

"Were you asleep?"

That's not my mother's voice. I jerk my head up. Crud. It's Will.

"What are you doing here?" I move to the space between the door and the wall, cut off the view to the inside.

"You're . . . uh . . . cute like that. Bed head. Uh . . . can I come in?"
He moves a step closer and I smell beer on his breath.

"No." I change my voice to a whisper. "My parents are asleep.
They'll freak. What do you want?" I have got to get rid of him.

"Tuesday night. There's this thing for my dad. A party. And I'm taking you. I'll pick you up at six thirty."

"No." I say it because it's the first word that comes to my mind.
No. He's too . . . invasive . . . and I think . . . unsafe. It's all I can do to
even stand at the door.

"What do you mean, no? We have a deal. You're my fake-girlfriend."

"No."

"You want me to put the kibosh on the summer project?"

"Like you could do that."

"I could." Maybe he's watched a whole lot of intimidation tactics in cop shows or terrorist movies or something, but it's the way
he stares at me, convincing.

"You can't force me to go. And you showed up here without calling, that's against the rules."

He considers me. I see his jaw clench. I don't cave in, but I feel
goose bumps orange-peeling my arms.

I remind myself that every school year since the seventh grade
I have created a path from the beginning of my school day to the
end that ensures I will avoid Will. He is dangerous. Dangerous.

When he finally speaks, his voice is different, a little less commanding. "Just . . . just come for my mom, okay? That's the only reason I'm going, for her. She likes you."

I remember: but I have a plan. He can't hurt me.

"I'm drunk. I have no pride."

Even though my stomach is in knots, I agree. I can do this. "Okay.
Tuesday night."

He smiles and with that smile I know I've been had. It's the same
smile he put on the night of the party right before he attacked me

with that kiss and his tongue. Disgusting. But this time it will be different. This time I'm in charge.

I fight the lump in my throat as he tells me among other things to wear a dress, and mascara and lip gloss, and sandals. At least we'll be in a public place. And what could go wrong at the Moose Hall with his mother and his dad both at the table? My one assertion, "I'll meet you there," comes at the end of Will's instructions. I close the door and lock it behind me before he can dispute it. Then I turn my back to the door and scrunch down to the floor, until I am a tightly held ball of doubt.

What am I doing? This will be the second date of my lifetime. Again, with the person I dislike the most.

I wonder how I should spend my last night of freedom. Correction: my last few hours, since my mother will arrive at ten tomorrow morning.

Nigella, what would you do?

Follow your heart, darling, and waste not another promising minute. Worry is an emotion you can easily live without.

• • •

It's either foolishness or courage that propels me off the floor twenty minutes later and guides me to the pile of baking implements and ingredients. I carry them to the garage and settle them into the trunk of my dad's SUV. I set the I Like Him, I Like Him A Lot Cake on the floor of the passenger's seat. The keys, found in my dad's desk drawer, jingle merrily. Or maybe they jingle a bad omen. Either way, I start the ignition, press the garage door opener, and put the car in reverse.

I've driven my dad's car five times as practice for my driving test, which I haven't taken yet. So, technically, what I am doing is illegal. I back out six feet and press the button to close the garage door. I shoulder check before I ease out of the driveway, push on the brakes, and shift the car into drive. My dad would say that at this second I'm definitely at the line between right and wrong. My mother would say I crossed the line just thinking about driving my dad's car. However, at 1:27 A.M. with less than nine hours before her arrival, I need to make the best use of my remaining minutes. My plan is to stick to the less traveled roads, to drive just under the speed limit, and to keep the vehicle going in a straight line at all times, except when I have to turn. If I get stopped, I'll tell the police officer it's an emergency. And it is. Without space to bake, I will be forced to revert to the old me.

Chantal

· · · · · ·

The Final Delivery.

I make four turns, stop at five stop signs, cross one highway, and navigate through two stoplight-controlled intersections. Other drivers honk at me four times and six vehicles pass me. I give them lots of room. I drive mostly on the shoulder of the road. I know this is attention-getting driving, but my fear of oncoming traffic keeps me away from the middle of the lane. Fortunately our town policemen are probably monitoring the last of the Friday night cruisers, not driving along Third Street where they could easily spot a girl without a license. I park in the driveway of the little house my dad uses for his office. I unlock the back door, walk through what used to be the mudroom for the railway men who lived here when the house was built.

In the tiny kitchen, I find the one-door refrigerator. I add my buttermilk and unsalted butter to the empty shelves. The KitchenAid barely fits under the sink but the flour and sugar fill up the empty cupboards. The baking pans are next and as I search for a place to hide them, I remember there's an oven here. I touch the dial for the oven, the dial for the temperature. A month ago, I wouldn't even have noticed this appliance. I pull out the drawer underneath and set my nine-inch round, eight-inch round, and Bundt pans on top of the broiler pan. I only remembered a microwave here, but maybe that's because all

I've ever eaten here is popcorn, after school. I doubt the real oven even works, but I turn a burner on, and twist the oven dial to 350 degrees.

"If you can resist this," Nigella said in one of her cooking shows, "you do not deserve to eat." She was talking about fried chicken, but I know Nigella. She'd say I can love cake more than chicken. She'd say I can love whatever I want.

I imagine the KitchenAid on one end of the small counter, leaving just enough space for a decorating station. The air above the burner is hot and inside the oven my hand definitely feels warmth. But my mother wouldn't let me bake here any more than she would at home. It's a matter of principle she'd say. *Only yours, only yours.* I turn the stove and oven off. It's nearly 2 A.M. and I've still got to deliver a cake and clean up the kitchen back at my house. I need to focus on my first plan instead of dreaming up a new one.

• • •

I wear black for the delivery. I am in my dad's car on Third Street, ten blocks from the home of Lauren, my next cake messenger, when I see what I least expect: a ball cap I recognize, a flip of hair that is only his. He's walking to his car a block ahead of me on the right-hand side. I have seconds to react. I crank the wheel right at the intersection, but I forget to press the brakes, and the speed and the panic combines and two wheels of Dad's car are riding on the curb and I'm headed for a bush. A big bush with, crud, don't let it be true, a telephone pole on the other side of it. I slam on the brakes and the bumper hits something, but I can't stop to look; what if Mitch heard the noise, what if he's walking toward me. I find the R on the shifter and I press the gas pedal enough that I roll back. In D for drive, I manage to get off the curb and I'm driving forward. At the end of the block, I take a left. At the end of that block, I take a left. I pull over to the side of the road. I remember the cake. It survived the incident (I can't admit it was an accident) although the frosting on one side is going to need some repair work. *I need to get out of here. I need to get out of here.* This was my final delivery and instead of feeling victorious and calm, I'm panicked. I turn right and try to recalculate how I'm going to get to Lauren's house. That's when I see Mitch's car up ahead.

The only way to explain my next choice is to point out that in my perfectionist brain, I try to find a way to compensate whenever something goes wrong. For example, if I miss three questions on a math test, I'll not only correct my mistakes, but ask the teacher for extra credit to make up for my less than 100 percent. Tonight my extra credit is Mitch.

I think about what would happen if he knew I was the Cake Princess. Would all that radio love he sends out for her transform into long, meaningful looks? Or my first real date? I'm so focused on my daydream, I've almost forgotten my near crash. I follow him at a safe distance all the way to his house, a trip that takes me through town and up into the subdivision near the ski hill. He parks in his driveway. I drive up two blocks and park on the street. My adrenaline-fueled panic has turned into an anticipation that flutters in my stomach. I get out of Dad's car, walk around to the passenger's side, and rescue my cake. I repair the frosting on the side of I Like Him, I Like Him A Lot Cake with my fingertips and start sneaking my way to Mitch's front door with the cake.

His street is at the edge of town where the houses emerge from the forest, their wide lawns plonked with rock fountains. It's too far out for streetlights, so tiny lanterns sprinkle the paths from driveways to front doors. The inky darkness out here nearly blinds me. I'm not afraid of the dark, but I'm terrified of what lives in the dark: bears, coyotes, cougars. Mostly. As I approach Mitch's house I hear his car door opening, closing, feet on driveway.

I move deeper through the shadows until I reach the edge of his yard. The porch light is off. I step lightly on spongy grass to the door. I could set the cake down, put the cardboard box over it, and dash in the darkness. I could be home in ten minutes. I set the cake down with the secret admirer note attached, cover it with the cardboard box, and sneak across the street to a black spot in the neighbor's yard, where I can . . . what? Spy on Mitch.

A light shines in an upstairs room. It's got to be Mitch's bedroom. The curtains drift in and out of the open window. I sit on the grass beside a massive rock fountain and wait—a slightly troubling moment of unrequited like.

Come close to the window.

His shadow moves, arms stretch up and out. His shirt flies past the window. His shadow bends.

A pair of jeans is next. The curtains get in the way, then, clear.

The shadow moves. Oh God, it's not a shadow. It's him, his naked back and his white boxers. Right in front of the open window. I hold my hand over my mouth to keep all sounds from leaking.

And he's dancing. Dancing? His knees dip, he moves side to side.

Well, he is in drama, right? Maybe all actor boys dance by themselves at 2 A.M.

And his right arm is moving up and down. Repeatedly. In rhythm. No. Oh. No.

Oh. God. He's going to face me. Well, not his face, but his . . . I hold my breath, squeeze my eyes shut. And then force them open.

God.

It's a guitar. I breathe again, all in one rush.

He's playing Guitar Hero.

In his boxers.

I watch as he spins around and strain to hear the song he's playing, but now I see he's wearing headphones. I could probably call his name and the neighbors would come out running before Mitch would hear me. If I threw rocks at his window, I'd have to break the glass to get him to notice. But I want him to notice.

Jillian

· · · · · ·

The Morning.

The boys are waiting in the van, the towels and picnic lunches, hockey sticks and nets already packed. The Hat Trick in the backseat read comic books my grandfather sent them years ago, when they were still too young to read. The Double Minor has the Dr. Seuss books that used to be mine and baby Ollie chews on the corner of *Good Night, Moon.* I added the reading material at the last minute, when I remembered that good sisters make sure their brothers read.

Parker arrives at the passenger's side door wearing the same smile he had on yesterday, as if nothing has changed.

"The heat must have gotten to me last night," he says as he pulls the seat belt across his chest. "I was out cold by nine thirty P.M. How about you?"

"Same," I tell him. "Right after the boys were asleep, the night was over." I concentrate on the road, driving.

"Yeah, I woke up in this fog, thinking I was supposed to call or something last night."

"I don't remember that." Now, I allow myself an eye exchange that forces me to look away.

"No? Okay."

I know the reason I'm lying is to protect the boys. I suspect Parker is trying to protect himself. It's disappointing, I think, like when my mother says she's going to take me shopping in the city and leave the boys with a babysitter, but it doesn't happen.

Parker

· · · · · ·

The Unbearable Morning.

I know I screwed up last night and I'm kicking myself for not being up front with Jillian. But I got there and she was already in the van. And the boys were in there, all kumbaya on the reading, and I knew if I said anything, we might end up in a fight and if that happened I'd feel even worse. And I can make this up to Jillian, anyway. She will know, by my unselfish actions, that I put the boys and her first.

When we pull into the parking lot, I'm out first and I've got all the kids rallied around me before Jillian can say a word. I've got baby Ollie in one arm, I carry the cooler that's so heavy it's like it's full of rocks, and the Double Minor trek right on my heels. I'm in a full sweat by the time we reach the tree at the top of the hill.

"Oh, hey Parker!" It's Annelise. She's just arrived and she looks, as my brother would say, like a cool drink of water. I've always liked her smile. "Can I hold the baby . . . uh . . . Ollie for you?"

I look back. Jillian must still be in the parking lot organizing the Hat Trick. If Annelise took Ollie and kept an eye on the Double Minor I could run down and help. "Come here Ollie." She reaches out and takes him from me before I can say no. "Don't worry," she says. "I love kids. We know how to have fun!" I think it's a bit strange that she's there so early and without any of her friends, but right now I've got some ass kissing to do.

I am halfway down the hill when I meet up with Jillian. I take the bundle of towels from her and she thanks me and continues on, carrying the orange cones. I think it's all going to be okay. We get within sighting distance of baby Ollie, who is gnawing on Annelise's cell phone, and things change. Jillian walks fiercely. The Hat Trick start acting up, trying to hit each other with the hockey sticks. And I trip over an old guy tanning his wrinkles.

I reach the blanket just after Jillian and I'm ready to run interference when she says, "I'll go set up the cones for the drills." She leaves before I have a chance to do the right thing. Anything right. I follow her, pulling the Double Minor and the Hat Trick along with me.

• • •

An hour later the sun is baking us all, especially me and my sick stomach. The kids run their drills, knocking down cone after cone. Jillian tells them they can have a sixty-second water break. She keeps her eye on the timing watch.

"Jillian," I say. "Let's see if Will's cake is here. It'll be a good break."

"Is that what you want to do?"

"I think that's what the boys want to do." I point at them. They're on their stomachs, chests heaving, their hair plastered to their heads.

"You know, Parker." She targets me with her look. "What's the point, really? So we're going to have a hockey tournament in a couple of weeks. So what? It's not going to change their lives if they play hockey. We raise a little bit of money. So what? What if it's not worth all this work? I didn't realize I was signing up for hockey bootcamp."

My stomach is on fire. I need Gatorade, or milk, or pink medicine. "I don't know how you can even question this. This is about putting effort into something bigger than us. We can make a difference, Jillian."

"No offense, but you sound like Chantal."

I thought Chantal was her best friend. "Grass roots. And we're starting with your brothers. The kids are going to benefit the most from this. I guarantee it." I do, don't I? This is about them, isn't it?

I convince her that the kids need a real break and we need to join the others, because I have a plan that is going to make this hockey tournament *the event* of the summer.

• • •

I'm the first guy to witness the scene at the blanket, but I wish like hell I wasn't. I wonder when my punishment will end. Annelise has been babysitting Ollie who appears to be wearing a T-shirt of hers. It's pink and she's got it sort of belted below his baby stomach so that really, he appears to be wearing a dress. This is a minor issue. His hair, usually curly, sticks out from his head in dozens of ponytails. His lips, even from here, shine in bright red lip gloss. His eyes are blue and pink rainbows. His cheeks glow orange-red. And then it comes to me, a way to save my fate. "Oh, look," I say. "Annelise has dressed Ollie up as . . ."

"Her identical baby sister . . ." Jillian says.

"I was going to say a clown."

"But my joke was better." She punches my shoulder. I realize it's the first time she's touched me, purposefully, since this morning.

"You're not mad?"

"At Annelise's makeover?" She shakes her head.

"No, at me."

"Not about this." And she walks ahead of me. I watch how she strides with confidence, purpose. We make a good team, Jillian and I. I need to tell her that.

By the time I get to the blanket, Jillian has taken baby Ollie to the bathroom to get cleaned up, leaving me to referee her brothers. They are digging into the cooler, and soon I figure out why.

Will sits up from his tanning position. He keeps telling us he's saving his energy for the massive hours he'll have to clock at the tournament. "No cake today. I've been telling everyone I have no idea who this girl is or if a cake is going to come at all, but they don't believe me. Some rumor got started that I know who the secret admirer is . . . As if that would make sense."

"I told you someone must have the cake and they're late getting here. I'm texting everyone right now. Hardly anyone's here. I guess you two weren't the only ones having a late night out." Annelise catches me looking at her and she winks. "Danielle saw you and Will weaving home."

No. She is the wrong person to have that information. "Annelise." I make sure that Jillian hasn't come out of the bathroom yet. "Can you go for a walk with me?" I really need to do something about my stomach; it's killing me.

Annelise follows me in the opposite direction of the bathrooms, farther up the hill. I'm not sure how I'm going to approach her, but I need her cooperation.

"Parker. That baby is so cute, isn't he?" she asks.

"Yeah. It was really nice of you to help out like that." I wince. It's like a fist is squeezing my insides.

"Do you really mean that?" She stops and I don't have a choice. Now we're standing uh . . . chest to chest. The discomfort doubles. "I really want to show you how helpful I can be and that, you know, I really like kids and stuff."

"Oh. I totally see that." Oh God. She's got those big eyes and I'm remembering the day I broke up with her and how she was convinced I showed up to surprise her. Her eyes are big with expectation. I remember that she's going to benefit from the ultimate plan, too, she just can't know how, yet. Right now, it's all about getting the right people all in line. "But I need your help in a different way. I need the Cake Girl . . ."

"She's the Cake Princess now, we changed her name."

What a surprise, Princess Annelise. "Oh, I like it. Anyway, I really need her to keep delivering cakes to Will."

"I think the cake is just late today." She pulls her phone from her pocket, reads the latest news.

I watch her closely as I reveal my strategy. "Well, let's hope so.

But we need to keep the cakes coming, all the way up to the hockey tournament."

"I guess I could put a message on the fanpage." Was she always this good at deception?

"Great. And, could you do me another big favor?" I touch her shoulder and she instantly loses interest in the phone. "I mean, this is so important and it will be so great for you."

"For me?"

"Yeah, if this works out, you'll get exactly what you've always wanted."

She takes a deep breath. And her chest . . . it really expands. "What is it?"

"The night of the hockey tournament, I want the Cake Princess to reveal who she is. Everyone will be there and she'll be the most popular girl there."

Her eyes shift from one of my eyes to the other, then over my shoulder. She's thinking. My stomach pains double. I knew it was going too well. "But what if Will doesn't really like his secret admirer? Won't she be crushed? I don't want her to get hurt. I like her."

I know the "her" we're talking about here is Annelise and she wants to know if I'm going to pick her at the end of the game. I have to find a way to tell her without telling her that she should trust me. "Well, she'll bounce back. Think about the *Bachelor* and how he picked that girl, but it turns out she wasn't the one. And then she got her own show."

She nods. "The Cake Princess can get her own show. Very clever, Parker . . . I'll work my magic."

"Thanks for helping me out here." I rub my stomach. "You have no idea what this is going to mean."

"Actually, I think I do." She winks at me. "But it will be our little secret."

I can see Jillian's returned to the blanket. "Oh and the part about me being out late last night with Will, can that be our secret, too?" I explain that we were strategizing and I don't want anyone else to know about it.

"Got it. I'll go to the blanket first. You follow later. Just like old times." I wonder if all the big game players get gut aches when they're making the most important moves. The greater good has got to be someone's vision, a future for the boys and a legacy for the high school. And the coach has to keep the team motivated; that's all I'm doing. Annelise will get a payoff. Not my girlfriend. But girlfriend of the class president.

Chantal

· · · · · ·

Sugar, Sugar Hangover.

I smelled her first: coffee, mint gum, and Burt's Bees hand cream. The smell of organized efficiency. I stayed curled under my comforter, my eyes delicately closed. I wanted to feel what she would do. Her feet stepped across my carpet quickly enough that I got the sense she was glad to see me. And her hand, I know from the overwhelming smell of shea butter, hovered over my forehead. She was indecisive about whether to caress my forehead the way she did when I was small and I had nightmares. The air shifted and I knew that she'd lost her nerve to be the mom she used to be.

I opened my eyes. "Hey, Mom." She turned around.

"Oh . . . Chantal. I was . . . I was . . . going to let you sleep a bit."

I yawned and stretched, watching her observe me, my tangled hair, the pimple on my chin. I saw something in her face, disappointment or regret, but it was gone too soon to know for sure. She'd only been away for a week, but she looked different. The worry she always carried around was still etched in the tightness of her shoulders and jaw, and now I sensed something else. Sadness. Hurt. I was about to ask her if anything was wrong, but she spoke first.

"I brought you something." She reached into the pocket of her Audrey Hepburn capris, and pulled out a rock. Gray with a white circle around it. I sat up and cradled it in my hands.

"You brought me a rock?" Her usual gifts of umbrellas, slippers, and pajamas were practical. "This will make a great paperweight." I smiled. I was determined that I would find a way to make at least this morning pleasant. I thought about Mitch. My smile grew wider, even if it was misplaced.

"About the rock." My mother pulls the end of a thick strand of hair through her fingers, in front of the first finger, behind the second, over and over, in a pattern that makes an eight or an infinity symbol. I long for cupcakes; my mother twists her hair. "That rock." She points at it. "It felt right."

"Oh." Now she was sounding a bit like Jillian's mother who claimed she felt the pull of the moon and the tides so acutely, she could feel the earth turning on its axis. "Thanks." I smiled.

"I picked it up and it felt right." She stared at her rock, my rock, while she talked. "When your father and I were dating we'd go on walks, down by the Columbia River and he'd choose a rock. He'd say, 'This one feels like it's meant for you.' He knew what I needed. A rock lasts forever. And I needed that then."

So it wasn't just a rock, there's some kind of lesson I'm supposed to learn. Or she was giving me a concealed message like she's leaving my dad. Maybe he's secretly gone to Lettuce Loaf on his own to avoid the conflict, the separation of belongings, the negotiation over me. "I thought you went for some course." I knew my word choice—some course—would grate on her.

"We had free time."

"And you collected rocks?" It was good to get her on another subject. We could argue about the rock instead of its hidden messages.

"I went out on walks. Like I used to. I needed to clear my head." Again with the strange look on her face that I couldn't read. This time I didn't want to ask her what was wrong. She shook her head, tried on a smile. "It's good to see you. To know that everything's okay. Everything is okay, isn't it?"

"Yep." If I'd even imagined I might tell my mother how I'd changed my life in the past week, all thought of that was gone. I'm not some teenager who is under the misguided assumption that her mother would freak when she'd actually understand. We have a track record. And my mother has issues.

"Oh . . . good. So . . . there you go. A rock."

"A rock."

We smiled.

• • •

Two hours later, she's at her office and I'm biking to Williamson's Lake. We sort of agreed this morning that I wouldn't tell her what's really happening and she wouldn't tell me. One day she'll hunt me down, grill me with questions until she's satisfied that I'm not the worst she fears: about to get fat, get pregnant, get a B in any subject, lose my interest in intellectual pursuits, or reject her.

My dad used to tell me she was high-strung. As I got older he used words like perfectionism and anxiety, phrases like, it was tough for her growing up. Someday she'll tell me a piece of the truth about herself, offering up some explanation for her behavior. Maybe she'll tell me that story again, the one that always makes me cry inside. When she was ten, her mother left her in charge of her four brothers and a sister who was two years old, but didn't tell her where she was going or when she'd be back. My mother was afraid to ask her dad, since he was worried about his business having already gone bankrupt once. She did what she had to do. She lied to the teachers, told them all the kids were sick and she couldn't go to school. After a week passed without even a phone call from her mother she thought she'd never go back again. *I wanted to go to school,* my mother says when she tells this story. *I was only ten years old.* That's the part that gets me the most. Eventually her mother came back but my mother, her daughter, never stopped worrying about when she'd leave the next time. My mother keeps things inside and she worries over everything, but she would never give up on me. Just like she never gave up on her siblings. At least that's what I want to believe.

Suddenly I'm imagining how badly I'd get hurt if I rode my bike over the next steep drop or crashed into the snack shack at Williamson's Lake. The longer I ride and tell myself that there is no problem, the faster my heart races. My hands begin to sweat. *Crud. Crud. Crud.* I haven't felt this, panic, so acutely since before I started baking cakes. I need Jillian. She can always talk me down. I pedal faster. I do not look down.

Will

· · · · · ·

Batons?

It's hotter than two rats making out in a wool sock, but Team Popular forces me to stay on the hill. Annelise's texting has convened more than thirty kids, all of them waiting for the next cake. And if it doesn't show I'll be the guy whose secret admirer dumped him. My head pounds and the five bottles of water I've consumed don't seem to be helping. You can understand why I want to go for a swim. Since the Facebook announcement that the Cake Princess will show us who she really is at the hockey tournament, plans have gone guano.

"Two cakes," I told Annelise, "that's it." I tried to keep my eyes focused on her face instead of her chest to show that I was sincere. "You need to slow the chuck wagon down."

"Will." She set her phone down to add another layer of coconut oil to her skin. "Enjoy the ride. This is as close to the paparazzi as you're ever going to get."

Even with my sunglasses on and my back against the towel I can feel the rush of the crowd when someone we know starts up the hill. The whispers start. Is she carrying something? No, it's Chantal. No cake.

Chantal. I ease myself up to sitting. Last night's convo with her definitely went sideways. I wasn't so drunk I don't remember it. And what I remember was her frickin' attitude. As if she thought she was better than me.

"You didn't get the cake, either?" Annelise asks.

"Cake?" Chantal raises her eyebrows.

Annelise reminds Chantal of the biggest event that's happened since the forest fire that got us all evacuated three years ago. "And . . . the Cake Princess is going to show us who she really is at the hockey tournament. It's on Facebook. Everyone is going to be there."

"Fun." Chantal says. She glances at me and I know she's thinking that I don't deserve to be the object of some girl's affection. She's thinking she wishes the secret admirer would end it all by Tuesday so she wouldn't have to go out with me. Whatev. She owes me.

Now Jillian, Parker, and the rug rats join us for the lunch break and all those boys spread throughout the crowd acting like they belong here with the high-fives and the hockey talk. I revert to my behind-the-shades and on-the-towel pose, hoping no one can tell that I'm as jumpy as a rabbit being chased by a dog through a bowling alley.

Annelise's phone pings and the five or six people nearest me go silent. *Maybe this is it*, I hear one of them whisper. "It" is the message that reveals who has the cake and why they haven't gotten here yet. We wait. Finally, Annelise speaks, "Guys? Quiet everyone. Quiet. Oh. Wow. This is unbelievable. Okay. Listen to this."

Annelise loves to be the center of attention. Obviously that's why she's baking all these cakes. "As you know, my dad is on the tourism board. He's been talking to the mayor and some other people about our summer project. And they're going to turn it into a tourism *event*. We can have it downtown. They're going to block off the street and bring in floodlights from the high school and bleachers for the fans. The Dairy Barn is going to sell ice cream. And that's just the beginning."

Conversations erupt. Some girl four people away from me says she'll organize a halftime show with baton twirlers. It's hockey, I want to yell. There is no halftime. My head pounds. I need water. Lots of water. Some towns have strawberry festivals or theater days or regattas on the lake. Ours has a charity hockey tournament organized by high school kids and some crazy girl baking cakes. I know I'm supposed to be celebrating. Parker's over there giving me the nod like I told you this was going to be great.

For real? This could be disaster.com. I'm supposed to be happy about this, my chance at class president and Annelise, but I'm thinking if the secret admirer has backed out, that wouldn't be so bad. I wouldn't get what I want, but I also wouldn't have to suffer any embarrassment on a plan that goes wrong.

I'm composing my exit speech in my head, for the moment when it's clear that the cake isn't going to show.

Then the crowd's energy shifts. The cake has arrived.

Chantal

· · · · · ·

Rule Change.

𝓘 make sure that I'm at the back of the mass of kids as Mitch approaches. It's hell to be sort-of-short in this situation. I have to look around people's heads to get a clear view of the cake and Mitch. His hair is perfect today and he's simply dressed but interesting—rolled-up jeans and a plain T-shirt and a new ball cap. He's so . . . noticeably unnoticeable. I Like Him, I think, I Like Him A Lot.

"Chantal." Jillian pulls my elbow, moves me closer to the center of the action.

"She Likes Me, She Likes Me A Lot," Will says as he studies the card.

"Told you. Told you," Annelise taunts.

"Strange you were right on that one. Like maybe you had some insider knowledge . . ."

Annelise looks at me. Ever since the day I sat in her car and gave her advice on how to get Parker back, she thinks I've got the answers. She doesn't know I'm the Cake Princess, but right now she's looking at me. At me! And everyone else does, too. *Crud.* Now . . . they're going to think I'm connected. I feel a brain rush and the words form a defense line that I may regret later.

"What's even stranger is that some girl is choosing Will to secretly admire." I glance at him for only a second and then at everyone else. "Just kidding."

And they all laugh. They laugh because a crowd always looks for someone to be different, someone to target. Today it's Will.

"Bitch." Will says it playfully, as if we're on some MTV show, but it doesn't feel like we're friends. Not even close.

"Aw . . ." Mitch rubs Will's shoulder. "Don't be such a prima donna. You're the one getting cakes. All the guys are jealous . . ."

Will shakes off Mitch's hand, faces him with fists clenched. He's going to fight Mitch?

"Let's have some cake." Parker pushes between them. As he whispers to Will, Jillian starts slicing the cake and Annelise pulls out the plates, napkins, and forks. Soon slivers of cake are dispersed.

"Chantal." Mitch is next to me. The sound of his voice sends reverberations of I Like Him A Lot through me. I'm not kidding. The sound of his voice, warm and rich with resonance, reminds me of a cello being played. An Italian cello. "You have to try this cake." He drives a fork through a corner of it, holds it up for me. "It's amazing," he says.

"You really think so?"

He nods as the cake tickles my tongue, the delicate crumbs dissolving so pleasantly with the frosting. "Oh. It really is good. I wonder where the Cake Princess bought it." I hope that my lie is believable.

"This is definitely not from a mix," Annelise says. "And I think we need to send the Cake Princess a message that she's got to take pictures of the cakes from now on, before she delivers them. Like, I think we need to make sure no one is going to, like, copy her." She looks at me. Again. I stare at my fingernails.

Now I have to document my deliveries. If I make any more.

"Yeah, Will only needs one girlfriend," Parker says.

Will punches Parker in the shoulder playfully.

"Or video," Mitch says. "She could make a video and it'll be like the Oscars. And the winner is . . ." Mitch has never spoken this many words in a group. Giving him the cake must have given him permission. As if the cake said, you're one of us.

Jillian suggests that the Cake Princess might be working alone and, therefore, creating a video would be difficult. Mitch turns to me and says that one person could not make a cake a day and have it be this great. I nod in agreement.

"Okay." Annelise stops chewing the end of her pen. "The Cake Princess is going to make a video of herself. We'll show it at the hockey game. I'll let her know."

"I'm sure you are in close contact with her . . ." Will leans in close enough that surely Annelise can smell his hair gel.

"Facebook."

"Right." Will sits back, defeated.

I can't object. They'll suspect me. Maybe I should just tell them now. It's me. I'm the one. Then I won't have to make a movie or keep this a secret from my mother. Mitch will know I like him. That will be enough, won't it?

I start to feel a bit faint, maybe from the heat or the excitement or the sugar rush. Did I even eat breakfast today? I think I was too nervous, worried that I would miss Mitch delivering my cake. That was all I wanted today, Mitch delivering the cake.

A sudden gust of wind catches me mid-fantasy. "Chantal." Will is next to me, squeezing out Mitch. The smells of vanilla and sugar disintegrate, overpowered by hot peppers and rotting wood. "I just wanted to talk to you about Tuesday night."

"Uh . . ." I'm trapped. I can feel my skin losing the glow of happiness.

"I'll be at your place at six thirty P.M."

"Uh . . ." I already told him I'd meet him at the Moose Hall, but I can't speak. I look at Mitch, who doesn't hide his look of disgust. He can't believe I'd be going out with Will. He thinks I should know better. I should know better. I hang my head.

"So. Tuesday night." Will leans into me and kisses my cheek. "Can't wait."

I can't look up. I'm trapped by a deal I never should have made and now I'm paying the price. My armpits start to sweat. No. I'm fighting back. With cake. I'll turn Will's humiliation right back at him.

When I finally look up, Mitch has gone and Jillian and Parker are off again with the boys to the hockey field. Annelise is throwing away the empty cardboard platter of the I Like Him, I Like Him A Lot Cake. That leaves . . .

Will. He's in his usual pose, hands behind his head, sunglasses on, chin up to the sun as if it's shining solely on him. He thinks all he has to do is sit on the hill and a cake will show up. I think it's time for a new set of rules and a new way of doing things. He wants to be the king of the cake. Well, he's going to have to earn the privilege. I'm the one who sets the price.

Parker

· · · · · ·

The Non-Fight.

Jillian and I are united on this: we are here for the Hat Trick, Double Minor, and Ollie. Now that the boys know the whole town will be watching them play hockey, they're motivated. I think the Hat Trick have convinced each other that talent scouts are going to show up because, you know, scouts are always watching seven-year-olds. And I'm not about to burst that bubble. Kids like them need hope in their lives.

About Jillian and me. We haven't argued. She hasn't broken down crying. She doesn't demand that I explain where I was last night when I stood her up. We are the perfect couple, really, focused on a goal. Everything is okay, I tell myself. Extraordinary.

I don't know why I feel so uneasy then, like I forgot to turn the lights off in my car and I'm going to go out to a dead battery. I focus on the hockey drills; this is where the improvement happens. You have to put in the time every day to build your skills, get the passing and the communication moving. Playing the games is just about seeing how the practice is working.

Jillian
• • • • • •
Dad 4?

I blame the heat when Parker and I pull into the driveway.

I need to cool them off, I tell him.

I'm worn out, I say, from the heat.

I wouldn't be much fun.

No, I don't even want to watch a movie.

I stop short of saying the truth; I want to be alone. I kiss him good-bye as if nothing is wrong because, really, it's just me. I'll get over it. I simply need some time by myself. Normal, I tell myself, this is normal.

I send the Hat Trick to take showers, give the Double Minor a package of saltines and a DVD in my room, and set Ollie in his playpen with a bowl of O's. I'm on my way back to the kitchen but I stop in the living room, in front of the fan. I meditate to the oscillating blades.

"Need some help?"

I follow the trail of a man's voice.

A man with blown-back hair, wide-set eyes, and a shadow of a beard sits at the kitchen counter. He's the sort of man you see on a Harley at a stoplight and you wonder if he's ever been in prison. I've never met this guy, but I know who he is and I don't want anything to do with him. Main resolution of this debate: this family does not need a Dad 4. This family needs a Mom 1.

"The name's Keith." He raises his coffee cup as if offering up a toast to me. "You must be Jillian."

The coffee cup is mine, created for me by Chantal during our summer pottery project. I walk to the kitchen. I wish I hadn't. This close I see that Keith is naked from the waist up. Dark hairs curl on his chest and his stomach is mostly flab free. My mother goes for the fit muscle men.

"You . . . uh . . . need something?" He sits back, sets his hands in his lap. He's only wearing boxer shorts. His right shoulder is tattooed with notes playing across a musical staff. *Not a musician. Please, not a musician.*

It would make sense for me to walk away. But I hope I can scare him off. "So . . . you know my mother."

"We work together." He runs his hands through his hair. Once. Twice. Trying to use that blown-out hair to get him out of this mess. He doesn't look like the type who'd work at a nursing home.

"Doing what?"

"Uh . . . assessments . . . mostly." His too-wide-set eyes remind me of a bulldog's. What does she see in him? What does he see in her?

"You know she has seven kids, right? From three different fathers?" I count us off my fingers, Jillian, Travis, Thomas, Trevor, Josh, Stevie, Ollie.

"We've been friends a long time." He winks at me and takes another sip of coffee.

What? My debating skills aren't prepared for . . . what is he saying? How does he define a long time? Or friends?

"Jillian. What did you need?" My mother walks, no, she floats, toward us in her hippy dress—no bra, a loose and flowing skirt. When I've told her she can't wear that dress around my friends, she says she won't get rid of something that transforms her into a princess.

"You're not working. And Keith's here. Just met him." My brain is telling me to calm down, but my mouth is in charge. "Did they close the nursing home down? Ebola? Bird flu? Send you guys home with strict orders to avoid cavorting with the outside world?"

"Jillian."

"I . . . uh . . . better go." Keith walks past me to the sink with my coffee mug.

"I'll take my mug."

He hands it over. "Sorry, I didn't know."

"You can only use that excuse once around here," I say.

"She's a teenager," my mother calls after him on his way to the bedroom to find his clothes. "It's a good excuse for almost anything."

I wash my cup in full-on-hot tap water, keep my back to them as they kiss their good-byes at the front door. Finally, my mother shuts the door.

She leans against the closed door with her eyes lowered to dreamy. She sighs. I don't want to think about what she's been doing with him. Today. While I've been taking care of her other kids.

"Couldn't you have at least made dinner?"

"Relax. We'll order pizza." She grabs her hair into a ponytail.

"I don't want pizza."

"Chinese, then."

"I don't want to order."

"No." She wraps the elastic around her hair three times. "You want to be unhappy."

I grip the countertop; let the sharp edges dig into me. It is happening. Again. "I don't have a choice."

"You have a choice, darling." She comes toward me. Her hand trails the side of my face. She stares into my eyes, trying to hypnotize me. "You always do."

Chantal

· · · · · ·

Two Days. Two Cakes.

$\mathcal{I}$t has been easier than I expected to disappear for several hours each day and to slip out of the house unnoticed after my mother has gone to bed. Altogether too easy. How could she not, for instance, hear me trip down the stairs right outside her bedroom at midnight last night? And she doesn't even come into my bedroom in the morning to tell me to get up and start my day. Since she got home from her training she hasn't once asked me what productive activities I have planned. I'm suspecting brainwashing occurred in Oregon. I'm not complaining per se; but I'm the type of girl who wants to know if it's a category 3 or category 4 hurricane well before it hits land.

I snoop. I look in her desk first. I find a card from my mother's mother. Unopened. Birthday cards from three of her siblings are simply signed: *love, Bill; xox, Jenny; Happy birthday, Stephen.* I haven't seen any of them since the summer after third grade.

Her underwear drawers hold only underwear and bras, no love letters. The shoe boxes in her closet, only shoes. Her bedside table, a book, lip balm, and a square card, printed on one side with a complex labyrinth and on the other side, some words: *when you are truthful with yourself, you start to see everything as it is, not the way you want to see it.* What the hell? I position the card exactly as I discovered it and close the drawer. I swear the temperature drops by at least five degrees. I almost leave, but I know one more place to look. The medicine cabinet in the bathroom where I find two bottles of medication. Google search reveals that my mother is taking an antianxiety medication and a sleeping pill. Bingo. That's why she didn't hear me, the elephant on the stairs.

I transform into Nancy Drew on a bike as I try to solve the Secret of My Mother. What is happening to her? I lean over my handlebars and address the roadside grass. The grass does not answer. Cake might very well help the subject in question, but she would be resistant. I'll have to call my dad tonight, after the worst night of my life, the date with Will. Maybe I'll talk to my dad about more than my mother and the hot weather. Maybe I'll tell him that his office kitchen is now a bakery of delicious revenge.

I'm fairly certain that while my dad would question the wisdom of keeping my secrets from my mother, he would find the idea of the Cake Princess amusing. Everyone else has. Except Will. Objective reached. We're now a group of about thirty regulars and Annelise is in charge. No better way to keep the spotlight off me. She's taken over my clipboard and I doubt I'll see it again. Kids check in with her for their specific jobs: hockey camp support staff, Ollie duty, photographer, Twitter assistant, lunch preparation and cleanup, and of course, cake spotter.

I check the time. I'm five minutes away from the hill and about ten minutes away from today's cake delivery. Annelise has requested that each cake recipient arrive at the lake at 10:30 A.M. to present Will's cake. She even noted that she would be happy to pick up the cake and/or the cake recipient to get him/her to the lake on time. It makes me wonder if she's just a little bit more excited about acting as the Cake Princess's manager than in stoking Parker's jealousy. He is so busy with the hockey camp that he only joins us to eat cake or lunch. Which means I hardly see Jillian because the two of them are inseparable. I miss her.

I lock my bike in the stand near the snack shack, and start the hike up the hill. I can only stay for a couple of hours today—I've got to bake the next cake early. Ugh. My stomach aches at the thought of the date. The crowd has swelled to forty today and I'm glad I made a Bundt cake; it's easier to slice. Tina's not here yet, so I know the cake hasn't arrived.

I sit on the blanket, making small talk with Annelise, even when I see Tina shyly walking up the hill. No one notices her yet; she's not someone they'd expect since she just moved from the Philippines last year and she may have spoken to two or three people, tops. Since Mitch, I've decided that the quiet people deserve a spotlight. If I like getting attention, maybe they will, too. Sunday was Cheryl's turn with the Puppy Love Cake (chocolate cake with a vanilla butter-cream spotted with chocolate circles). Jason delivered the Bliss Is You and a Banana Cake yesterday.

Finally, the crowd parts and Tina stands in front of Will, who has remained seated on his towel throne. "I believe this is for you." She holds out the cake. The crowd laughs at her careful pronunciation, at the way she sort of bows, at her shy smile. "I'm not late, am I?"

"No. No," Annelise takes the cake from her. "You're perfect. Hey, you're the new girl, aren't you?" I wonder if this nice Annelise has been hidden or if she's been influenced by all the sugar love. "Do you have the card?"

"She can keep it." Will's intimidating eyebrows, his unmannered jaw, his thug posture tells it all. The frustration. The embarrassment. The anger.

"'I'm Coconuts for You,'" Annelise reads. "'Wear your specially made chest protector out to the floating dock. Get a picture of you, going coconuts for me, once you're out there. From: Your Secret Admirer.'"

"Chest protector?"

"Oh, yes, wait. I have it." Tina reaches into her beach bag and takes out a bra made from coconuts and string. I'm so handy with a hammer and an awl.

"No way," Will says. "I've done enough keeping everybody entertained."

The crowd disagrees. They've enjoyed it too much, the price that I've been extracting from Will each day. On Sunday, he had to find a dog to lick him on the lips—and have a piece of cake in the picture. On Monday, he had to stand next to a tourist (he chose a gray-haired man in long black socks with sandals), strike a monkey pose, and stick a banana in his ear. I'm getting almost as much enjoyment from the pictures on Facebook each day as I do from delivering the cakes. Both feel productive; giving a quiet person a chance to shine and giving a jerk an opportunity to show he's an ass.

Once we are down to the sole piece of cake that Will has to display in his photo of the day, he takes off his shirt and Annelise helps him into the coconut bra. The gray cloud that normally travels over Will's head darkens to black with intermittent lightning bolts.

I break away from the crowd as they make their way to the beach; even Parker, Jillian, and the boys have joined in for the jeering. I wonder what Jillian thinks of the latest development in Will's cakes. She's been so busy with Parker and the boys we haven't talked. Against all predictions, my life is Hollywood-starlet busy even if no one else knows: I have a cake to bake, a video to film, a mother to worry about, and the thing that any celebrity should not have to deal with: an obligation for a disaster date.

Will

· · · · · ·

The Cake Bitch.

This whole photo thing is about as funny as a fart at a funeral. I pull Annelise aside, after the photo shoot of me in the coconut bra, and demand that she cease and frickin' desist.

She tells me it's hot that I'm not threatened by a little fun. No more, I say. She says she doesn't know who the Cake Princess is so she can't do anything about it. Right.

We both know that making me the center of attention is all part of her plan to make Parker jealous enough to dump Jillian. I wonder how dressing up like a hula dancing monkey could make Parker jealous.

Parker sees me arguing and gets in the middle of it. "Relax, man. It's just for fun. Look, the Hat Trick and Double Minor are lovin' the pictures."

"So why don't you do it, dude?"

He comes right up into my face, just inches away and I know he's trying to shut me down. I'm so close to shoving him away. "You're the secretly admired, not me. Keep your eyes on the prize." And he winks. The prize. I'll be the top guy soon, the one that Annelise will put on speed dial. I want the next ten days to be over. Over.

Chantal

· · · · · ·

Dilemma[100]

The dilemma: I must pretend to like Will through an entire date at the Moose Hall to increase his stock value from his parents' point of view.

The dilemma[3]: Meanwhile, I am on a private campaign, that will soon become public, to embarrass him. I can only imagine how angry he'll be when I back out on this date and worse, when he realizes our original agreement was all a sham.

The dilemma[100]: It's 5:22 P.M. and I haven't found a cake to bake. Accidental? I think not. It will be impossible, now, to bake a cake and meet Will at 6:30. Impossible. I have to give up one or the other. I need to make a decision.

And yet, I continue to read cookbooks. Here I am with *Nigella Christmas*. I flip to the index and toss out the idea, none too soon, for a yule log cake I would title I'm Burning Up for You. Some other Cake Princess will have to choose that one. I'm about to close the book when I stop at the introduction. Nigella's cookbooks are so much more than recipes. I want to spend time with her. So I read.

"Everything I believe in—essentially, that warmth and contentment and welcome and friendship emanate from and are celebrated in the kitchen . . ." she writes.

That's the secret to solving my baking block.

Nigella's words tell me, instantly, what is wrong. The kitchen is about warmth, contentment, welcome, and friendship. Here I've been focusing on Will, who brings the opposite feelings into my life. No wonder I can't find a cake. When I think of the messenger—Cheryl loves dogs, Jason dressed as an ape for Halloween two years ago, and Tina, well she's new and I thought this might help her break the ice—I find the perfect cake for that person. That's why I've been able to do it. Today I've been so worried about this awful date that I can only think of Will, and he blocks out everything.

That's enough of that.

Will is unimportant. I'm going to forget about him. Avoid him. Starting tonight.

Darling. You've come round to good sense now, haven't you?

Nigella? I stare at the photo in front of me. She's in her crimson sweater set holding a red bowl, about to scoop flour into her KitchenAid. I half-expect her to look up at me. I detect the smell of vanilla and a citrusy sweet perfume and, if I'm not mistaken, sugar carmelizing on the stove.

Jillian

· · · · · ·

Sinking.

As I'm hiding out in my bedroom, the fan blowing the last drop-lets of water from my shower dry, my body is sinking. I could talk to someone about this. Correction. I could listen to someone talk, let the wind of their problems paralyze my own and stop the spinning pinwheel in my head. The issue, of course, is that during the listen-ing, I would be tempted to reveal the facts I'm facing. Better to wait. Usually things improve. The longer I do nothing, though, the lower I sink into my plaid comforter and the more I can feel the atmospheric pressure threatening to crush my skull. I could be depressed.

I haven't felt this lonely since before Chantal and I met in the third grade. We used to talk every night if we didn't see each other, even when she went on vacations with her parents, but this summer, well, we've been busy. That's what happens between friends, I think. It's never happened between us before but it could be that it's normal. Chantal was afraid this would happen if Parker and I dated, and I wonder if she knew the one who would be loneliest would be me.

And now Keith has all but moved in. Meeting Keith will confirm to Parker that despite his valiant efforts the kids in this family are bound to be screwed up.

I am also limiting my Parker time because I can't get over the fact that he stood me up. I think about it and my skin starts to itch.

Chantal would say I might be allergic to being betrayed. And she might be right.

In my house you accept what you cannot change. That means I'm powerless to get rid of Keith, for one thing. Now that Parker has shown me that he has the potential to let me down, I've accepted it, too, but I'm not going to leave myself open. I am not my mother. I will not make the same mistake over and over and over and over. So, I sink.

The ringing phone rescues me. I check the caller ID and discover that Chantal must know even from across town how much I need her right now. After we say hello and tell each other that we are fine, she starts in on her not-so-fine status notes.

"It's about my mother." She adds that her mother's back and that she's got an issue at work. "She's been asked to um . . . attend a work event . . . but it's against her principles."

I wonder why we're talking about Chantal's mother's work, because it is not something we've ever talked about, but already I'm feeling relief from the pressure. I ask a clarifying question, "An event at the hospital is against her principles?"

"It's sort of at the hospital. It's actually at the Moose Hall but it's to . . . uh . . . celebrate a guy who has always put her down, and other people, too. He's never been a nice guy. And some people pretended that they liked him because, you know, he had power and he had powerful friends. My mother put up with him but she definitely doesn't want to go."

"Your mother is asking for your advice?"

"I know. Weird." Chantal tells me that the strange behavior began with a rock from Oregon. "She told me it felt right."

"Not a rock," I groan. "That's something my mother would do."

"She feels that if she doesn't go, this guy will for sure notice and he might even, you know, try to get back at her."

"She shouldn't go." She's an adult. She can do whatever she wants.

"Should she call him and tell him she's not coming? He might talk about her to try to damage other people's perceptions of her."

"She could or she couldn't call. That's up to her, but she shouldn't go." This is all sounding a little too weird from Chantal and I wonder if we are really talking about her mother. "Why hasn't your mom talked to your dad? He's the therapist."

"He's in Saskatchewan at the Lettuce Loaf."

Ah. That explains a lot.

"It's that easy though?" Chantal asks. "Just don't go?"

"It's not easy. But you have to live with yourself. And it sucks when you realize you sort of hate yourself for going along." Surely if Chantal's mother can refuse to go to a family gathering every summer, she can say no to a retirement party. All this thinking about Chantal's issues has me practically floating above my mattress. It's possible that giving good advice is a small substitute for acting responsibly on your own behalf. I hear her sigh and I think that something else is going on. I'm on the edge of asking a probing question when she cuts in.

"Thanks. Um, my mom thanks you and I thank you for her." I imagine her lying on her twin bed, across from the perfectly matched and made twin bed that's mine. That's where I want to be right now. Escaped from confusion central. "We've hardly talked," she says.

"The hockey tournament." I sigh and, like a submarine, I drop.

"A summer project that's snowballed. Even Annelise is in." She pauses. "Are you mad at me about that?" She must be feeling guilty that she was the one who asked my boyfriend's ex to join the party.

"No. It's not even an issue." And because we're talking about Annelise and not about me I can tell Chantal that all Parker is interested in is the hockey tournament and ensuring my brothers reach their full potential.

"Hockey potential, right? Like, he's not going to parent-teacher conferences next year?" She laughs and when I laugh, my butt nearly hits the floor. Last year my mother sent me to the elementary school as her "parent representative"; not even Chantal knows that the principal called me into her office the following week and drilled me about what was going on at home. It is possible that once the summer is over, Parker and I could be talking about Travis's poor spelling and Josh's temper tantrums at day care. He could be my partner in all of this. And I'm so close, so close to telling Chantal *I'm confused* but her words come first. "I was wrong about him, Jillian. I want to say this now. I didn't trust him, but he's turned out to be a good guy."

"He really tries to do the right thing," I say. That's all. I change the subject, talk about the weather, it's been hot; the cakes from the Cake Princess, amazing; and, finally, I say I hear Ollie crying. "Good luck with your mom," I say.

"My mom? Of course. Thanks. Um . . . for everything." We say our good-byes even though we both sense that a gust of wind would blow down the carefully constructed bridge between our secrets. And yet, this is enough. She is my best friend, after all, and I know that even though I didn't tell her my worst fears, if I had she would have listened.

I scramble my way out of the middle of my mattress and pull a pillow and my comforter onto the floor. Tonight I'll sleep without feeling like I'm suffocating.

Will

. . . . . .

The Ten-Pound Tumor.

Inside the Moose Hall, it's hotter than a firecracker lit at both ends and outside it's not much better. I'm pacing between the table where my parents wait for my amazing date to arrive and the sidewalk where I watch for the shadow of a dress and heels.

"Your father is so happy," my mother told me as I helped her with her pearl necklace. "It's the biggest night of his career and we're showing off our best." By career she means my dad's job as hoghead for the railroad and by our best I guess we're each wearing new clothes. Though I doubt I could increase the Ogre's happiness, I couldn't be more willing to make my mother's night perfect. I'm carrying around a corsage for Chantal.

I check my phone. It's now 6:25 P.M. and the polka band is warming up the crowd. A union rep hands out a welcome drink to the adults and a program with the Ogre's name in bold font. The men call his name and form a handshakes-and-backslaps line. They don't know him like I do. I see my mother leaving the end of the receiving line, weaving her way through the thinning crowd, lit from behind by minilights. Soon I'll have to face her worried, disappointed eyes. I've already failed her because I'm not standing at the end of the line with the girlfriend that would complete our family portrait. She's always missed not having a girl. And tonight, it's looking like she's out of luck, again.

My phone rings. And I don't recognize the number. Chantal says a shaky hello. She gets as far as *I can't make it* when I cut her off.

"Food poisoning?" I say as my mother reaches my side. "Of course you can't. Oh . . . no . . . that's fine. Oh, yeah, I understand. Well, take care of yourself. I'll call you tomorrow."

I slide the phone into the inside pocket of my suit jacket before my mother can hear Chantal's protests. "She's sick," I say.

"Why did she wait until now to call? That doesn't seem like her."

"Yeah, well it is. If I'd known she wasn't going to come, I could have found another date."

"I told you how important this was."

"Out of my control."

"Oh, Will. Your father will be so disappointed." But it's my mother's hopelessness that weighs me down with a ten-pound tumor in my gut.

"I know." I walk into the Moose Hall, right up to the Ogre and hold out my hand. He can't refuse it in front of his railroad comrades and I hope my mother sees that I'm trying. The Ogre gives me a strange look but shakes my hand and dismisses me. I stand next to my mother and wait out the last of the straggling partygoers as they head through the receiving line. I know Chantal set me up. The back-out call at the last minute is all the proof anyone would need, but she'll never know I gave a shit.

We're at the head table with an empty chair that mocks me all through the pickled vegetables, overcooked meat with horseradish and mashed potatoes, and apple pie. After all I did to help her. This is what I get in return. She's now officially dropped from my existence. Her loss.

My dad stands up at the podium and dread sticks to my skin like a wet T-shirt. He's accepting an award for fighting the good union fight, for not backing down under extreme pressure from management, for giving generously to his brotherhood. His speech is excruciatingly boring, not because I'm absent from his remarks, but because he's talking about hard work and sacrifice. The two words that he attempts to hammer into my head. He also appears to forget his wife. Doesn't even thank her for her support all these years. My mother shreds a tissue. I snake my headphone into my right ear, turn the volume up high and smile, as the music takes me far away.

Chantal

· · · · · ·

Fallout.

It's been a week since I backed out on the date and Will still ignores me. I expected him to get mad. I thought he'd shout and I'd defend myself. I thought I'd hang up, justified. By accident, judging from the sounds of the muffled voices, I witnessed the fallout.

I heard his mother's voice, "your father will be so disappointed." And I knew what she didn't say; I am so disappointed. In you. I couldn't listen any longer. It's been bothering me ever since. Except when I remember what he did to me.

Will doesn't suspect anything. If it weren't for the daily cake delivery, I probably wouldn't look in his direction; wouldn't notice that he's reached maximum tan, and that he is the king of cool with his sunglasses and a surrounding bevy of fans. I suspect he realizes it's the cake they come for; because now he strives for creativity and the unexpected in the photo challenges. While I'd hoped they would embarrass him more, his popularity has spiked. This doesn't upset me. Will is going to do a belly flop from the high dive of his ego someday soon. The cooler he thinks he is, the better. At least that's what I keep telling myself.

You musn't beat yourself up. You'll take all the fun out of it. Nigella's voice is inside my head again. Instantly I feel sunshine spreading through me even though it's dark outside. I'm inspired tonight by a cake she made in her "Weekend Wonders" show.

The KitchenAid motor buzzes and the whisk attachment forces air into heavy cream, whips it until it drops in soft peaks. I add eggs and whip them until the color is light and consistent. The sugar is next, followed by the vanilla. I mix only until incorporated. Today's cake is a repeat, but so popular it deserves a second date, this time with the glamour treatment. Instead of seven-minute frosting, this whipping-cream cake is going to the cake salon for an updo. Honey buttercream with chocolate toffee crunch highlights.

I sift flour, salt, and baking powder in a second bowl and add it to the cream and eggs. I slip my spatula between the back of the bowl and the whipped eggs and cream, keeping a slight angle (approximately 30 degrees) as I slide it along the bottom and up the side facing me. I fold my wrist over when I reach the top, allowing the creamy lemon mixture to fall onto the dry ingredients. I repeat, and in five folds the mixture is homogeneous but not deflated. Exquisite. Two cake pans. A 350-degree oven and a timer set to twenty-five minutes. The cake is *finis*!

With my favorite pink Sharpie I add the cake to the list:

1. Crush on You
2. Epitome of Refinement Chocolate Cake
3. I Like Him, I Like Him A Lot Cake
4. The Puppy Love Cake
5. Bliss is You and a Banana Cake
6. I'm Coconuts for You
7. Spice Up Your Life Cake
8. No Fear of the Devil's Food Cake
9. Smile at the Sunshine Lemon Cake
10. Chips O' Joy Cake

11. Go for It! Surf the Mint
12. Peach for the Stars
13. *Bee Yourself Honey Cake*

Lovely, darling, lovely.

I knew you'd think so, Nigella. Her voice always comes at the right times, helping me to avoid panic. Speaking of panic.

I check my phone. It's 10:55 P.M. I turn the radio up and I'm not disappointed.

"Hello cats and kitties, dogs and puppies, here we are again. Another smokin' hot day at the hill—and another gift from the Cake Princess who wants us to Peach for the Stars. Five-star effort, Princess. Two more cakes and we'll know who you really are. Check out the Facebook page for details. And Cake Princess, this is for you."

Our song, "Sugar, Sugar" comes over the airwaves and I tingle with interior firefly lights. His goofy radio commentary is new to me, but I like a guy who doesn't mind showing a little bit of his inner nerd. I think it holds promise for a relationship. With me.

I have always thought that my future one and only would be good looking but not rock star, enjoy documentaries about science but not WWF, and listen to music that has intelligible lyrics not that screamo punk. Mitch, I think, scores high on my list of requirements. I might be sending these cakes to Will, but Mitch has become the hidden object of my baking affection.

• • •

The song ends. It's time for the buttercream. Over simmering water, I whisk together the egg whites and sugar until the sugar is no longer grainy and move the mixer bowl to the KitchenAid. I beat on medium speed until the meringue has cooled and doubled. I add butter chunks that measure a total of one and a half cups of unsalted butter and beat until smooth and thick. Nearly ten minutes later, I add lemon juice, vanilla, and the feature ingredient, honey. I pull out the paddle attachment and lick the sides. Oh . . . it's heavenly, a perfectly rounded flavor of sweet and fat that is decadence defined. My mother would die if she knew what she's missed out on her whole life.

I'm proof that baking and eating the occasional piece of cake does not make one fat. In fact, I've lost ten pounds since school let out despite my taste tests. Not that my mother has noticed. She's been distracted in a way I've never seen. My dad assured me over the phone that their relationship is intact. "The new job is stressful," he said. "Just be patient. I'll be home on Friday." I trust my dad—he said he'd keep the baking at the office a secret from my mom for as long as he could—and I'm glad he's on his way home, though I am concerned that he's arriving on the night of the hockey tournament. He'll insist on coming; he'll say it's a great family event. If I'm lucky, my parents will leave before the Cake Princess is revealed.

My changed mother is at the office early and all day. We only meet at dinner. While I clean up the kitchen, she closets herself in her room with a book and a sleeping pill. When she's asleep she doesn't hear my bike slip out of the garage to go to Dad's office to bake. Not that I'm complaining. Not really. I thrive on structure and routine, especially when it's self-imposed.

You have every reason to be supremely happy, Nigella reminds me.

Yes. It's true. Two cakes from now, I will be crowned the Cake Princess.

A title you are deserving of, rest assured.

"Thanks, Nigella." I press play on the Nigella video on my laptop; it's sort of like having her watch over me as I construct my cakes. I slide one layer cake onto a cardboard circle and spread the top with the honey buttercream. I sprinkle on smashed-up chocolate-covered toffee candy bars and add the second cake layer. Now comes the dance of buttercream along the sides and top.

Nigella talks to the camera and she's so real. Herself. That's what I want to be: the real me. I haven't even started making my video yet; I'm so terrified of looking . . . stupid. What if stupid is the best I can do?

The thing about the twenty minutes following the hockey tournament is that it's going to be big. Literally. On the big screen. All me. In a video where I have to explain myself. I've got a whole lot of people to be worried about.

If Mitch thinks that I am secretly hot for Will, he might not be interested in my subtle flirtations. My mother might ban any future baking. Jillian might be mad I've kept her in the dark. Even Annelise, the queen of publicity and perhaps the biggest fan of the Cake Princess, may want to Tweet obscenities about me when she realizes that I've tricked her, too. I'm now at 759 friends, four of them, inexplicably, from Iceland; that's a lot of people to piss off. I'm hoping the crowd will be asking themselves how it is possible that socially awkward Chantal has baked her way into our hearts? Not, how could we let ourselves be tricked by a strange girl who figured out how to bake a cake. This is serious. It could go wrong. Very wrong.

"What I recommend," Nigella says on the computer screen in front of me, "is that you take the weight off your slingbacks, relax, and eat."

I hear you, Nigella. I make myself a peanut butter and jelly sandwich. I eat. And I breathe.

Parker

· · · · · ·

Negotiation.

It's a puzzle I'm trying to solve, sliding tiles into a frame to create a picture. One shift creates the need for more moves.

We were driving home from the lake this afternoon. The Hat Trick and I were reviewing plays while the Double Minor told me their worst knock-knock jokes. Then I realized that Jillian was silent. Distracted. I tried to remember the last time she initiated a conversation with me, or the last time I really kissed her and she kissed me back. I waited until the boys climbed out of the van and ran into the house.

I reached for her, but she backed away. "Let's do something to-night."

"Tonight?"

"We haven't seen each other outside of the lake."

"The heat has been hell. The boys are so worn out after the hockey." She kept looking away from me.

"You're sure that's all it is?"

She nodded.

I watched her. Waited. She bit her bottom lip. Sighed. Scratched at a bug bite on her ankle. Stared off at the distance.

"Look," I said. "On Saturday night, I'm taking you out. Just you." I told her I'd get Chloe and her friends to come to the house to watch the boys.

"Okay." She shrugged. "I've got to go in." I leaned down to kiss her and my lips landed on her cheek. I wanted to stop her again, on her way into the house, but I didn't know what to say.

Now I'm driving home, the sunroof open and the radio on, but the music isn't the magic it usually is. I'm two days away from my hockey tournament, the first of my altruistic innovations and I feel like an ass. Irony sucks. I stop the car at the park near my house, turn off the engine, and recline the seat. I stare up at the cloudless sky. My meditative state is interrupted by my phone. It's Will. I consider ignoring it, but it's Will. I need my friends. Especially now.

"Dude, the posters aren't here." He's ripping through some kind of paper from the sounds of it. Annelise brought the posters for the hockey tournament, he explains, but the other posters are missing.

"What posters?"

"The ones I had printed. You know, you suggested it. WILL FOR CLASS PRESIDENT."

Did I suggest posters? "Print some off the computer."

"They won't be the same. Those were posters."

"Print fliers. We can hand them out." Problem solving is time-consuming.

"I don't know. I don't know about this anymore."

What? Now I've got to rah-rah Will? I can't let this whole thing fall apart. "Listen, man. Success is in the palm of your hand. The cakes. The photos on Facebook. Your face time is skyrocketing. I'm almost jealous."

"Right."

"Seriously. Man, you know what? You don't even need fliers. Annelise is going to play her video and we're going to find out she's been your secret admirer all along and you're going to go up there and give her the big oh, we're-a-cute-couple kiss and you can take the microphone and say . . ." I trail off at the thought of Will with

Annelise. And me, without Jillian. I want to spend time with her after the hockey tournament. Lots of time. Just Jillian and me. That's the only way to fix this.

"Say what?"

Right. I slide away another tile of the puzzle in order to concentrate. "Say, 'Thanks. And if you want me to be class president, I'll make sure we have cakes. Lots of cakes. After all, I've got the connections.' People will laugh. It'll be online in minutes and once it's viral, you're in."

"Perfect. So that's what you want me to do?"

I hesitate. Now I'm in charge of his life, too? I wonder what Annelise would say if she were in on this conversation. Guilt tunnels through me, rises like a worm looking for water. "You don't think Annelise would want to be class president, do you?"

"Dude, she'd be terrible. We'd have leopard-print tablecloths at graduation."

"Yeah . . ."

"What? You don't think it's going to be good."

"No. No. It's good. All good."

"What's with you, dude? The rug rats wearing you down?"

"No, man. They're great. Really great. It's just, well, I guess I've got a lot on my mind in other ways. But. It's nothing." I hang up the phone a few minutes later, turn it off. Jillian's right; the heat is exhausting, and I'm done. I drive the rest of the way home.

When I pull into the driveway I realize I am not as done as I'd like to be.

My mother is coming out of the house with her tennis racket and she runs to the car as I turn the engine off. I get out quickly trying to avoid her expectation, her critical eye.

"Parker. Join me for a doubles game." She twirls her racket.

"Mom. I'm exhausted. Can I get a rain check?"

"Parker." She waits until I'm looking right at her. "You've been spending too much time on this hockey tournament thing, with those little boys and that girl."

"We're raising money for kids in Africa," I remind her.

"I understand that's the good cause, but I've had enough of you being gone all the time. And we will be playing tennis next week." She winks at me. "I've booked a villa for us at the Waves and Wishes retreat. Remember we went there when you were little?"

I want to say I'm not interested. You can't make me. I'm not a kid anymore. Instead, I stare at her and nod.

"We're leaving on Saturday. Two weeks in luxury. Me, you, and your dad."

Damn. This is so like my mother, she decides what she wants to do and nothing is going to get in her way. Damn. And I'm like her. A lot. Pushing forward, like I know what's best. During this whole hockey tournament I've been focused on the boys and me, and what I'm going to get out of this. No wonder Jillian's upset. "Can we postpone it? For a week? Or a few days?"

"You know how I feel about family time, Parker." She lays her hand on the side of my face. "You've had your fun with your friends."

I try to protest.

"This isn't a negotiation."

This is how it is with my family. They only give you so much room to move.

Jillian

· · · · · ·

This is what I have discovered. When you are stuck in a too-small sweltering house with six little boys, you think. About your potential, and theirs. Parker is clearly the expert when it comes to hockey skills. But I worry, you know, about deciding that hockey is the best investment you can make when you're young. Statistically speaking, few kids end up playing hockey as a career and a really small number of them are successful beyond the old-timers' community league. And, statistically speaking, your best investment in your brain is learning to read. Kids who read at fifteen are more likely to graduate. That's a debate fact. So I'm making my investment in my brothers. Post-it Notes, smelly markers, and a game.

"Living room is done!" Travis shouts.

"Living room is done!" Thomas echos.

"Living room is done!" Then Trevor.

I hold my fingers to my lips as I walk in the room. I remind them that Mom is sleeping and we've got to be quiet, but cannot help squealing at what I see. "Oh, it's perfect!"

The Hat Trick have created their first Word Room. Pink, green, yellow, and purple Post-it Notes label every piece of furniture, the walls, the stir-fry of odds and ends in the living room.

Couch
Window
Dirty laundry
Cracker crumbs
Television

"It's time for the Around the Word in Nine Minutes!" I proclaim. "Everyone line up!" Their mouths, still smeared with jam and peanut butter from breakfast, spread into wide smiles, teeth and gums showing. Baby Ollie jumps, jumps, jumps. I lift him out of the playpen and he gets in line behind Stevie. They wait for me to throw my arm down, for the race to begin. I start and then I stop. Their eyes are on me. On me. Holding my gaze. They love this. They love me. Isn't that worth everything? I drop my arm and the boys begin the tour.

Thomas and Trevor lead the Double Minor from one sticky note to the next. Travis buddies up with baby Ollie. The Hat Trick says the word, the Double Minor and Ollie repeat it.

Old pizza crust
Little cars
Video game

We move as a flock from word to word, branching into the kitchen. Thomas opens the refrigerator.

Milk
Jam
Penis butter (Thomas! I take that one off and crumple it up.)

The cupboards reveal more words:

Stuffing
Rice
Noodles
Ketchup

We are an amoeba that grows with the words we eat. We spread out, searching for more, the Double Minor hand in hand, trying to sound out words on their own. Ollie is our pseudopod tail, dragging his blankie behind us. We blob down the hallway (carpet, wall, picture, hole) to the end. After a stop in the bathroom (poop, pee, diaper, stinky) we all gather in the area outside our bedrooms. The end of the Around the Word Tour. The beginning of quick, get dressed, we're going to play hockey. But, they aren't ready. Travis, Thomas, and Trevor each have Post-it Note pads and they continue to write down words. The boys' names on their doors, my name on mine.

Love. Travis writes that word and sticks it on my door.

I feel warm now, and comfortable, and important. Valued. In a way I haven't for a while. This is *my* project. I've decided what the boys need. Words. I want to grab Post-it Notes and write down important words for them. Stick them where they can never lose them.

Freedom
Independence
Responsibility
Pride
Courage
Kindness
Compassion
Love
Hope

They're finished writing words now, and it's time to move and instead of an amoeba, they decide we are a pack. A pack of hungry wolves. I follow the pups through the house. I howl in a ghostly whisper. Baby Ollie grips my leg and slows me down. I almost miss the moment.

The boys are in front of Mom's bedroom door and before Travis or Trevor or Thomas can tell the Double Minor the words, Josh points at the first word and says, "Mom." Stevie points at the second and says, "Door."

The Hat Trick explodes in a wolf pack/hockey chant celebration with high-fives and howls. I join in, too, I can't help it. The first day. The first day. And they are already reading. I hug them and the Hat Trick let me hug them and we know, we know so clearly, that we are a team. A word team. But our celebration ends.

"What the hell?" My mother's voice comes through the door even before it swings open. We back away from the heat of her words. "You know I worked a double shift that ended last night, don't you? And what the hell is this? A crime scene? What are you doing with them, Jillian? Playing *CSI*?"

"We're teaching Josh and Stevie how to read." Travis sticks his jaw out and I wonder if he understands the word courage even better than I do. He pulls Josh and Stevie in front of him, makes them stand in front of her. "They know this word means door and this one says Mom." She tilts her head at Travis, does a quick survey of her audience, me included. I almost think she's going to shut her door and let us alone. But I am wrong. Again.

"Oh whoopity dippity do!" She throws her arms up and gives a fake sort of smile. The Hat Trick are still gullible, they think she really is happy at their genius. "Give me that marker." Travis hands the Sharpie to her. Now they think she's joining in their game, that somehow she's changed.

She turns her back to the boys and she writes on the dingy white paint of her bedroom door. The boys are open-mouthed. I grounded them all two months ago when I caught them drawing on their bedroom wall.

Her letters are big and looping. And she's laughing. Giggling at how funny she is. I'm thinking oh, no, now she's going to be creating a permanent chalkboard of I-love-you-messages-to-Mom on her bedroom door. That's so like her. Take anything good around here and make it about her.

Finally she's finished and she backs away. The boys' eyes widen with expectation.

"I'll give you twenty dollars if you teach them to read that by the end of the day."

Inside the outline of a huge heart, she's written a message. She underlines each word with her hand as she reads it out loud.

"Shut The Hell Up."

She laughs like it's really funny. Because it is, to her. And she holds out her hand for a high-five from the Hat Trick. Thomas responds weakly. Travis and Trevor turn away from her. "Hey, get back here. Travis. Trevor." She forces them to high-five her.

"Mom," I say. "That isn't very funny."

"Jillian, you and I have different senses of humor." She takes me on. "I accept that you're boring. You'll have to accept that I'm not." She laughs again and holds up her hand for more high-fives.

"It's stupid." Travis sets his hands on his waist, refuses to play along with her I-love-me-and-so-do-you game.

"Stupid," Trevor echoes.

"Stupid." Then, Thomas.

"Stupid." Josh.

"Stupid." And Stevie.

"Stoof-eh." Even baby Ollie tries it.

"Get out." She glares at me. She adds a fake smile. In her dirty bathrobe and her wild hair I see her again, and again, the real her: nasty and mean under a veneer of sarcasm. She is not the hippy mother who is a little scattered. That's just a part she plays. She is more the character from a bad sitcom that no one believes is actually a mother, only a placeholder for cruel jokes.

She opens her bedroom door and Keith lolls in the background in his dopey plaid boxer shorts. He looks at me like a sheepdog, with a drooping moustache that he's been growing ever since he saw the pictures of Dads 1, 2, and 3. They all had facial hair because my mother finds it manly. I hope my real dad is a grown-up now with a clean-shaven face; I imagine he's moved on to all sorts of cosmopolitan choices by now.

I wonder what made my dad stop thinking about saving me and start thinking about escaping my mother.

Chantal

. . . . . .

Cheetahs Always Get Caught.

Folding my dry ingredients into a dark chocolate cocoon of batter showers my brain with a tiara of sparking synapses.

I read the line twice. I try to say it out loud spontaneously, Nigella style.

Crud.

It's like I'm talking with a mouthful of M&M's and that thing I'm doing with my hair, tossing it over my shoulder, it's too . . . not the real me. I try the line again, adding in pauses, trying to be Nigella instead of just acting like Nigella.

Better. This time I don't even touch my hair.

"Darling, you're brilliant." Nigella's voice arrives at just the right time.

"Oh, you're here. Listen to this . . ." I start my introduction from "Hello, Chantal the Cake Princess here," but my pace is fast and my gait wobbly. I gain confidence through the bit about how Will is my target and then, I lose my momentum. It feels too long, too constructed, too complicated, like a cake with contradictory flavors. The white cake, vanilla frosting version is this:

I detest Will. With good reason.

I baked him some cakes.

He thought someone liked him.

No one does.

The end.

I try to rework the two paragraphs I've got about Will, but they fall flat, every time. I thought this part would be easy, but I start in on that paragraph and I begin to feel ill. It must be my allergies coming back. Eventually, I move on.

I try to channel my inner Nigella again. "The final cake is a fabulous example of overindulgence. Much like my inspiration Nigella Lawson, I am a more-is-more kind of person. What could be more hedonistic than deep dark chocolate cake, layered with the finest ganache, spread with chocolate Italian buttercream and decorated with a daring dash of Cheetah spots. In the world of cake, Cheetahs Always Get Caught."

I glance up at the clock: 11:32 A.M. The Bee Yourself Honey Cake will have made its debut at the lake—it's probably gone—by now. My mother will be going on her lunch break and will call my cell phone before she remembers the note I left her this morning that my cell is dead. My dad will know that I can be reached at his office only if there is an emergency. Jillian and her brothers are all engaged in practicing for tomorrow's big tournament. I should be motivated to produce this video.

Revenge, darling, I imagine Nigella's wise words, *is only useful to get you started. If you've given in to it, you may spoil the taste of every cake you bake from now on.*

"Nigella." I need her to listen to me. "It's all about revenge. I can't separate the two. Not now. I am the Cake Princess because I've set Will up."

Cinderella's fairy godmother warned her about midnight . . .

"But Cinderella was trying to get Prince Charming. I am trying to get rid of a frog. Evil Will."

Darling . . . her voice persists in my brain.

"Enough, Nigella. I am in charge. Stop." I command it and it is done. As if I were a real princess. I survey my ingredients and implements: white and pink bowls of measured flour, sugars, baking soda, baking powder, eggs, melted unsweetened chocolate, and buttermilk. Metal mixing bowls, whisks in two different sizes, the mixer with the paddle attached, a pink spatula, my prepared cake pans, and, finally, my pink gloves.

I stretch my pink dishwashing glove, trimmed in fur over my fingers. It's crafted from materials I found in the hardware and scrapbooking store. Shimmery stick-on letters spell CAKE on one glove and PRINCESS on the other. I press the record button on the camcorder and rush to the stove. I turn the knob slowly to 350 degrees. The shot over, I run back, rewind, check it. Nope. Not perfect. I have to do four takes to get it right.

I set up for the second shot: the whisk is in the gloved hand. Hold it upright. Two seconds. Whisk. Ten seconds. Eggs blend. I lift the glass cup toward the camera, showing off the beaten eggs. Drop the whisk back in the measuring cup. Take off the pink glove. I race to the camera and press pause. I rewind fifteen seconds. Play.

It's not perfect. You can see my arm, and I've stuck my other hand in the picture, and I've forgotten to put on the second pink glove. I rewind. Pull on the gloves. Move to record. Again. Again. Again.

On my fifth take I whisk vigorously to add more action in the shot. I lift the measuring cup. The shot is finished. The take is perfect until the view of the eggs: black strings from the faux fur trail through the lemony goo.

I pick them out and I see more black. Stick-on S's and C's are floating among the eggs. I drop the whisk into the eggs. Now, I've got to reconstruct the gloves.

I lean against the cupboards. I need a break, maybe a permanent one. I drop my head in my hands. Idiot, my emotional editor screams.

I don't recognize the tapping on the window above my head

until it is a pounding. What? Who? No. They've tracked me down. I pull off the pink gloves, shove them under my shirt, crawl like an army soldier along the cupboards where whoever is spying on me shouldn't be able to see me. The pounding stops and when I think I'm safe, it begins again on the back door. Now, I hear a voice.

"Chantal. Chantal. It's your mother. Let me in."

We are in a standoff for a few minutes, me pretending I'm not in the kitchen, her telling me all the typical things like, I know you're in there. I'm worried about you. She moves into specifics: "I talked to your dad. He told me you're here, but he doesn't know what you're doing."

And now questions: "Where have you been going every day? Who are you hanging out with? It's not drugs, is it? You're not using drugs, are you?" Then, pleading: "Your dad told me we needed to talk. We can work this out." The panicked edge to her voice gets to me, but not enough for me to open the door. And then she tells me she's going home to get Dad's spare keys and she'll let herself in. I stand up, open the door.

"Chantal." She moves into my space.

"Mother." I back up. "Everything's okay. I'm baking cakes. That's all."

She couldn't look more stunned if I'd just told her I was the Tooth Fairy's assistant. Before she starts her litany of questions I tell her the details. Everything. When I baked my first cake, who I gave it to, where I've been baking, what kinds of cakes I've been baking, and why I started in the first place.

She moves to a counter stool, sets her arms next to the mixer, drops her head.

"Mom?"

Her shoulders shake. She's crying. My mother. Crying.

"Mom? Mom. I'm sorry. I didn't mean to upset you. I didn't . . ."

"I . . ." She looks up, her eyes raccoon circled from her mascara and eyeliner. I hand her my dish towel.

"I thought it was about me." She wipes her eyes. "I thought you were trying to push me out of your life."

"What?"

"The secrets."

"Mom." I've seen my mother tear up before, but it never *hit* me. Not like this. Usually she cracks when I'm not doing what she needs me to do. Get all A's, eat healthy, clean my room. But this is not about controlling me. My eyes begin to fill up, too, and my throat aches. I matter to her. *We* matter—as in our relationship. And that's enough for me to let her in on my plan. A little.

We sit on the floor, our backs against the cupboards. My voice shakes as I tell her selected highlights of how I came to be baking cakes in Dad's office. She listens.

"Baking is part of who I am. I have learned how to communicate in a language that people accept. They really love my cakes." I pause because honestly, I'll start bawling if I say more.

She lifts an eyebrow. Sniffles. Is that disapproval?

"I was desperate," I say. "And I didn't think you'd understand."

"Desperate." I think she is going to begin a lecture that will never end. It will blow up the kitchen, Dad's office, and my entire life. But she doesn't. She just gets quiet. "Desperate," she repeats. "I understand desperate."

I stand up, move to the counter, and drag a fork through the beaten eggs, pull out a C and a P. I stay silent. Maybe she'll leave if she thinks I'm uncooperative. Dad will be home tomorrow and he can be our mediator.

"You don't have to do this," my mother finally says.

"Do what?"

"Bake for them. To make them like you. You don't have to prove anything."

"Um . . . okay." Do I tell her I'm not doing it for them?

"It's okay if you just want to be good at one thing. Just because they expect something more out of you doesn't mean you have to conform to their ideas of who you should be."

"Mother, who are we talking about here?"

"You."

"No, we're not. Because no one asked me to be the Cake Princess. I invented it. It was all my idea. I found Nigella Lawson on the TV and I wanted what she had. Fun. Love of food." She stares at me, her mouth slightly open, as if she is surprised. This is me, I want to yell. This is me.

"Nigella says that when she sees someone who is overweight she doesn't think, oh what a pity. She thinks, wow, I bet that person has tasted some amazing food in her life. I like the way that sounds. She doesn't have as many rules." And I realize that's what's wrong with my video. Not enough Joy, too much Take That, Will. Now, I really need my mother to leave so I can finish it. My brain is rocketing with new ideas. A new script. A new angle.

"And this woman, Nigella, you met her on TV?"

"I found her. She's a domestic goddess. She has her own TV show. She cooks. She . . . um . . . she says great things like, 'Isn't this butter-cream utter gorgeousness' and . . ." I see a slice of a smile in her face.

"And she talks about needing a squidge of something and she calls . . . uh . . . her children *darling*." My mother's face startles at the accent I've added. "She's British." I go on, telling her every episode I remember of Nigella Lawson. I expect that Nigella will start talking to me, but her voice is silent. The more I talk, the more this concerns me. I sent her away earlier and suddenly she seems more of a TV star who lives in Britain and less of a fairy godmother. Did Cinderella ever see her fairy godmother again? I slip into silence and my mother and I mirror one another, chins in our hands, thoughts flying about to other places and people. My mother talks first.

"We need to collect some rocks."

"What?" I have no idea where she's going with this; maybe it's part of a new fitness regime.

"You and I need to go for walks and find rocks, take time for peace and beauty. You know, we work too hard." And her face settles into despair. I remember her medication. I remember how she's been sleeping or working, little else.

She surveys my bowls and video camera, my pink dishwashing glove—the evidence that I'm in love with things that she despises. If she knew how I compare her to Nigella, she'd be devastated.

"Fine. We can collect rocks."

I notice a slight shift: her right eyebrow lifting, her jaw relaxing.

"But can I finish my video first?"

"You're making a video? A YouTube thing?" Her face registers shock that I would be putting myself on the Internet, but she composes herself quickly. "I suppose. Yes, a video is fine."

My mother doesn't have any confessions to offer, she doesn't make any apologies, she doesn't take me in her arms, and we don't break down crying in each other's embrace. Real life is mostly, well, real. All of the above my mother doesn't do. But what *does* she do? She picks my shot list off the counter. Pulls my script off the fridge. She studies them both. I bite the inside of my lip, chew a hole that will take weeks to heal.

"Okay," she finally says. "I'll be the camera operator," like we've been planning this all along.

"Great," I say. "But first I need to make some modifications to the script."

Parker

· · · · · ·

Bee Yourself. Really. Bee Yourself.

𝓘 notice what I have failed to see since our project began: Jillian is separate from me, from the boys. She is always willing to help, she is always encouraging, she is always so damn perfect at knowing where the juice boxes are, finding the Band-Aids, filling up the water bottles. But the real Jillian is missing.

Today, the delivery of Will's thirteenth cake has him wearing a headband with two bopping antenna, a yellow shirt striped with black duct tape, and a piece of black doweling protruding from his . . . posterior.

Everyone is laughing at this photo shoot. Everyone. Ollie is laughing so hard, his cheeks must hurt. Jillian told me last week that Ollie should be walking by now and that her brothers said at least a few words when they were fourteen months. I reminded her that all the girls carry him around. They do the talking and the walking for him.

Jillian didn't laugh then and she isn't laughing now. Even if I get the boys into the NHL Hall of Fame, my legacy will be tainted. The one girl I wanted to make a difference for is only marginally impressed by my efforts.

I look over during the afternoon practice and she's on her back, watching the clouds streak the sky. When I gather all the kids in a final huddle, she sits in the center of them.

"We're going up against kids who are bigger than you, played more than you. But we've got what they don't. Tell me what that is!" I say.

"We can run like hell!" Travis says. The rest of the team cuts up.

"Yep. You can run like hell. And there's something else. It's about working together as a . . ." I wait for the right answer, but the boys are shouting out that they can shoot the ball, they can deke the goalie, they can tell them to stick-a-rubber-hose-up-their-rubber-nose.

"Jillian—you want to help me out?"

"What was the question?" she asks.

"Team. We're a team," I say. I finish my motivational speech before they start wandering off. "Get some sleep tonight. Drink lots of water." We end with a final cheer that half the mountain can hear. When they've run off for the playground, I sit next to Jillian, wait for her to talk first.

"They all need new shoes," she says, finally. "Travis's big toe is sticking out of his, but he hasn't complained. Not once."

"I'll get them new shoes," I tell her. I put my arm around her, but it's like she doesn't want to acknowledge I have a limb touching her shoulder. "Jillian, what about you? What do you need?"

She doesn't answer and I realize that things have gotten so bad I'll be crawling my way back. "Can I call you tonight? I'm worried about you."

"Um . . ." The pause is so long I lose my confidence. "Sure, if you want."

"I won't let you down." It's not much, but it's a beginning.

Chantal

· · · · · ·

Delicious, with a Delicate Crumb.

*M*y mother is a not-bad camera operator. A little bossy, but not bad. We finish the footage in just under two hours and I tell her she has to leave.

"I have an eye for detail," she says. "You need a good editor." Just when I was thinking things between us might shift.

"Nope," I say. "I've got one. Me."

I walk her to the door and shut it behind her, after, of course, I agree to turn on my phone and take her call tomorrow. With any luck the next time she sees the Cake Princess will be after the hockey tournament. My dad will be next to her in the stands.

Dressed in my black delivery outfit, I balance the Cheetahs Always Get Caught Cake in my bicycle basket. The last delivery. The final cake. Parker's house. It's midnight.

I swing my leg over the middle bar and start pedaling.

"Chantal?" I hear a voice and from my left I perceive a shadowy figure emerging from a nearby bush.

Oh God. Someone knows. A guy. He's after me. I press the right pedal down and now the left. I'm traveling in the opposite direction.

"Chantal?"

I look back to see who it is. It's . . . it's . . .

An odd, but perfectly predictable thing happens when the handlebars of a bike are pointed at an angle. The wheels of the bicycle follow that direction—they make a slight turn and collide with a rock that stops the wheel, creating a physics phenomena that I like to call frozen momentum. The rider of the bicycle is thrown over the handlebars, though she lands in the grass. But the contents of the bike basket are not so fortunate. The Cheetah cake lays broken and damaged, chunks of chocolate cake and buttercream, a mockery of utter gorgeousness.

I want to crawl away when I hear the footsteps—I can't believe what a fool I've just made of myself—but I'm in shock. This is it. My failure to function in a social setting has finally caught up with me.

"Chantal, are you okay?"

"Mitch?" I try to be calm, normal. "Why are you downtown in the middle of the night?"

"What do you mean? Why shouldn't I be downtown? I was at the radio station. I parked my car in a different place tonight because I've had this feeling that I was being watched when I left work."

"Weird." I look down and see what he sees. Me in black. A cake that's gone splat.

"And you're downtown in the middle of the night. On your bike in a black . . . disguise?" I watch him put the pieces together. "Oh, no, that was the cake? The Cake Princess cake? You were going to deliver it?"

I nod my misery. Now I've got to bake another one.

"You're the Cake Princess!" He smiles. It's like happy birthday and you've won the lottery all in one. "I think you're great."

"I know." I smile back and I'm sure my eyes are sparking like a waterfall of fireworks. "I listen to you on the radio."

The only logical solution is to regroup, restrategize, and start over with the assistance of Mitch. Could this be a more perfect situation for a Cake Princess about to be crowned? I so want to call Jillian, but I'm afraid that the magic is time-limited, situation-specific. Mitch and me! Me! And Mitch!

Twenty minutes later, I've measured out the ingredients and Mitch is stationed at the kitchen counter with the laptop. We are masters using our tools. The butter plops into the mixing bowl, sugar cascades over the top, and the motor runs. Since I can't rely on my ability to judge time right now, I set my timer for three minutes. I stare at him. The nerdy black plastic eyeglasses are a pleasing contrast to his short faux mo. He's one of those kids who gets good grades, but not great ones, because he likes to have fun.

"I've got to tell you something." He scrunches his nose to push his glasses closer to his face and yet he never stops moving his fingers along the keyboard. A multitasker, too!

He presses a button and turns the screen toward me. It's the final shot, the only one with my face in it. Everything else is about the cake. "You're great," he says. "Exquisite. Splendid." He throws in a British accent.

A multitasker and he thinks I'm splendid! Nigella would be so proud. "You're just saying that because you made me wreck my bicycle, and my cake."

"Nope. You could have your own show. I'd be your producer." His voice gets a little shaky and the air between us vibrates in wind chime music and whispers of vanilla and chocolate. Oh. I want him to kiss me. But he's watching the video.

"That isn't my real life."

"Your whole life is your real life." He says it as if it's a simple truth. He's adding in photos from the lake. We've already come up with an extra bit that he's going to tape, something that will make the Cake Princess's debut warm everyone's hearts.

Your whole life is your real life. I thought I was acting, you know. Pretending. But maybe I've been creating.

When he looks up at me I like that it seems as if he sees more than curly, unmanageable hair and my obvious plainness.

Darling, he's perfect for you.

Nigella, you're back!

I wouldn't miss my youngest protégé domestique! But tell me, this young lad who fancies you, will he appreciate your culinary artistry?

"Mitch, have you ever baked a cake?" I ask.

"I burned out my mom's old-school Easy Bake Oven when I was ten. Put my GI Joe guys in it to melt them down—it was supposed to be the aftermath of an atomic bomb."

"Would you like a chance to redeem yourself?" I hold out a wooden spatula.

Jillian

. . . . . .

Special Delivery.

Chocolate, butter, and vanilla smells continue to drift in through my open window. My stomach grumbles. Not that I'm complaining. I just wish my baking neighbor knew that I am here, alone in my room, wishing for the companionship of a brownie or a chocolate chip cookie. I am not afraid of calories today; I want chocolate. Chocolate would get me started in the right direction.

For the first time in a month, my mother has taken the boys out with her, leaving me all alone. Not that any of us should be fooled into thinking she's changed her ways. No. She found out that the big hockey tournament is today (even though I told the boys we could keep it a surprise) and when she insisted that she was coming to watch, when she demanded that we all go out for breakfast to celebrate, when she said we are the biggest, happiest family in town, I said, "Screw that. I'm not going. And they all need new shoes."

So I am alone. Not pretending we are a family we are not. Contemplating my next move. I know the pros and cons of what I am considering. I've listed them, scrunched the paper into a ball, and put it between my mattress and the box spring. The phone is next to me. I've found the phone number and I tried it yesterday, pretended

I was a telemarketer to confirm that the number matched the person I am, now, getting the courage to call.

I hear a car pull into our cul-de-sac but when the door opens the sound of six little boys high on sugar doesn't follow. Even though they should be home by now, I bet they'll be gone for another hour.

Now, the sweet smells from before grow stronger, as if they're blowing toward me. I turn off the fan and listen. I hear footsteps.

"Jillian. Jillian." A whispered voice reaches me through the window. I open the curtains.

"Parker?" What is he doing here? He was supposed to phone first. Ugh. I don't need more complications.

"I brought us a cake. Can I come in?"

"A cake?" And like that, something shifts. I don't want to be alone. I don't want to sit on the sidelines. I want companionship; well, cake can be companionship. But will he think I'm weak, that all it takes is a little cake to woo me? "Is it chocolate?"

He runs his finger through the icing, licks it off his finger, nods his head. Oh, what does it matter if he thinks I'm weak? Maybe, right now, I am.

"Okay. Go around front, I'll open the door," I tell him.

"I want to come in through the window." He sets the cake down and I see he's dragged an old ladder from the shed. He props it against the house.

I almost tell him that it doesn't make sense; that he could drop the cake, but I keep my mouth shut. The guy is made to be Prince Charming. It's just who he is.

• • •

The cake is the absolute best. The name, though, Cheetahs Always Get Caught, makes me think Annelise really could be the Cake Princess. She's in animal prints every other day and she has a message to send to Parker.

I wonder two things:

1. Could she bake a cake that tastes this delicious?
2. What would she think of Parker secretly bringing it to me?

"Isn't Will going to be ticked off that we've eaten a big chunk of the cake you're supposed to give him?" I ask as I fork my last bite.

"He owes me."

I run my finger along the plate, squeegeeing the last of the frosting. "I really needed this."

"Great. Great." He studies me. He motions for me to close the space between us. I move next to him so that we're sitting on the floor, shoulders touching, with our backs against my bed. I hope that this is enough, because right now, that's all the contact I want.

"Jillian . . ."

From the way he says my name, I know I'm doomed. He wants more than a shoulder against a shoulder.

"I feel like I've done something wrong but I don't know what it is."

I'm at a loss to say anything, but eventually I come up with some words to fill the silence. "That sucks, doesn't it?"

"What?"

"I don't mean to be flippant, but it's just, I guess, I understand what you're saying." I do, don't I? Isn't this one of my complaints about my mother, I never know how I've screwed up.

"So what can I do about it?"

"You have to communicate. Set it down in point form. Make it clear." I visualize the crumpled list wedged under my mattress.

"Okay." He reaches for my hand and turns his body enough so that he can watch my face. Hold eye contact. "I really, really, really, really like you. Like, I really do."

I hold eye contact for as long as I can but the more *really*s he throws in the harder it gets, like looking at a bright sun that I need to turn away from. "Articulate." I smirk. His bottom lip shakes a bit and I realize that I've gone too far. I punch his shoulder. "I'm kidding."

"You win. My apologies." He punches me back. "I didn't want to scare you off."

It's the words *you win* that swing a punch into my stomach. He's putting up with me.

"We need to start over," I say. "I am not tough. I don't normally punch boys and I apologize for the sarcasm. I have never had a boy-friend. And I am scared. And not because there was one too many *really*s."

While I sneak in deep, cleansing breaths, he tells me that from the beginning he's wanted to date *me* and that he's sorry he got so focused on the boys and their hockey skills.

"They're more important," I say. "Everyone knows that. They're so little and vulnerable."

"Wait. Not more. Just as important. They're so *noticeable*, but, Jil-lian, you are, too. You're smart, you're funny, you're beautiful, and, sometimes, like on our first date, when you looked at me, I saw past the puzzle of you and I saw you." He runs his first finger along the in-side of my elbow, makes tracks to my wrist and back again, and I let him. He makes eye contact and I don't look away. I don't look away even when I think we might resemble a cheesy romance movie.

"Go on," I say.

"I saw goodness and . . . a survivor."

"Right." I laugh.

"No. Really. A girl who isn't going to give up because her nail broke or she didn't get a free pass to the movies. You say you're not tough. I don't think that at all. Not at all."

He leans toward me. His fingers lift my chin. Oh . . . it is a cheesy movie scene. I give in. To him. To the kiss. To the feeling that it's okay to let him get close. It's good to be me, at least for now.

Will

· · · · · ·

Cheetah?

*C*heetah? She thinks I'm a cheetah. As in fast and sleek. All those extra workouts I've been doing must be working. If Annelise isn't the Cake Princess, than I am a doorknob. Maybe this will all be worthwhile in the end.

I won't deny that I was a little ticked when Parker showed up with a cake that had two pieces carved off—needed for his girlfriend emergency. And enough with the photos. Today I had my face painted as a cheetah and I had to pounce in front of the WELCOME TO OUR CITY sign. I'm drunk on chocolate cake and my imminent power player position.

I didn't share much of the cake today, because it was my last one, and because the rug rats were apparently resting up before the big game. In my false drunken state, I weave up the path to my house.

I find my mother in the kitchen, ask her to sit at the table. I pull out two plates, two forks, and a knife to slice the remaining cake in half. "You're going to love this," I say. "For a whole shitload of reasons."

I show her the note from my secret admirer, I tell her the story of a guy who has become the most popular boy at the beach, the one who is surrounded each morning by dozens of kids, the friend to all who is not only going to be publicly hailed as the object of the Cake

Princess's affection, but who will begin his campaign for class president with the most stunning girl beside him.

"This is delicious cake," she says. "How do you think she got those spots on there? You don't think Chantal's baking this cake?"

I stare at my mother.

"I guess I don't know her that well, but she seems like the kind of girl . . ."

"Who would stand me up for a date and be my secret admirer? I don't think so."

My mom dives her fork into the next bite. "All of the cakes were this good?"

I ignore her. Instead I focus on what I want. "You guys, you and Dad, you need to be at the hockey game Friday night. I want Dad to see it happen."

"Oh, I don't know, Will. Your dad isn't into all that flashy stuff."

"He is when it's about him. They had a head table, Mom. A head table. He gave a speech."

"Right. After twenty-seven years of service. I just, I think you might be trying too hard." She's got that look of pity on her face and I want to hold up a mirror to show her what she looks like.

"You could come. Without him."

She looks up, only for a second though. "I don't know."

What was I thinking? I should have known she'd choose him over me, again. I don't know what to say now, so I eat cake. And so does she.

Chantal

· · · · · ·

More Than a Ride.

𝓕riday morning I wake up shivering, my armpits prickling with anxious sweat. A million hammers pound my head in simultaneous Morse code. SOS. Only one thing can help me: cake. Baking cake. A whole lot of it.

I call on Nigella but she must be busy this Friday morning making eggs in a cup with toast soldiers for her Bruno and Mimi. My own mother is still in bed so I'm on my own. And I know where to go. The grocery store. Then, the kitchen.

· · ·

I'm outside the store, next to the bike rack, attempting to problem solve how I will transport an entire grocery cart of baking ingredients on two wheels when an unlikely heroine in a shining convertible stops next to me.

"Hey. You need a ride?" It's Annelise. She's wearing a hot pink top with PRINCESS emblazoned in sequins, white short shorts, and huge sunglasses that match the white convertible, all accessorized with a leopard print scarf.

"Out for another test drive?" I don't even have a sneer in my voice, because Annelise is the sort of girl who grows on you. Pretty. Rich. As harmless as the stuffed Bengal tiger riding shotgun on her dash.

"It's mine, now. I was supposed to get it after my senior year, but my dad bought it early."

Shoppers swerve around the car and stare at her. "Hey, get in."

"I've got my bike . . ."

"Can you lock it up and get it later?"

"I think I'm going to need it." I reach for my grocery bags.

"Well, at least it's clean." She opens her car door and before I can decide that I don't want her help, she's picking up my grocery bags. When I carefully put the bike in the backseat I notice sugar and pastry flour labels are clearly visible. How many more clues is it going to take before Annelise knows who I really am? Crud. I decide I have no choice but to play it cool. She doesn't say anything about the groceries though, not even when we're driving out of the parking lot.

"You know, Chantal, I've been thinking. Parker is just too complicated. Like with the kids and all that? He's like Mr. Mom and he's sixteen. I want to have fun and travel around the world. And honestly?" She turns to me for so long I almost beg her to keep her eyes on the road. "Don't tell anyone I said this because they'd think it was shallow, but I don't want to wreck my figure by having kids. I mean, I work hard at this, you know, over an hour a day." I nod. I sort of respect her attitude; I spend time baking cakes or studying, therefore I'm a great baker and I get A's. Annelise wants to be fit. Different goals, same persistence. "Do you get that?" she asks.

"I totally get it," I say. "You need to know who you are before you become part of a couple."

She stops at a stop sign. Turns to me again. I can see my reflection in her big sunglasses and I look almost like I belong in a convertible. Relaxed. "You know that's smart. Oprah smart." I laugh and she does, too, and it feels strangely comfortable. As if because we think something good about each other we can hang out, even if we're not the same in other ways. "Okay, where to? It looks like you've got some work to do." Annelise is the one playing it cool, she shoulder checks and keeps driving.

As I give her the directions to my dad's office I wonder how much she knows.

"You know," she says as we're transferring the groceries from the car to the back step. "That Cheetah cake yesterday had my name all over it." She fluffs her leopard print scarf. "And another thing, the Cake Princess delivered her first cake to me. Because she liked me. Every person who got a cake was nice, even if they weren't all popular. She didn't have to do that."

"Interesting . . ."

She waits for me to say something more, but I outlast her.

"You know, if I could talk to the Cake Princess I'd tell her something." She leans in close to me.

"Yeah . . ."

"I'd tell her that one of the most popular girls in the school has her back." She points to herself. "No matter what Will does." She backs away, makes a 90-degree turn on her leopard print heel, and continues her catwalk to her car.

Jillian

· · · · · ·

The Debate.

I hear the boys return from breakfast and my mother yell at them to go outside and play. Doors slam shut.

"Jillian," my mother shouts. "I need to see you in the kitchen."

I stop my daydreaming about Parker, check my reflection in the mirror, and reach for my bedroom door. A final debate with my mom is coming.

My mother is in the kitchen. "I'm going to get my hair cut, get a new skirt for tonight." She slurps loudly from her coffee. "I'll be in the stands cheering those little monsters on. Why didn't you tell me they were so good? Travis says a talent scout is going to be watching and, by Christ, they've sold two hundred tickets."

I wonder where Keith is, if he's working or if she'd kicked him out last night. I'd like to know the chances of him appearing suddenly to take her side, but I decide to hope for luck. "Mother." I wait for her to give me her complete attention. "I don't want you to come," I say.

Her response is quick. "I am their mother," she says. "I am your mother."

We're within throwing distance of a coffee cup or a jar of mayonnaise. I've been waiting for something to send me over the edge and now I'm looking over a cliff, prepared to jump. I made the phone call after Parker left. Everything is in place for what I am about to do.

"You are a mother in name only." I recite the second point on the list that remains under my mattress. I remain calm. Calm. Calm.

She begins her counterattack. "You don't talk to me that way," she hisses. She reaches for my wrists to shake me until I beg her to stop, but I know this trick of hers. I move out of her reach until she stops grabbing for me. I wait for her rant to end. "Don't you judge me." She throws her coffee cup and it shatters in the sink.

"In fact." I take a steadying breath, remembering bullet point number seven. "This isn't about you. It's about my brothers. And me. I've got some people coming to help you."

She relaxes a bit, leans against the counter, thinking I'm on her rescue team. It's always about her. She doesn't consider that the boys or me are in need of saving.

"They'll be here for dinner tomorrow night. They're bringing it with them. Roast chicken. Gravy. Mashed potatoes. The boys' favorite." I nearly choke as I'm saying it because even though I hardly know my grandma, she cared enough to offer dinner and she wanted to know what the boys loved to eat. She said it would make it easier for them. She said it was the boys, the boys and me, who were most important.

"You got Parker paying for a maid and a cook?" My mother laughs. I think it might be the last time I hear her mean sarcastic laugh.

"It's Grandma and Grandpa. They're staying here to help with the boys." I watch her face change as the reality sets in; this was the grandma who brushed my hair in the hotel room, the one my mother ran away from and then refused to talk to after we moved into the house on Columbia Street.

"As in my mother and father?" My mother's face is pale. Nothing is funny now. She erupts in a story of self-pity. She tells me how they oppressed her as a child, how their rules wrecked her self-confidence, how they expected too much and gave too little. "What makes you think you can invite them here, without asking me?"

I'm as prepared as I can possibly be for this question. My final argument is distilled in one sentence. "Either they come or I call child services."

She reacts in stunned silent rage. She takes a knife from the drawer and begins slashing the cutting board, leaving deep groves, chipping off chunks of wood. I wonder if she's seen this in a movie; it seems so . . . psychotic. I back away, closer to an escape route. The longer she obsesses with the knife, the more I want to run or call for help, but I don't. I'm numb. As if I'm stuck in this place where she has defeated me before, and it's about to happen again. She continues her intimidation, doesn't look up when she seethes, "Where are they going to sleep?"

"In my room."

"And where are you going to sleep?"

"With Travis until Tuesday and then I'll be in Vancouver."

She continues lifting and slamming the knife on the cutting board, missing every now and then and hitting the counter instead. The knife kicks back and I wonder if it's going to break, if the blade will snap off and hit her in the jugular. I know she's figuring out that I'm going to see my dad. Dad 1. That I got his address from the child support checks.

"He said you were ugly." She stops slashing the wood. She stares me down. "And he was right. You're ugly through and through."

Her words are acid that burns away the numbness, revealing cracks and rivulets of hurt. I hug myself. My only defense. I want to be good. I want to be good. The cracks expand and I'm breathing in deep, holding my breath. I recognize this mother. This was the mother I was trying to protect myself from. I remember her now; she's the one who made the cracks.

"That's a lie," I say.

Until this moment I don't know the power of the words you tell yourself about who you are or the way someone else's words can change you. Who you are is all about what you want to believe. This, I know is true: I could tame a grizzly.

Parker

· · · · · ·

The Hockey Tournament.

"Check. Check. Check." My voice echoes over the sound system and two guys Will recruited from the broadcasting class give me the thumbs-up. Heads turn toward me. The scene is smoking. Not only is it still hotter than Hades, we have got an epic crowd. They fill the bleachers the city crews set up on either side of the blocked off street, courtesy of the town council and a phone call from Annelise's dad. We're wearing team jerseys, too, donated by the Sporting Life. My dad and mom take front row seats in the VIP grandstand with their friends.

To calm my nerves I've got my iPod playing in one ear. When the music kicks in, my adrenaline pumps and the nerves smooth out. I hold up the earphone to the mic, blasting the beats.

"Something for the people!" I shout. "In the place to be!"

Will pumps his fist and before long everyone is into it. Everyone younger than twenty anyway.

"Hey O!" I holler.

"Hey O!" The crowd calls back. I look over at my mom. She's swaying her arms with the crowd.

This is the best part of being popular. You have the power to get a whole crowd liking something you like. I know the party belongs to me.

"Dude." Will pulls me away from the microphone. "You know what this is? Flying without a parachute! This is our night, man."

We punch fists and I make the announcements.

"We're here for two reasons today: to support our kids in sport and to raise money for Read On, the Africa Literacy Project. We want kids to play hockey!" The boys whistle and shout from the players' bench. "And we want kids all over the world to have access to books!"

Will steals the mic. "Reading is fundamental!" He pumps his arms to get the crowd into it and they follow along. The power trip is off the charts. Finally, the noise settles.

I make the introductions, and ask the mayor to drop the puck so the hockey tournament can begin. It's the Pee Wees of the Summer vs. the Sled Dogs of the Winter. I didn't want to play my kids against each other, so I convinced the community center to sponsor a team to play against us. We have all the youngest kids, they have the next age group up. It looks like it could be an unfair match, from the size difference, but that's exactly what I want. For everyone to underestimate my boys.

My team is set to exceed all expectations, and they do. They deke, they score, they lay down to block shots on their own goal, and they run like hell. Training over the hot summer has given them ten times the endurance as the community center team. We rule the period.

At the break, Annelise and crew collect more money for the Africa Literacy Project. The crowd gives and gives, inspired by the little kids in jerseys sweating on the sidelines. Jillian works the electrolyte drink patrol, sponges the boys down with cold towels. Mitch is on the sidelines, taking pictures of everything and I stop him, ask him to snap one of Jillian and me.

"Nice," he says after he checks the image.

"It's better than that." Jillian laughs. She laughs.

The second period starts with the big kids remembering that they're big and throwing their bodies around. Travis, Thomas, and Trevor each serve time in the penalty box for slashing. The crowd boos each time the referee pulls one of them from the game. I shrug my disbelief. Survivors fight back. I also know that this is okay for the game. People want an underdog to cheer for and they'll open their wallets if we end the second period with a losing score.

The bench is quieter after the period, the boys sunken into themselves; little Josh and Stevie are barely holding back tears. I ask Jillian to talk to them while I rile up the crowd to give big.

"You're the coach," she says.

"We're a team, remember? Remind them that they have skills."

"They can run like hell?" She smiles.

I kiss her forehead. "Start there," I say. When I turn to the crowd, the first face I see is my mother's and her dismay is unmistakable. *Yes, Mom, Jillian is my girlfriend. Her brothers are part of my project.* This morning I told my mom she could either change our vacation week to later in the summer or she could go without me. She nearly threw a tantrum over changing the plans. I wouldn't tell her why, but she knows now. I'm at the center of something big.

Mr. Tourism, Annelise's dad, welcomes all the visitors in the crowd. They cheer as if this is their town, their kids, and their hockey game. They cheer for me, too. Hyper-buzz. I wait for the applause to die down and then I talk about my team, who they are and where they come from. I focus on the Hat Trick and Double Minor, share their story of perseverance. "It's up to us to show children all over the world that if they persevere we will support them. No matter if they're in small towns playing road hockey or small villages trying to learn to read. Please, give generously."

And that hyper-buzz I had a few minutes ago has wormed deep inside me and the weirdest thing happens; it's like I'm an atom that's splitting and the chain reaction speeds through the people in the stands. The crowd is on its feet. I see my mother in the front row applauding.

"Dude," Will yells in my ear. "You are on fi-yah!" I guess that's true. He takes the microphone to introduce the kids who have volunteered their time to make tonight possible. The list is long, but necessary. Share the spotlight, I told him; you'll get more votes. When he mentions Annelise's name, she yells out and waves two hundred-dollar bills, recent donations. The crowd erupts in applause.

By the time I'm back at the bench the boys are vibrating in place, they're so ready to get out and play.

Chantal

· · · · · ·

Hiding.

I watch the game's last period on the big screen from my hiding place under the speaker scaffolding. The box seats Mitch devised behind the black curtain are two chairs wedged inside—mine, and his. We peer through a slender opening in the black fabric, shoulder to shoulder and sometimes, hand in hand, and once, leg against leg.

The Hat Trick is nothing less than fireworks wearing shoes in the way they zoom in and out, strike at the opposite goal. Their enthusiasm mesmerizes the crowd. And Josh and Stevie? The other team doesn't have a chance. The Double Minor literally, and I'm not even exaggerating a little, fly between the legs of the other players, swipe at the ball, and serve it straight to their older brothers. Only Jillian and I know that these techniques have been well practiced while jumping on all the beds at home.

And Jillian. She's on the sidelines, so composed, so wonderful and encouraging with her brothers.

The Pee Wee team is up three goals with two minutes left to go when I have an unbearable urge to . . . pee. It's nerves. I know it is, but the more I try not to think about it, the worse it gets. And I know that I've only got minutes between the end of the game and the start of the Cake Princess video. But, I can't wait.

"Mitch." I lean over and whisper in his ear. "I need to . . . um . . ." I

can't finish my sentence. I can't think of another emergency to substitute and I don't want to say the word.

"Pee? Do you have to pee?"

"Yes, how do you know?" Please tell me it wasn't obvious.

"I do, too. Nerves."

"Okay, what do we do?"

"Hold it."

"I can't hold it."

"You have to. Think about something else."

I shake my head.

"No chance we are risking getting seen or missing your part.
You've baked too many cakes. And I spent nine hours editing the
video."

"But what if they boo?"

"We're not going over this again, Chantal. Anyone who matters
will love the Cake Princess. The rest don't."

"But . . ." I have a list in my head of all the other things that could
go wrong and I've detailed them for Mitch, many times now.

He leans toward me and his hand comes very close to touching
my thigh. "This might be my only chance for fame."

"Excuse me?" He only helped stir the batter.

"Everyone will know that I'm going out with the Cake Princess."

It's a perfect moment.

Will

Holy Shit.

The Pee Wee team wins. People are still throwing down their money as the rug rats toss their hockey sticks in the air, climb all over Parker, cheer, and dump pitchers of yellow energy drink over each other's heads. It's the end of Super Cup I, the Tournament of the Littlest Underdogs. I'd be more into it if I could get myself Zenned. The sorry truth is that I'm shaking worse than a Chihuahua in a bathtub.

Now, the team lineups form and the opposing team gives the new hockey heroes high-fives and the people in the stands are still on their feet. Parker holds Jillian's hand. All this from a man challenge. Parker and me. Awesome. Awesome. Awesome. I push myself forward and take command of the microphone. Now, it's my turn to shine.

I thank the mayor for coming and the town councilors, Mr. Tourism (who I expect to meet after Annelise publicly changes her secret admirer status) and all the tourists, and finally, my subjects—the students of Revelstoke Senior Secondary. They go wild. Not like *Girls Gone Wild,* but you know, they hoot and they scream and rush the stage as if they've sprung a free weekend pass out of juvie hall. I explain for those who haven't been on Facebook this summer or who missed Annelise's Twitter-feed fest how cake has shaken up our summer and that the Cake Princess is about to reveal her true identity.

"It's a bit embarrassing to tell you all, but I am the one she admires." I feel the shake in my top lip. "She's sent her cakes to me." The crowd *aws* and I drop my chin. It's all an act, but they like it. I name the cakes starting with Crush on You and ending at Cheetahs Always Get Caught. The crowd laughs at each cake title and it's like they're with me, on my side. "And I truly do not have a clue who she is." I search the crowd for Annelise so that I can nod to let her know that, soon, we'll be sharing the podium, but I don't see her. "So . . . let's start the video."

The big screen shows a video feed about to start, a black screen, and then, two pink-gloved hands with fur and black letters. Oh, that's Annelise. Then the song, "Sugar, Sugar" plays in the background (not Annelise's style, really) while the hands whip eggs, add stuff to bowls, turn on the mixer. Finally, the song fades and a voice, technologically altered, speaks.

"What do I admire about Will?"

Photos fade in. My photos.

"You toughed out every photo challenge."

More to the point, photos with me making an ass of myself. There's one of me at Grizzly Plaza in Mickey Mouse ears and a red bow tie, me on the floating dock wearing a coconut shell bra, and that awful one of me dressed as a bee in front of the WELCOME TO OUR TOWN sign.

The crowd laughs. At me. Some admirer. Is this Annelise's idea of a joke?

Finally the photos fade to a black screen.

Her voice speaks, "I also admire that you always shared your cake."

Dozens of photos flash—first, of the cakes being delivered at doorsteps, then, the messengers at the lake delivering them, and finally, pictures showing people eating the cake. Now, I'm really wondering if this is Annelise. Who collected all these pictures? And who made this video? I scan the crowd. I don't see Jillian. Or Parker. It's beginning to look like a setup. As if I'm the object of some challenge. Even though the air is heavy with heat I'm colder than a penguin's ass. This is not how this is supposed to go. She's supposed to say, "Ta da, Will's great, eat cake." I consider making a run for it.

The screen fades to black. I'm hoping that this is the end, the moment where I am crowned the new king. "But what do I admire most about you?"

A photo of me, chilling out on my towel with my sunglasses on takes up every inch of screen space. "Your cool factor."

I hear a man choke and I swear it is my dad. I wanted them to see my victory. Not this.

The misery does not end. Photo after photo of me fades in and out—all in the same pose looking lazy as a raisin waiting to be scooped. Could this get any worse? And where is Parker? Is this a joke? I look for hidden cameras. And my agitation grows so that I'm pacing. This was supposed to be my moment. I can't look at the screen anymore.

"Will . . ." Suddenly the voice is unmasked and I know that voice, even though she's talking with a strange British accent. "Thanks for letting the Cake Princess discover a passion that everyone loves. You really are sweet."

A silver tiara sparkles in her hair. She's wearing a pink apron. She holds the Cheetahs Always Get Caught Cake in front of the camera.

The screen fills with Chantal.

The crowd cheers, girls' voices scream in high pitches, chant the name of their new celebrity crush.

Chantal.

Holy shit.

Jillian
••••••
Never Underestimate a Brainiac.

"Chantal! Chantal! Chantal!" I add my voice to the chant. This must be what it's like at a concert, a mass of people cheering for a chance to see an idol. Listen to me, Chantal, an idol!

Parker nudges me with his elbow. "Did you know?" I read his lips because I can't hear above the noise.

I shake my head.

I feel the tears welling up in my eyes. She's amazing. Amazing. And even though I'm surprised like everyone else, it doesn't surprise me. She had all the ingredients for greatness, she just needed a reason. I don't know what it is, but I'm glad she found it.

Chantal

On Stage.

I trip twice trying to get to the microphone and each time I hear gasps from the crowd. Finally I am next to Will, my face projected on the big screen behind me. I reach for the microphone, but Will refuses to hand it over. His eyes are like flesh-cutting lasers. The way he's gripping the microphone, it's like a weapon that he wants to smash into my face. I haven't told anyone what he tried to do to me, but I'm not about to let him wreck this moment.

"Speech! Speech!" The crowd chants. I turn to them and smile and they go wild, again. "Speech!"

I hold out my hand, waiting for the microphone. My heart beats chaos.

• • •

It's grade seven all over again, my hands heavy with the fetal pig in a box. My ears pound with humiliation.

"Why?" I asked him, my voice shaking, tears starting to leak down my face. "What did I do to deserve this?"

He smiled. "I like to watch you freak out."

• • •

He deserves this moment. It's bigger than I ever thought it would be.

But he won't let go of the microphone. In fact he's lifting it toward his mouth. He's getting ready to say something. Something that could ruin everything. I can't let that happen. I grab the mic and his hand and pull it toward my mouth. We're so close now, he could spit at me.

"The Cake Princess is in the house!" I say in my British accent. The crowd laughs. Cheers for me. Again. And in that moment when he's disarmed, I yank the microphone free. I look back at myself on the big screen. I am beautiful. I really am.

"This is bogus," Will says.

I step away from him, toward my fans. My fans!

"I have loved baking for you!"

The crowd explodes again. Jillian and Parker are in the middle with the crew of boys waving their hockey sticks in the air. And strangers—all along the edges of the street, they applaud. They don't even know me. Mitch is out front, too. And now my dad is cheering and shouting. And my mom, too, I hear her voice the loudest. And I am overcome. Overcome with gratitude.

I am heard.

I am seen.

"Thanks," I say. "Thanks."

Will can't do anything to me again. Because I am myself. And they like me.

Will

Rat in a Trap.

I'm like a rat in a trap—I'd chew through one of my own legs to get free—but the crowd is on her side. I shouldn't have given up the microphone. I should have handed out the WILL FOR CLASS PRESIDENT posters. Now, I'm screwed. The only person they want to see is the Cake Princess. I consider my exit options. Then I see Annelise.

She climbs onto the stage from the front of the audience. I smile. She's coming to help me out. She knows, she must know, that we are the *it* couple.

"Annelise," I call her over.

She holds up her hand to ask me to wait, and I know that things are about to change. So I'm willing. I cross my arms, lean back on my heels.

Annelise whispers in Chantal's ear and they go back and forth a few times. The crowd begins to get restless. I'm thinking through what I'm going to say about my campaign when Chantal speaks into the microphone.

"My friend Annelise . . . I think Annelise wants to say something. And . . . for the record . . . I didn't have any previous knowledge about this. I've just been baking cakes this summer. That's all. I didn't really have time to accomplish much else than that. It takes a long time, you know, baking a cake. Especially a delicious one. You have

to ensure that all the ingredients are at room temperature and . . .
okay . . . thanks for eating my cake and watching the video . . ." Chantal
the geek comes out full force, but the crowd laughs with her. They
love her. I just can't catch a break. My last hope is Annelise.

"Hey all!" Annelise takes the microphone and the crowd hushes.
"I'm just here to let you know that Chantal the Cake Princess is
officially—as of right now, this second—running as our senior class
president!"

I couldn't be more amazed if stars started falling from the sky
and made a halo around Chantal's head. Frickin' hell.

It's all a setup. To get me.

Annelise continues, "As the Cake Princess's campaign manager
I'll keep you updated on Facebook and the Twitter feed. Okay girls!"
A group of girls wearing big buttons that read THE CAKE PRINCESS FOR
CLASS PRESIDENT weave through the crowd, handing out campaign
buttons.

I need to get off the stage.

"Will."

It's Chantal. I take another step but I'm stopped by a massive
speaker. A speaker I set up for tonight, my big night. "Will!" I look out
and see the grade nine girls who fell in love with me on the hill holding up their camera phones. I move closer to Chantal and we both
look out, we smile and wave.

She whispers something to me.

"What?"

She clears her throat, says through a smile. "I'm not afraid of you."

I clench my jaw. Hold in my disgust for her. I plant a kiss on her
cheek. I'll get another chance someday. I just have to be patient.

Parker

· · · · · ·

Reaction.

*M*an. This is so not what I thought was going down tonight. I mean the hockey tournament was kick ass, but the thing with Will? Chantal baking cakes? I never saw it coming. I'd have bet money it was Annelise. Good money. And Annelise backing Chantal for class president? Whoa. That's a whole lot of pink princess power.

But what are you gonna do? Live with it. Move on. I'll wait to talk to Will, though. The crowd is intense. Annelise is on the microphone telling the audience that they can line up for autographs. Autographs. Class president. That's a slam-dunk. But me as vice president is still a possibility. I'm dating the future class president's best friend, right? Even if I'm not VP I can still lead a special project that puts me in the spotlight. Nothing can stop me now.

The energy of the street is like a power surge. I want to move. Maybe I should get the boys to grab their sticks and we'll go into the parking lot where we were practicing earlier. I look around for them.

"Travis. Thomas. Trevor." I call them but I don't see them. "Josh. Stevie." I don't hear any of them, either.

And then Jillian is coming toward me. "Have you seen Ollie's stroller?"

I shake my head. "The parking lot. Where we were practicing. Maybe they've gone there." I hope like hell I'm right and that nothing has gone wrong.

Chantal

. . . . . .

Finally.

I couldn't hold it any longer. I told Annelise that I needed to get off the stage or I was going to pee my pants. "Okay," she said. "I'll take over. Make a run for it." So that's what I did. And I feel so much better.

Annelise said she had my back. And that whole class president thing was to overthrow Will. Apparently, he let Annelise in on his plan too early. Ouch. The guy has been dumped by more than the Cake Princess tonight.

I should be calm now. It's over. Everyone knows. I shouldn't be trembling like this, but, oh, I'll just come right out and say it. I've been kissed. By Mitch.

Right before the video ended, I felt his hand on my arm and when I turned to him, I knew. I knew he wanted to kiss me. His eyes searched mine for my silent agreement. He finished his kiss and backed away, checking to see if it was okay, and I went for it. I kissed him back. It was the first time I've really kissed anyone and it was as addictive as chocolate buttercream licked off the beaters. We kissed full on, until my voice came over the video and we realized we'd exceeded common sense. The next thing I knew I was talking into a microphone.

I've got to cross through the parking lot to get back to the stage from the bathroom and that's when I see the commotion. Jillian. Parker.

The Hat Trick. The Double Minor. Baby Ollie. And Jillian's mother. I can hear her, because she's yelling. "I told you. I am their mother."

"Chantal! Chantal!" I look back and my parents are waving, following after me. They are hand in hand. Joyful.

"I'll be right back," I call out and I break into a run for Jillian.

Jillian

• • • • • •

Saved by a Tiara.

"**M**other. You're not driving them anywhere." The boys are in the van, but the windows are rolled down and even though they could yell out and we'd hear them, they only listen. What other things have they heard, I wonder.

"You're right." She slurs the words and it's clear she's been drinking. I wonder how she got here, if Keith drove her. "I've been waiting for our chauffer. You. We're all going home."

"Stop. Please, stop." Parker reminds her that the boys won the tournament, tells her we're celebrating at the Pizza Shack. "Don't take that away from them."

"I'm not taking anything away from them. I am their mother. They want to be with me." She takes a step toward Parker and he backs away. "I already told them I'd have pizza delivered. And wings. And as much pop as they wanted. They're fine with that."

Fine. The word causes the boys to slump defeated in the van and I can feel the knife of you-can-accept-less chipping away at my toughness. We all know (even Josh and Stevie) that our mother will never give up in a fight with me. I consider tricking her: driving her home and sneaking the boys back down here, but she'd follow. She'll always follow. Finally, I say the only thing that comes to me, "I need help."

"What the hell?" my mother asks. Before I can repeat myself I hear footsteps pounding from behind me. Seconds later Chantal is beside me, out of breath, her tiara in her hand. The boys wave when they see her.

"Hey boys! Congratulations! You won! I watched it all on the big screen! Did you see me?" She puts the tiara on her head.

"You're awesome!" They yell out through the windows. "You make great cake!"

"Chantal?" My mother weaves slightly. "What are you wearing?"

"You mean my apron and pink sneakers?" She models her outfit in a surprisingly confident pose. "Or my tiara? Oh . . . uh . . . Mrs. . . ." (It's obvious that she has no idea what last name my mother is currently using.) "Can the boys come with me? You guys want to make some cupcakes?"

The boys start unbuckling themselves from their car seats and Travis and Thomas have the van doors open faster than my mother can object.

Chantal

· · · · · ·

An Unlikely Heroine.

I may have freed Jillian's brothers, but it's only temporary. Jillian's mother is shouting for the boys to get back in the van. It's unfair that this woman should have so much control over this night, so much control over my friend. And I want to say it out loud, but I know my magic is used up. The last thing I want is for her to turn on me.

"Chantal!" My dad and my mother join our glum party. "We caught up to you!" I hug them and they tell me how proud they are. They ask me what I'm going to do with the rest of my night.

"Well," I say. "I'm not sure." I nod toward Jillian's mother. Maybe it's a mother's sense about mother-daughter bonds, or maybe my mother is a mind reader in disguise, or maybe she's reaching out to me in ways I would never expect. Whatever the motivation, my mother steps in as a problem solver. I stand open-mouthed and watch a master at work.

"Teresa." My mother smiles at Jillian's mother. She channels the power-mom, the woman who makes things happen. "It's been a long time since we talked." They move away from the group to a spot behind the van. Through the windows I see Jillian's mother is crying on my mother's shoulder a few minutes later.

I promise myself that later when the two of us are out collecting our rocks I'll thank her for being in the right place at an opportune time.

Parker

· · · · · ·

Facing Will.

Jillian, Chantal, and I decide that we will take all necessary measures needed to avoid another ambush by Jillian's mother. It seems she'll be sleeping off her bender in Chantal's family's guest room, but we've found a secluded spot to order in pizza, wings, and all the pop we can drink. If I understood Chantal correctly, there will be cupcakes, too.

The plan is simple. Jillian and Chantal will go to her dad's office to bake cupcakes. I'll round up the boys and take them there a bit later. But first, I have to talk to Will.

Will

. . . . . .

On My Way.

$\mathcal{I}$ find a dark doorway where I can lick my wounds while I watch everyone else celebrate. Feeling lower than a mole in his hole in January, I start inventorying what prized possessions will fit in the backpack I'll take with me when I hitchhike out of this town. Tomorrow. My plan so far is to find a park bench to sleep until the middle of the night when I'm sure the parentals will not wake up. I'll go to my room long enough to collect my shit and then I'm gone.

Some girl in a pink T-shirt spots me, offers me a campaign button.

"Go to hell," I snarl. Could my life get any worse? I shove my earbuds in my ear, consult my playlist; anything with whiskey in the title sounds about right.

"Son? Son?"

I look up.

"It's Will, right?"

Annelise's dad, Mr. Tourism, with his side-parted hair and nerd-shaped glasses has his hand stuck out in front of me. He's a car salesman and a high school principal all rolled into one. I grab it weakly and he shakes it hard. I grip harder. "Yes . . ." We let go and I pull out my earbuds. He asks if I have time to talk. I shrug.

"Will, I've been thinking. We need more of this." He gestures behind him at the crowd that still fills the street. "Bringing young people and families together with the tourists. You know tourists love a small town that, well, feels like a small town. They stay longer. Spend more money. And they sometimes move here if they've had a great vacation. The town could use a few more taxpayers. What do you think?"

I struggle to catch up. "You mean about taxpayers?"

"Sure. And about doing more of this sort of thing."

I'm stunned. Did he not witness my humiliation? Has Annelise plotted to twist the knife in my back so my death is more painful and obvious? I shrug.

"Look. I respect you, Will. You were willing to put yourself out there, to well, let's face it, make a fool of yourself. And that's not a bad thing. It shows potential. The Tourism Association could really capitalize on your success."

"Okay . . ." My success. Capitalize. I start to listen, really listen, and ask questions. I begin to imagine the difference the right director might make in my life. I shake hands with Mr. Tourism and agree to meet him in his office on Monday morning to discuss my future. My future.

• • •

"Parker!" I find him rounding up Jillian's brothers. "Dude!"

"Will! Man!" We fist punch and the awkwardness of where-were-you and what-the-hell-happened-there sets in. I almost give in to it, too. I almost get mad, because I could, you know, I'm totally justified. Except. I can't stop thinking about my future, about how, now, I have a choice.

"Dude! Mr. Tourism wants to hire me."

"Annelise's dad? To do what?"

"To be the youth ambassador of the town! Is that golden or what?"

"Man! That's great. It's great. It's really, really, really great." And he's got that I've-got-everything-I-want smile.

And I turn mine right back at him. I am on my way back. On my way.

Chantal

• • • • • •

The Perfect Friendship.

Baking is chemistry. It's about incorporating air, activating gluten, and using leavening and binding agents to maintain the integrity of the air pockets. Recipes are formulas, and if you mess with a formula that works, you end up with a mess. The same can be said about a friendship. My friendship. The one with Jillian.

She sits on a counter stool, her attention far away from the kitchen and the bittersweet chocolate cupcakes that wait for frosting. Her eyes cloud with worries. I've heard her whole story and I understand that she's been struggling while I've been off becoming a Cake Princess.

"It would have been simpler," she says, "if we'd just done a summer project. We could have both been Cake Princesses."

My eyes sting. She would never have agreed to bake cakes with me as a summer project. Never. "Let's face it, that would have only happened if Parker and Will wanted to bake." Even I'm surprised at my statement. I thought I was over her dumping me for Parker. It's clear that becoming the Cake Princess hasn't fixed everything. I busy myself with measuring sugar.

"And now I'm leaving for Vancouver." Jillian continues as if I haven't said anything. "What if my dad doesn't like me?"

I turn the burner on for the caramel. I can't even look at her. We should be talking about us. Why is she talking about her dad? "You'll get over it. Eventually."

"Chantal." She pulls the spatula from my hand. "What's wrong?"

Maybe I should tell her that I know all about getting over something. I could also add the real reason Parker started dating her. "Nothing." I shrug.

"No? So is this insensitivity a piece of the Cake Princess? If that's the case I want the real Chantal back."

I turn the burner off. She knows so little about what I went through this summer. It all looks good now, but it was difficult. Damn hard.

"Please, tell me what's wrong," she says.

I choose my words carefully. "I'm glad the Cake Princess project was mine."

She bites her bottom lip. "And . . ."

I could tell her how lonely it is when you are different from everyone else. I remember the scene with her mom, the last of so many that I can't remember them all. She knows what lonely is. Isn't that why we're best friends? I wish I could take back my revengeful thoughts about uncovering Parker's challenge. "Rejection won't be the end of you," I say. "It wasn't the end of me."

"But is it the end of us?"

My breath catches. "Do you want it to be?"

"I let you down. Parker's great, but I should have handled it better."

"True. But . . . I learned a lot. About being on my own."

"You love to learn." She smiles and the world begins to feel right again.

"I do."

"We're good then?"

"Yes." I take back my spatula. "We will speak no more of it."

We share stories as we create the caramel cream-cheese

frosting. When it's time to frost I demonstrate the technique for squeezing the bag while swirling frosting on the cupcake. "Your turn." I hand her a second bag of frosting.

"This is so you, the perfect mix of technique and art."

We work in concentrated silence.

When all the cupcakes are frosted Jillian asks, "Can I name them?"

"Well . . . you can suggest a name." It took me hours to come up with my first name, Crush on You.

She swirls a pile of frosting into her open hand, licks it off. "You're gonna love my suggestion."

"Let's hear it then."

"Nah, maybe I'll save it for my own cupcakes someday."

"Jillian!"

"The Perfect Friendship."

"Delish."

We each bite into our signature creation. The flavor pirouettes across my tongue like no other cake I've made.

Acknowledgments

Many people gave time, space, and/or financial resources that helped me complete this novel.

Thanks to the Alberta Foundation for the Arts, and Canada Council for the Arts, for their financial support.

Thanks to the Banff Centre for the Arts, for their scholarship and amazing mountain retreat for artists.

Thanks to my agent, Rosemary Stimola, who saw something sweet and challenged me to dig deeper.

Thanks to my wonderful editors, Liz Szabla and Kate Egan, for their patience, encouragement, and refinement.

Thanks to my writing group, Caterina, June, Debby, Naomi, and Lori, who read, discussed, and helped me to believe. To Rosa, for helping me understand.

Thanks to my family. My daughter, Callie, inspired the first sentence, and encouraged me through to the last. The boys in my life: Cameron, Chris, Gavin, Andrew, Brenan, and Ben all inspired and helped me refine the male point of view. The girls in my life: Danae and Linda kept the faith, and Ashton inspired one particular character. Thanks to Shirley and Paul, who have opened their hearts wider.

Thanks to Dennis, who could not have known when he married me what a roller coaster he'd be on, and he's still with me.

Thanks to all the taste testers, blog readers, and lovers of cake.

Go Fish!

MAR'CE MERRELL

What did you want to be when you grew up?
I wanted to be on Broadway, singing and acting, after I saw *The Sound of Music*. I always knew I wanted to be a mother, though, and I couldn't see how I could do both.

When did you realize you wanted to be a writer?
Like many writers, I can credit a teacher for my initial interest in becoming a writer. Mrs. Bowman at Tipton High School, in Tipton, Indiana, asked me to read my short story out loud to the class. I was the only one who read, and when I got to the end of my unfinished work, my classmates asked me to finish it, so they'd know how it ended.

What's your most embarrassing childhood memory?
So much of childhood is embarrassing when you're there, but I've developed a whole lot of compassion for that awkward girl that I was—someone who knew a lot about many things, someone who wanted people to like her, and someone who didn't easily give up.

What's your favorite childhood memory?
I spent much of my childhood reading. I remember the book fair in third grade and buying my first book—*Charlotte's Web*—and my mother bringing home boxes and boxes of hardcover books from the secondhand bookstore in Easton, Maryland. I still have my copy of *The Bobbsey Twins' Adventure in Washington*.

As a young person, who did you look up to most?
I read Harriet Tubman's story when I was nine. I have never forgotten how I cried and I demanded an explanation for why any human would treat any other human that way. I admired people who survived and who lived honestly and gave back, always.

What was your favorite thing about school?
I loved French in the eleventh and twelfth grades. It was me, a novel, and a French-English dictionary. For two years, I translated *Le Petit Prince* and Jean Paul Sartre's *Les Jeux Sont Faits* (The Chips Are Down.) My best friend, still, was in my French class, too, and we had fun despite our French teacher needing obedience at all times.

What was your least favorite thing about school?
The unexpected realities of teenage relationships. I had such difficulty navigating a world with little stability in relationships. It was so rare to find someone I could count on and so common to hear how often I was being trashed. Being the new girl every year or two makes school life a nightmare.

What were your hobbies as a kid? What are your hobbies now?
As a kid, I, big surprise, read constantly. I was also a singer and actor and I LOVED to bake! I don't sing or act much these days,

but I am still a baker. I also love to create things with my hands. I never had enough money to buy all the craft supplies, and every time we moved, art supplies were one of the first casualties.

What was your first job, and what was your "worst" job?

My first job was my worst job. I was a cornfield worker the summer I turned 13. I stood in a basket suspended from a large frame that was attached to a farm tractor. The crew boss drove the tractor down a one mile-long row of corn without stopping until we reached the end—over an hour. My job was to pull the tassel out of every cornstalk. They were planted about six inches apart from each other. I lasted less than a month at that job, but I still went back the next summer.

What book is on your nightstand now?

Don't you mean books? Fiction: *The Sisters Brothers* by Patrick deWitt. YA fiction: *You Against Me*. Teaching Resource: *Making Thinking Visible*. Nonfiction: Jon Kabat-Zinn's books on mindful meditation.

How did you celebrate publishing your first book?

With cupcakes, of course! And at my launch, I took time to acknowledge and thank my wonderful husband and children, and my friends for their sacrifices, love, and support. Books are not created in isolation.

Where do you write your books?

I have written at my kitchen table, at a small desk in my bedroom, and now I have a large attic that is all mine. With five kids in a small bungalow, it hasn't always been easy to find space, so I have gone to the Banff Centre for the Arts for many a long retreat.

What sparked your imagination for *Wicked Sweet*?
A rejection letter came for a novel I'd spent two or three years writing, and I was in my mourning bathrobe when my teenage daughter came home. I told her my woeful story and she said, "Why don't you write about something that makes you happy?" I started writing Chantal's story that day.

Are you a good chef?
I wouldn't use the word "chef" because that implies a level of professionalism that I'm not sure I'll ever attain. I am inspired in the kitchen, though, and I love creating things that taste good.

What would be your favorite cake out of all of Chantal's cakes?
I love anything with salted caramel and chocolate combined. Oh . . . and coconut lemon. And fresh-picked, pureed strawberries are truly amazing. And let's always remember the value of a Swiss-meringue buttercream—light, yet sturdy, slightly sweet, and so amazing on the tongue.

What challenges do you face in the writing process, and how do you overcome them?
The challenges shift the more I write. At one time, it was dialogue, then it was scene work, and then it was plot. I'd say the biggest challenge right now is the overall narrative arc and how all of the characters weave together. I write from four (or more) points of view at once and that's challenging. I overcome the narrative arc challenge by writing pages and pages from the first-person point of view that detail each character's life story, their thoughts, their fears, their beliefs, and the things that make them most happy.

Which of your characters is most like you?

I think we are all driven by two things: finding a way to avoid or get over the things we fear/hate most, and finding a way to do the things we love. Jillian and Chantal are each composites of me: Jillian has to survive and get away from a home life that isn't pleasant, and Chantal is moved to bake so that she can find that joy in connecting with people.

What makes you laugh out loud?

All of my children and my husband. They are the funniest, most engaging, most honest and authentic people on the planet. They know my story and I know theirs, and the level of joy is over the moon.

What do you do on a rainy day?

I love to bake and make plans for the next sunny day.

What's your idea of fun?

It always involves creativity! I could be in the kitchen with one of my sons or my daughter baking or making dinner, or playing Scrabble in the living room, or sitting on a beach talking about the important things in life. Or I might be alone and that's fun, too. I'd say the times when I am experiencing the most joy is when I am present in the moment.

What's your favorite song?

Right now, it's "Home" by Phillip Phillips of *American Idol* fame. I love the lyrics and the music.

Who is your favorite fictional character?

Fern from *Charlotte's Web*, followed by Charlotte from *Charlotte's Web*. Both are strong women who stand up for what is right, and together, they save a pig from being slaughtered. Did I mention that I don't eat pork?

What was your favorite book when you were a kid? Do you have a favorite book now?
Charlotte's Web was my favorite book as a child. And one book I would recommend to any young person to read is *The Giver*. I've read it out loud to each of my children, and I always choke up on the last paragraph or two.

What's your favorite TV show or movie?
I love watching *The Good Wife* because of the complex lead female character. The writing is terrific and I have always been interested in the law.

If you were stranded on a desert island, who would you want for company?
My children and my husband.

If you could travel anywhere in the world, where would you go and what would you do?
If I had months of travel available, I would want to choose a place where I could give back to the community and, over time, become a member of the community. If I had weeks, I'd choose a place where I could learn the culture, ingredients, and cooking styles through classes and eating, of course. I would probably pick somewhere warm, too. I live in northern Canada, where we experience winter for about eight months of the year.

If you could travel in time, where would you go and what would you do?
I would travel back to see myself when I was nine and ten years old, and living was difficult. I would tell that little girl that

she was strong and that she was going to grow up and live in a family where she wouldn't be afraid.

What's the best advice you have ever received about writing?
I had a mentor tell me that I was going to be published one day and that I knew how to write. That belief got me through a whole lot of bathrobe mournings and mean critiques from other writers later on in my career.

What advice do you wish someone had given you when you were younger?
Of course you are smart enough, you just can't give up.

Do you ever get writer's block? What do you do to get back on track?
I have struggled often and watched my colleagues in my writing group struggle, too, and I think universally, we get through it by talking through it. When we listen to our allies reflect back what they're hearing and give insight into the struggles we're having, we are able to put them into context and move forward. Sometimes by an inch.

What do you want readers to remember about your books?
My characters are survivors. They are smart, resourceful, and capable young people who can provide a light to get past the teenage years. And they are all out to find the things that make them happy.

What would you do if you ever stopped writing?
Talk more?

What should people know about you?
I am committed to doing good in the world.

What do you like best about yourself?
I want to hear what other people have to say.

**Do you have any strange or funny habits?
Did you when you were a kid?**
One of my quirks is that I love to sing when no one else is around. I have memorized all the words of many songs, whole albums, and when I am waiting in line and not text-messaging, I am singing in my head.

What do you consider to be your greatest accomplishment?
That I can consistently experience a massive amount of joy.

What do you wish you could do better?
That list is too long! I am a lifelong learner and that means that I'm always seeking ways to do everything I do better. I've been to pastry school and I've baked hundreds of cakes and I still believe I could bake tastier, fluffier cakes.

What would your readers be most surprised to learn about you?
I want to be a filmmaker one day.

ALSO AVAILABLE
FROM SQUARE FISH BOOKS

Even with the odds against them, these girls never give up hope.

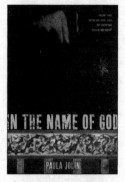

In the Name of God
Paula Jolin
ISBN 978-0-312-38455-5

How far would you go to
defend your beliefs?

Make Lemonade
Virginia Euwer Wolff
ISBN 978-0-8050-8070-4

Fourteen-year-old LaVaughn is
determined to go to college—she
just needs the money to get there.

A Room on Lorelei Street
Mary E. Pearson
ISBN 978-0-312-38019-9

Can seventeen-year-old Zoe
make it on her own?

Side Effects
Amy Goldman Koss
ISBN 978-0-312-60276-5

Isabelle is living a normal life
until everything changes in an
instant when she is diagnosed
with lymphoma.

Standing Against the Wind
Traci L. Jones
ISBN 978-0-312-62293-0

Patrice dreams of a first-class
education, but right now she's just
got to survive the walk to school.

Under the Persimmon Tree
Suzanne Fisher Staples
ISBN 978-0-312-37776-2

Two people trying to
find their way home find
each other along the way.

you'll find laughter, love, and wit in these great reads!

AVAILABLE FROM SQUARE FISH

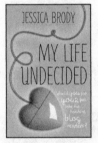

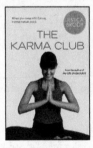